Tru

A Southern

Ella Sher

Cover Art Design by Kellie Dennis at Book Cover by Design

Editing by Rory Olsen

Formatting by Matthew Wade

Dedication

To Jack.
You barged onto the page the way you barged into Maddie's
life, and I knew then that this would be a wild ride. You really
are the perfect hero.

And to my mom, who taught me what it means to stand up
when life has thrown you down.
I love you, Mama.

Chapter One

Jack Quinn hit the heavy wooden doors that led into the Halftime Bar like a runaway train on the downside of a mountain. Even the hard slam didn't help his frustration. His muscles swelled with it, his skin so tight it could burst. He wished it would so he could finally get rid of the feeling that he wasn't at home in his own body.

He didn't recognize himself anymore, and deciding what to do about it was a drive pushing him closer and closer to the edge. Tonight might just tip him over.

The crash of music against his senses as he crossed the uneven planks of the floor into the darkened interior of the country bar was a welcome reprieve. The beat pounded in his head, his body, matching the adrenaline-laced rhythm of his heart and telling him he wasn't alone in his need to pound something. Preferably his best friend, Con.

The minefield of dancing couples was lighter than usual tonight. Jack didn't swerve; he made his own path straight to the bar. Anyone in his way could take one look at his face and see they needed to be the one to move aside. They moved. He saved a civil nod for Taylor, the tall blonde waitress who so often served him, as she wove her way through the tables on the far side of the dance floor. Most of them were empty, save a few clustered around the three high-definition TVs hanging along one wall.

Ignoring everyone else, Jack zeroed in on his favorite bar stool, the one that should have the shape of his ass tattooed on its surface considering how much time he'd spent on it lately. The stool was the only one positioned where the long mahogany bar top took a sharp turn into the wall. The short span on that end and the wall at his back meant no one shared his space while allowing him to see everyone and everything around him. His guard could stand down and he could relax for just a little while.

Maybe. If—and that was a big-ass *if*—he could stop wanting to punch Con just one time. But then Jess would complain about her pretty-boy husband's black eye, and Jack wouldn't hear the end of it for a while.

He sighed as he sat on his stool. Probably wasn't worth it after all.

"You're early, Jack. Run out of asses to kick? People to intimidate?"

Jack grunted at the big bruiser of a man making his way down the bar toward him. John, Halftime's regular bartender, had the shoulders of a defensive lineman, football pads and all. Except he wasn't wearing any. Jack sometimes held his breath as he watched the man maneuver behind the bar, waiting for one wrong turn to throw John against a shelf and send bottles of liquor and glasses crashing to the floor. Tonight he flicked a bird in John's general direction as payment for the sarcasm and pretended interest in a couple of women preening at one corner of the dance floor.

Yeah, he was in a pissy mood. That wasn't unusual lately. Didn't mean Con had the right to send him home like a little kid. Time off wasn't going to help.

John laughed as he stopped in front of Jack. "If you're needing to relieve a bit of tension, they're probably up for it," he said, nodding toward the two women. "Pickings are otherwise slim tonight."

"I bet." Shirts a bit too tight, a bit too small, makeup a bit too heavy for the eyelashes batting his way. Not out of their early twenties, he'd guess. Way too young for him, especially tonight. Even at their age, he hadn't felt as young and innocent as they looked; he sure as hell didn't feel it now, at thirty-four.

Besides, quick and dirty and meaningless wasn't what his gut churned for. He'd seen the real thing now, every time Con and Jess were together—hell, every time the man said something about his wife or even thought about her, it seemed—and Jack had a bad feeling that meaningless wasn't going to do it for him anymore. If he had a sweet something waiting at home for him like Con did, Jack wouldn't have to be told to go home; he'd rush there voluntarily. But he didn't. Work was all he had, and if he wanted to put in extra hours to avoid the silence his house practically throbbed with? That was his choice, not his best friend's, business partner or not.

The best friend who was currently at home, probably curled around—or inside—his wife's warm body, while Jack was stuck with the occasional one-night stand or a not so satisfying handjob. Jack was damn jealous, not of Jess but of Jess and Con's relationship. No wonder he was spending so much damn time at the neighborhood bar.

He needed a life. A hobby. A dog.

Jesus, he was losing it.

His expression must've given his answer, because John snickered. "Didn't think so. What'll ya have?"

"The usual."

John nodded. Twisting to look over his shoulder, he yelled, "Maddie, Sam Adams."

"Who's Maddie?"

John turned sideways, showing what his bulk had hidden up till now. Jack glanced down the long service area behind the bar and almost swallowed his tongue.

A woman. A blonde woman, but not the same kind of blonde as the waitress, Taylor. This woman had a straw-colored mane, thick enough it almost didn't fit in the claw clip holding it in a graceful twist at the back of her head. Spikes stuck from the top of the clip to fall along the sides, pointing to the creamy curve of her ear as she bent her head to focus on the frosted glass she was filling at the tap. A slender neck led to a body encased in a tight white T-shirt and short black vest. The clothes silhouetted her tucked-in waist and a sexy strip of bare skin above Levi's he would swear were painted on. And boots; God, he had such a thing for boots on a woman. And this woman wore them with the ease of longtime use, confirmation that balancing on them was second nature. One look at those boots and his dick shot straight up and strained in her direction as if she were true north and he was a compass.

Damn.

"Roll your tongue back in your head," John told him, laughter tangling with the words.

Jack glanced at the bartender, over at the woman, back to John. Swallowed. "Right."

John shrugged, and his easy smile widened. "I had the same reaction. Heck, every red-blooded male that's walked through the door since she was hired Monday has had that reaction. She is something."

"Damn straight."

The towel resting on the new bartender's shoulder slid off, landing with a *plop* on the ground. She bent to grab it.

Both men groaned.

The woman glanced over her shoulder.

John startled, actually blushing. Jack kept looking, appreciating the view from the front as much as the back when the new bartender stood to face them. She had a sweet body with curves in all the right, mouthwatering places.

"Can I help you gentlemen?" she asked, interrupting his reconnaissance. Jack met her eyes, a brown so dark he couldn't tell iris from pupil, though the narrowing of her eyelids might've had something to do with it too. Her lips were tight, pressing together in a way that made him want to tug them apart with his teeth.

The brittle edge to her expression had him narrowing his eyes too. His mama had taught him manners, even if she hadn't insisted on them for herself, but it wasn't like he was leering. He believed in appreciating what was before him; nothing crude or ugly about that. Most women he knew basked in the attention.

And maybe you're getting a bit too arrogant, dickhead.

He answered her look with a wry smile of his own.

The dish towel got a toss into the nearby hamper as the new bartender made her way toward them, Jack's lager in hand. John tucked himself against the back wall so she could make her delivery.

"Maddie, this is Jack."

"Nice to meet you." Jack extended his hand to shake, the anticipation of touching her forcing his erection harder against his zipper.

Down, boy.

Maddie shoved his beer into his hand. "You too."

Her voice was feminine, husky, arousing. Which was a ridiculous thought, because she didn't sound like it was nice to meet him. John sniggered. Jack ignored him, bringing the cold glass mug to his lips.

The deep, earthy bark of hops settled in his nose as he took his first drink, but his eyes stayed on Maddie's. She didn't back down, didn't blush, just raised a brow and stared right back. Why in hell did that make him so hot?

When he set the beer on the bar, Maddie nodded toward it. "All right?"

"Absolutely, darlin'," he said, the endearment slipping out automatically.

The eyebrow got higher. "Good."

He kept staring as Maddie returned to her end of the bar. The spikes of hair sticking up from her clip bounced with every step. Jack imagined his fingers fisting the long length, holding her still for him. Taming the shrew, so to speak. He had not a single doubt that she'd be feisty as hell. Yeah, he'd definitely like to get his hands in that hair.

John's laugh sliced through his sexual haze. He shot the bartender a sharp look. "Shut the hell up."

John laughed harder.

Jack opened his mouth—to say what, he didn't know—but an angry bellow cut him off. The trailing cry that followed, high-pitched and feminine, had every muscle in Jack's body tightening. His beer hit the counter and he was off his seat long before the motion registered.

Maddie was faster, and she was closer to the chaos than he was.

Jack watched in slow-motion fascination as the small bundle of angry woman hit the hinged half door marking the end of the bar at a full-out run. She didn't even pause at the impact, just kept on going, across the uneven floor in those heeled boots, through the tabled area to the edge of the dance floor. He gained on her as the fight came into view.

One of the waitresses, Elena, struggled in the grip of a burly, obviously angry drunk, tears on her pale cheeks. She whimpered in his hold as her skin whitened around the fist enclosing her fragile wrist.

"I told you I want another. Now go get it, you little slut!"

Jack heard the waitress's muffled gasp in response as she shook her head no.

"Yes," the man shouted, shaking her in his grip.

Maddie closed the last three feet of distance between herself and the drunk with no hesitation, stepping right into his space. Jack's heart leaped into his throat, a warning rising to just behind his teeth…

Maddie gripped the drunk's thumb where it rested atop Elena's arm, one finger on the bottom joint and one sliding right up underneath—perfect positioning—and shoved back hard. The move forced the man to release his hold or have his thumb broken. He chose release.

"Ow! Damn bitch," the man growled, reaching with his other hand to make a grab for Maddie now.

"Bitch is right," she muttered, her voice rough with menace and a thread of satisfaction that had all of Jack's senses screaming to alert. She twisted to the side, slipping the drunk's hold easily. On the back swing, she clasped her hands together in a firm grip and used them as a brace to shove her elbow up toward the drunk's face. The three-inch heels on her boots allowed her to hit him square in the nose, which promptly gave way. Blood spurted in a crazy arc.

The whole thing took seconds. Jack watched, stunned, as the man's head fell back, as droplets of blood landed on the smooth expanse of Maddie's face. For a single moment the image of an equally beautiful blonde, long hair bloody and tangled as she cowered in a corner, hit him in the gut. And then the moment was gone and he was in arm's reach of Maddie and her drunk opponent.

"That's it." With a growl of his own, Jack grabbed the bartender around the waist and moved her bodily away from the attack, subduing her kicks and struggles easily with his six feet four inches of military-trained muscle. Maddie bucked in his arms, her head hitting his collarbone. Pain shot across his shoulder, and the hold on his temper, the one he usually kept with barely any effort at all, snapped in two.

"Stop!" Planting her firmly on the ground out of the way, Jack whipped her to face him. Wild eyes latched on to his, her face going red with impotent anger. He gripped her biceps before she could explode into violence. Maddie twisted her arms, trying to slip his grip the same as she had the drunk's, but he was ready for her and clamped down tighter, giving her a little shake. "Maddie, stop."

Her name seemed to register, but the anger was still there. One side of those full lips lifted in a snarl. Jack allowed every ounce of command he possessed to shine from his eyes, using attitude as much as strength to subdue her. Only when Maddie sank back on her heels did he let go.

"Stay!" His pointed finger told her where, though the way her mouth dropped open and the stunned look on her face assured him he only had moments to work before her surprise wore off and she came after him again.

Moving quickly toward the bellowing drunk now holding his bloody nose, Jack gripped the man's thick neck and pushed him onto the dance floor. The man pulled away with a loud grunt, swinging a shaky fist in the general direction of Jack's chest. Batting the hand away like a pesky fly, Jack twisted one burly arm behind the man's back, using it as a lever to frog-march him across the room.

"Don't," he warned as the man struggled in his grip. "I've got no problem fucking you up, asshole, and trust me, you won't enjoy it."

A carrot-topped head appeared through the crowd of onlookers. Troy, Halftime's bouncer, forced his way over. "Jack, no beatin' up the clientele. I told you that before."

Snorting at the man's sarcasm, Jack gave his prisoner another shove. "Not me. Blondie." He jerked his head in the direction where he'd left the new bartender. "This guy's drunk, and I'm pretty sure his nose is broken."

"She's got good aim," Troy said, eyeing the injured man. "Guess that'll teach you, huh, Bernie?"

"Dat bitch broke my node!"

"Yeah, yeah." Troy grimaced before taking Jack's place behind Bernie's back. "I might break something else if you don't come quietly, so come quietly."

"But—"

Troy gave the man's wrist a slight twist, forcing him up on his toes. "Quietly, I said."

Jack stayed where he was a moment, watching the pair exit the heavy double doors out front, trying to calm the fire of adrenaline racing through his veins, to get ahold of the fear that had threatened to choke him when Maddie grabbed Bernie's hand. To get the hot desire that had flooded him as her firm ass pressed against his cock under control. He inhaled, held the air for a count of ten, then let it out. Did it again. When he got the emotion down to a hard simmer, he turned back to the little troublemaker.

Maddie's position as she bent over to examine Elena's bruised wrist showcased her mouthwatering backside in a way that did absolutely nothing to calm him down. He circled the pair. "What the hell were you thinking?"

Her head jerked up, innocent eyes meeting his squarely. *Innocent, my ass.* "What?"

"You heard me," he gritted out through his teeth.

"Yeah, I did." She straightened, only to turn her stiff back on him, murmuring to the waitress once more.

"You didn't answer me."

"I don't answer dumb questions," she threw over her shoulder. Draping an arm around Elena's slender shoulders, Maddie urged her toward the kitchen. Halftime's owner, Tommy Ray, came rushing to meet them, his face a mix of displeasure and concern.

14

"What happened, girl?"

"Bernie," Elena said. She cradled her wrist in her opposite hand.

"Damn."

"Yeah, and now his nose is broken," Jack said sourly. "Troy's handling him."

Bushy black eyebrows rose in unison above Tommy Ray's dark gaze. "How did his nose get broken?" He eyed Elena's tiny stature uncertainly.

"Her." Jack nodded toward Maddie. "You got yourself a bundle of surprises behind your bar, Tommy Ray."

Tommy Ray looked to Maddie this time, surprise and a hint of amusement mixing with the concern. "Maddie?"

Jack clenched his fists, his entire body tense.

Maddie shrugged. "I saw Elena needed help, and I helped."

"You were reckless and damned lucky, you mean. I just don't get what you were thinking." The chaos in Jack's mind roughened the words to a rumble.

"What were *you* thinking? You were right behind me, jackass."

Jackass. Clever. He glared. "I'm trained for this. Most people at least hesitate."

She scoffed. "Not likely. No one's getting hurt on my watch if I can help it."

"Look—"

"Jack," Tommy Ray warned.

That cocky blonde eyebrow lifted in his direction. Again. "Who the hell are you, anyway?" Maddie asked. "My keeper?"

"It looks like you need one." He was not going to yell. He would not lose it that far. No matter how fast he felt his control slipping through his fingers. No matter how calm, cool, and condescending she looked. No matter how damn good she'd felt against him, and how much his body raged to jerk her against him again and take all this aggression out on her full lips and generous curves.

Not gonna happen.

Maddie leaned forward, mere inches separating him from her sweet breath. "You wish."

"Damn it!" Jack snarled.

Elena's shoulders began to shake with laughter. Tommy Ray rolled his eyes. "Now, children…"

Maddie squared off with Jack, the heels of her boots barely bringing her height to his shoulder. Her eyes blazed. "You can take your opinion and shove it up your—"

"Enough." Tommy Ray stepped between them, or at least his rounded belly did. He pointed a finger at Maddie. "You've got drinks to make. Get back behind the bar. And next time"—he lowered those caterpillar brows at her—"call Troy. That's what he's here for."

Jack rocked on his heels and watched her stalk back to her station. He waited, ignoring the sweat trickling between his shoulder blades, while Tommy

Ray sent Elena to the kitchen for an ice pack before turning back to him.

Jack shifted to keep Maddie and the bar in his sight. "Who is she, Tommy Ray?"

"New girl. John's needin' more time for his classes; she needed a job. It seemed like a good trade. She knows her stuff behind the bar."

"And in front of it too, looks like. Or thinks she does." He could still feel her glare burning through him. "Where's she from?"

"Don't know. Doesn't matter." The stubborn look on his friend's face said that was all he would share. It could be all the man knew. It wouldn't be the first time Tommy Ray had taken in a stray puppy with no paperwork. Jack's friend didn't care as long as she could do the job. So why did Jack care?

"I'd keep an eye on her. She's a firecracker waiting to go off, and you know what kind of damage that can do."

The other man laughed. "Yeah, I sure do. Too hot to handle, at least for an old guy like me." He patted his burly chest and turned serious. "I'll have Troy keep an eye on her, but if she can handle Bernie, she'll do fine."

"Tommy Ray—"

The man held up one huge paw. "You know I don't allow any trouble around here, Jack. I run a clean bar; otherwise you and a bunch of others wouldn't come here. But I'll keep an eye out."

Jack watched his friend head back to the kitchen instead of letting his gaze turn back to the bar. *Me too.*

Chapter Two

"Wow, Maddie. Heard you broke a nose tonight." Taylor was laughing so hard the last word ended in a snort. Several moments passed as she fought to get herself under control. "Three days. You know the record is two weeks, right?"

There's a record? Maddie glanced at the waitress as she leaned on the bar, elbows planted on either side of her serving tray, abundant chest still shaking with continued giggles. Taylor's friendly grin begged Maddie to share it, to come out of the emotionless cocoon she'd lived in for so long, but she didn't dare, not really. She'd already taken too many risks tonight.

Instead she pulled on the mask that earned her tips and hid her real self. The happy bartender, she called it. An easy smile, sympathetic eyes. Only with the mask firmly in place could she finally breathe, knowing she was safe from prying eyes, that her emotions were hidden away where no one else could see them, use them against her.

She shrugged one shoulder, a plastic smile glued to her lips. "I'm trying to get a jump on fitting in," she said. No one could know how true that was.

But Taylor wasn't buying it. Her brow creased, something soft and almost caring suffusing her expression. "You okay?"

"Of course."

"Of course," the other woman repeated, her words gently mocking. "I'm serious. You weren't hurt, were you?"

Jesus, these people saw too much. Maddie blinked, the second it took to slide her eyelids down and up just enough to force reassurance into her voice. "No, I'm fine. Seriously."

It was true, after all. She hadn't been hurt; she'd been the one hurting someone else. That fact should horrify her, but it wasn't horror churning in her gut, and certainly not over Bernie. No trace of remorse, either; just a deep, dark sense of satisfaction every time that moment played through her memory: crunching cartilage, spraying blood, Bernie's loud bellow of pain.

A sadistic bitch, that's what you are, Maddie.

This time her shrug was mental.

Taylor, oblivious to Maddie's internal gestures, glanced over her shoulder. Maddie followed the look, and, unwanted, her gaze settled on Jack, his brooding eyes staring straight back at her, laser focus tightening every last nerve ending in her body as he walked past. He didn't pause. His eyes held hers as long as they could, and then he was striding through the table area, the view of his broad back and shoulders filling the void he left behind.

Above his shirt collar, his short, military-style black hair ended in a crisp horizontal line. No stubble, no nonsense. Kind of like his attitude. He had to be a cop, or maybe a soldier. She didn't care what he did, exactly; her instincts told her all she needed to know: he was trouble. Even his easy posture was a warning

19

sign. The man didn't strut, didn't hesitate. He knew he was a badass, and everyone else knew it too. He didn't have to prove his badassness by forcing it down anyone's throat—except hers, apparently.

Jackass. The man infuriated her.

It wasn't until the front doors banged shut behind him that she was able to pull her attention back to work. Taylor's amused expression was waiting.

"Why, whatever did you say to make him look at you like that?" the waitress asked, her long eyelashes batting coyly in a perfect Scarlett O'Hara impression.

"Like what?"

"Like he doesn't know whether to tie you up and spank you or kiss you senseless."

"I think that's suspicion, not lust." She flicked her fingers toward the front door. "What is he, the bar police?"

Taylor shook her head. "Nah, he owns some company in Atlanta, something to do with finances, maybe? Ex-military." Her expression turned dreamy. "That's where all the muscles came from. God bless the armed forces is all I can say."

Maddie wondered if the poor woman would start to drool next. "Yeah, well, muscles or not, I still beat him to the punch. Literally."

John snorted somewhere off to her right. She fought the urge to shoot her supervisor a bird like Jack had earlier. Oh yes, she'd seen him. From the moment he'd walked through the front doors and begun his long journey across the room, she'd been aware of him, as if his sheer presence had changed the air on a molecular level she couldn't ignore. And that pissed her off more than him staring at her ass or even manhandling her out on the dance floor. In her line of work, men stared at her every damn night. They never put their hands on her, not if they didn't want to draw back a nub; Jack was lucky she hadn't had time to react or she would've broken *his* nose right after Bernie's.

But it wasn't either of those things that had her shaking in her well-worn boots. It was the memory of those long seconds when he'd held her, all that hard muscle bunching at her back, strong arms bruising her ribs, and the realization that what she'd felt hadn't been fear or a need to strike back. Far from it. She'd felt *need*, and that she couldn't allow. She was here for a reason, and it wasn't to open her personal Pandora's box of issues.

Elena signaled Maddie from where she stood near the tables close to the dance floor. Two fingers. Maddie nodded and moved to pour two beers. Gripping the first glass firmly, she tugged the tap with her other hand. The gold hue of the liquid reminded her of the amber flecks in Jack's eyes, the ones she'd seen clearly when he bent close, nose to nose, and told her to stay. Like a dog.

Jackass.

Only the icy shock of liquid hitting her fingers brought her back to reality. She bit off a nasty curse.

"Maddie." John eased up next to her. "Come on; you need a break."

She was already shaking her head before he'd finished his sentence. "Me? No. I'm good." She winked at him, mask in place, and dumped the beer like she'd meant to overfill it. John didn't say anything, just watched her start again, but a moment later his big paw landed on her shoulder for a gentle pat. The glass in her hand slipped. She barely managed to catch it in time. *Get your head back in the fucking game, Maddie.*

With deliberate care—and ignoring John's concerned frown—she stepped out of the bartender's reach and settled the thick glass onto a nearby tray. Her second pour was swift and sure, not a drop lost. Instead of signaling Elena with her order, Maddie hefted the tray and walked it over to the busy waitress.

"Thanks." Elena slipped her unbruised hand under the tray, next to Maddie's, and transferred the weight with seamless ease. Maddie gave her a smile and turned back toward the bar.

"That was quite the performance earlier."

Maddie caught herself before her smile could deepen at the sound of that oily voice. "Philip. I hadn't realized you were here," she lied.

She kept her muscles loose, ready, as the man moved in front of her, blocking the path back to the bar. Philip Montgomery had an abundance of blond good looks and money to throw around, as she'd discovered last night. She'd discovered other things too, like the fact that the only thing he enjoyed more than weakness was tearing down strength. His intimidation tactics put most barroom bullies to shame, though she noticed he carefully avoided the waitresses, maybe because he didn't want anyone spitting in his drinks. With her it wasn't spit he had to worry about, but he didn't need to realize that just yet.

Of course, after her earlier performance, he likely already did.

Bartholomew Symmons shifted at Philip's side, his curly brown hair and slightly overweight body marking him as the classic sidekick. Maddie peeked up at him from beneath lowered lashes, careful to keep Philip in her sights as well. "Bart."

Soft brown brows drew together over Bart's concerned eyes. "That was quite a hit you took at Bernie. You okay?"

"Of course she is." Philip slid a discreet tongue across his bottom lip. "She was magnificent."

"Magnificent is Milla Jovovich," she countered. "I'm just Maddie. I'm sure there are plenty of women in this town that could take down a drunk like that."

"Could they?" Philip asked. His tone discounted each and every one of the supposed *them*.

"Elena couldn't."

Maddie's gaze snapped to Bart, but the look he sent the tiny waitress held the same concern it had with Maddie.

"Bernie's always been trouble," he continued, seeming unaware of her scrutiny. "She should know that by now. A little thing like that shouldn't be working around drunks without a way to protect herself."

"Maybe I'll teach her a few tricks," Maddie said. She sidled around the men, careful to keep her body a firm distance away. Philip took his time giving her room, his gaze running over her like a grimy rag. Bart stepped aside immediately, his attention still on Elena.

The two men followed her across the room. Maddie swore she could feel Philip's breath on her neck, he dogged her so closely. For a moment she wondered if he'd follow her into the service area behind the bar, but John's brick-wall presence shielded her as she stepped through the half door.

She gave the men an encouraging smile as she made her way down the bar. "You guys seem to know everyone around here." Like most small towns on the fringe of a major city, Freeman—and therefore the Halftime—had its share of newcomers, people looking for rural living. But most of the people in the bar knew each other, called each other and the staff by name, their familiarity speaking of long acquaintance. She'd noticed last night that just as many people seemed to avoid Philip as greet him.

Bart settled himself on a convenient bar stool. "That's usually the way it is when your families founded the town."

"Is that how you two know each other?"

"Since birth," Bart chimed in.

Philip's chest actually puffed up. "That's right. Politics, religion—you name it, our families control it. My father and grandfather and great-grandfather were all pastors of the Freeman First Baptist Church."

Maddie almost choked. Somehow she doubted Philip planned to follow in his family's footsteps.

"Half the elders are blood relations," he was saying. "The city council, even most of the board members of Union Plastics are all from the same handful of families that settled here over a hundred years ago."

"The big manufacturing plant out on the highway?"

"Biggest employer in the county. My uncle is the CEO." He stared down at her, waiting for a response. She wasn't sure what response to give him, comments about nepotism notwithstanding. She didn't think that would keep him talking, at least not in a civilized manner.

She pasted on what she hoped was a suitably impressed look. "Oh."

"But enough about our families' silver spoons," Bart said. "Can I get another drink?"

"Right...sorry."

He gave her an indulgent grin and pulled out his cell phone. While he clicked away, Philip watched her begin filling what she assumed was their usual order since it was all they'd had last night: two Long Island Iced Teas.

"Have you thought about my offer?"

Maddie glanced Philip's way before pouring the rum. "To go out?"

Even concentrating on mixing drinks, she caught the tightening of Philip's lips. "I was thinking this weekend," he told her. "I have a friend with a house on Lake Lanier. Perfect for summer parties."

Maddie added ice and shook Bart's drink first. "I don't date customers, Philip. I told you that yesterday. Besides, I have to work this weekend."

"You could call in sick."

"My first week?"

"How about next weekend then?" He didn't work very hard to keep the impatience out of his response. "I have a home theater. We could watch a movie, take a ride into downtown Atlanta to visit one of the clubs. What do you say?"

That she wouldn't put herself in the dark or alone with this man for any reason, even if her instincts weren't screaming what a bad idea it was— and her instincts never lied. "I say I'm sorry, but I don't date customers," she told him, letting her own impatience peek through.

A spark of something distinctly uncomfortable lit Philip's eyes. "I'm not just any customer, Maddie." He reached across the bar toward her.

She stepped to the side, pretending it was so she could settle Bart's drink in front of him. A sip, a sigh, and the man grinned over at her. "Perfect."

She picked up the second drink. "I'm sorry, Philip, but I'm firm on that. I can't go."

Philip waited until the tall glass was placed on the bar near his hand before wrinkling his nose. "I think I'll change it up. How about a Sam Adams?"

Subtle he was not. Maddie stood for a moment, staring at him, reading the malice twisting his lips and narrowing his eyes. Eating the cost of the wasted drink didn't bother her that much, but the fact that he'd seen something between her and Jack that Maddie'd hoped no one but the other staff had seen... He'd been watching a lot more closely than she'd realized.

Hiding her reaction behind her friendly bartender smile, she reached for the drink without comment. Bart beat her to it.

"I'll take that." The glass was placed next to his first drink, awaiting his attention. Philip shot his friend a black look. Maddie grinned—internally, of course—and went to pull the man's requested Sam Adam's. *Definitely not subtle.*

His stare burned into her back the whole time.

"Here you go," she said finally, placing the mug on the bar.

Philip held her gaze as he lifted the beer to take a long drink. With Jack, that move had projected his power; with Philip, it made her feel like she needed a bath. His smile didn't quite reach those watchful eyes when he finished. "Perfect. That's what makes you my favorite bartender."

Flattery will get you nowhere, dipshit. She let her lips curve upward. "I've only worked here three days."

"And that's all it took for me to know you were irresistible."

A tray clattering on the bar startled her. "Maddie," Taylor called. "Two whiskeys for the show-offs watching golf."

Taylor's disgust permeated the last word, amusing Maddie, though she merely gave the waitress a businesslike nod. By the time she had the Jack poured, Bart had coaxed Philip into a game of pool and Maddie felt like she could breathe clean air again. A glance at the clock told her she still had several hours before the bar closed, a fact that elicited a groan Maddie couldn't suppress. She picked up a cloth and started drying dishes.

Taylor delivered the drinks and wandered back to the bar. Reaching across, she scooped up a clean towel.

"That's so not fair," Maddie said.

Taylor winked. "Being tall does have its advantages, but so does being short. I couldn't have made that shot you threw at Bernie; it would've landed on his hard skull and probably broken my elbow."

Elena stepped up on the low rung of a bar stool to grab a towel for herself. "Of course, you both know how to improvise rather well when it comes to dickheads."

Both waitresses glanced toward the pool tables, then to each other. Sly grins confirmed her suspicions. It seemed she wasn't the only one Philip had gotten aggressive with.

Taylor swiped her towel over her tray, a wicked glint in her eye. "You aren't the only one around here with a reputation."

Before she could protest that she'd barely been here long enough for a reputation, Elena broke in. "That's right. About two weeks after Tommy Ray hired her, some obnoxious prick had the gall to get handsy with Taylor. She broke every toe on one of his feet."

Taylor pouted. "Hey, he wouldn't let go."

Maddie couldn't hold back a laugh at that.

Elena laughed too, her white teeth gleaming against a flawless Hispanic complexion. "He let go fast enough then. I've never seen a grown man cry quite that hard."

"He got what he deserved. Jack's a good teacher."

The jackass again. She shouldn't ask; she knew she shouldn't. "Jack?"

Taylor smoothed the ponytail trailing down her back, practically preening. "I took one of his self-defense workshops. He didn't make it easy on us, either. Said we had to know what we might be facing. He even had a friend come in with all these pads and things on so we could hit him and not damage his…equipment." She waggled her eyebrows.

"Conlan?" Elena asked, obviously referring to someone both women knew. Taylor nodded. "Damaging that man's equipment would be a crime," Elena agreed.

Maddie's mind was buzzing in a different direction. "Jack teaches self-defense?" He was ex-military, Taylor had said earlier. His handling of Bernie had attested to training of some kind, but teaching women? She couldn't really see it. With his taste for sarcasm, she'd be more likely to catch him without padding just for a chance to do some damage to that arrogant head of his.

On the other hand, a class with Jack might be good training. There really was no preparation for the shock of being helpless in the face of a strong man's anger. She thought about facing Jack in a rage, and her heart stuttered.

"Strictly volunteer." Taylor turned serious as she looked down at her tray. "It was at a women's shelter, Hope Place. I…uh…had to go there a couple of years ago when my ex threw me out."

Hope Place. Suddenly the uneven thump of Maddie's heart seemed too loud, too fast. A sharp pang shooting down her arm forced her to relax her grip on the glass she was drying.

"He's a great teacher," Taylor was saying. "And like I've told him more than once, he can manhandle me anytime."

The flirty words fit Taylor's normal happy-go-lucky attitude, but Maddie sensed that, in this instance, they were more about drawing attention away from what she'd admitted about her past.

"No kidding," Elena teased. "I mean, God"—the petite waitress fanned her pink cheeks—"those thighs."

Taylor winked. "That ass."

And that was the last place Maddie's mind needed to go. *No thinking about Jack's ass.*

"Not to mention that face," Elena said.

"You mean the one with the smug male arrogance?" Maddie asked.

Elena's mini swoon mocked her. "Yeah, that one."

"Come on, Maddie," Taylor said. "Don't tell me he didn't push any buttons with you."

"Oh, he pushed buttons, all right." She clamped her lips shut before she admitted which ones. Instead she gave Elena a warning look. "You, on the other hand, you hit a big button."

"Not sure I would say 'hit' around here for a while," John put in, sotto voce, from a few feet away.

Maddie stuck her tongue out at his back. Taylor hooted, the hand over her mouth barely muffling the sound.

"How's your arm?" Maddie asked Elena when the amusement died down.

"A bit bruised, but I'll be okay." She rotated her wrist cautiously. "I'll keep an eye on it."

"Do that. You never know when there might be a hairline fracture." Maddie knew that from experience.

"So where'd you learn your moves, Maddie?" Taylor asked.

The ever-present shrug came to her rescue. "Here and there."

"Comes in handy in a bar," Taylor said.

"Back to work, girls!" Tommy Ray called through the window to the kitchen.

Taylor and Elena returned to the floor, their heads together, continuing the conversation between them. Maddie watched for a moment, an emotion swirling in her chest that she had no desire to identify but couldn't get away from: jealousy. She shouldn't feel jealousy, shouldn't feel need. Shouldn't feel any of the things that were raising their nasty little heads tonight. The only thing she allowed herself to need was justice, and to gain it, she had to keep her sights on what was important.

Uncovering secrets.

Finding the proof.

Emotion would only make her vulnerable, and vulnerable was as good as dead in her world.

Her feet and back ached like a bitch as she followed John and Tommy Ray out to the employee parking area after closing. Her bike received a quick, thorough check before Maddie dug out her helmet and climbed on the old motorcycle. She hated the heat of the helmet on her head, smashing down her hair, especially in the god-awful, sweltering Georgia heat, but having her head smashed in was worse, so she buckled it on with a grimace. When Tommy Ray's brake lights were lost from view and the lot was clear of everything but shadows, she centered her weight on the bike and started it up.

At first, when she'd been living hand to mouth and desperate for any mode of transportation, the bike had been a necessity, a sweet little crotch rocket that'd been rebuilt so many times its original make and model were indecipherable. Nowhere near as expensive as a car and much easier to learn to fix. But over time it had become her solace. Climbing aboard the sleek black-and-chrome racer, hearing that high whine as she revved the engine, was the only lullaby that could soothe her nerves on the nights when nightmares were too close and the darkness was a pressing void, empty of life and breath. Tonight, though, she craved a few hours of blessed oblivion.

The mattress on her bedroom floor was calling. Loudly. Too bad she still had work to do.

Her apartment, a tiny two-story building her landlord had somehow managed to divide up into four smaller-than-postage-stamp units, waited only a few blocks east of the Halftime. Still Maddie circled through a couple of stoplights, past a gas station lit only by its bright red price signs and a dollar store that constituted the only shopping on this end of town. Only when she knew she was alone did she head back to her place. The road her building was on stayed fairly dark, nothing but a streetlight at each end of the three-block distance to dispel the shadows. Maddie did a slow drive-by, checking the darkness for anything unusual, but nothing stood out. With a tired sigh she pulled around the far side of the building.

Her bike fit easily in the space between the alley exit and the fence to the neighboring property, half-hidden by a large flowering bush Maddie had yet to identify and a massive weeping willow living off the drainage-ditch water. She parked facing the road, tucked out of sight, and circled to the back to enter her apartment through the rear door.

Her keys and cell phone were stowed safely in her backpack. Bypassing the fridge—one of the perks of working with a generous heart like Tommy Ray was free dinner—she flipped on the lamp situated on the aluminum '50s dining table and sat. The pack went on the floor next to her chair. Paranoid or not, she never let the thing get more than a few feet away from her except at work. Everything she needed to start over was in there; she wouldn't risk being caught without it.

The surface of the table was covered in papers, thick file folders, and more than one thumb drive. Every piece of information she'd managed to gather over the last four years. Her reason for living. Maddie clamped down on the rush of tears that burned the backs of her eyes, begging to be let out, and instead picked up the newspaper clipping taking center stage at the moment.

It was the first article she'd found. The others, detailing the area, the town and its people, the movements of significant parties, had come later, after she'd seen this: the picture of a sweet coffee-colored face. Vaneqe Wilson. So young, barely into her teens. Maddie stroked a finger down the black-and-white image of the girl whose kidnapping had been front-page news in the *Freeman Daily*—and fifteenth-page news in the *Atlanta Journal-Constitution*. She had shoulder-length black hair, the curls a riot around her head.

Just like Amber'd had.

"I'm still looking. I promise."

Vaneqe had disappeared three weeks ago without a trace. In her previous life, Maddie wouldn't have believed it—how could anyone just up and vanish? Her years on the run had taught her better. The thinly spread state troopers that covered tiny towns like this had quickly ruled the girl a runaway. Maybe, with their limited time and resources, that had seemed the best call. They knew the people and the area, after all, but they didn't know what Maddie knew, or suspected, at least. The key was Hope Place, the shelter Vaneqe had been living in when she "ran away." If Maddie could make the right connection, uncover the right clues, hopefully she could find the proof she needed, both to rescue Vaneqe and stop the monster she believed was behind all of this. It was taking time, something Vaneqe might not have much more of, but Maddie didn't know what else to do than keep trying.

She set the article aside and rifled through her files until she found what she needed. Hope Place, technically Hope Women's and Children's Center, was a nonprofit, and nonprofits were always looking for donations. That meant keeping donors informed, and one way they did that was through a quarterly newsletter, which they posted to their website. A newsletter that included the names of board members and a few employees. It wasn't much, but it was a place to start. She grabbed a pen and the list of names she'd made and settled into the chair.

Bartholomew Symmons. He was the son of Freeman's mayor, a board member for Hope Place. According to Google, Bart had no record that she could find. His social-media presence was an open book, though—profiles open for anyone to read, frequent check-ins or mentions of places he was or was not. None of it was too smart if he had anything to hide. Bart's name got a check mark, along with notes detailing their meetings and what little gossip she'd learned about him and his family at the bar. She'd heard the same thing over and over: he was an

35

okay guy, if more of a follower than a leader. Which explained why Philip led him around by the nose.

Philip Montgomery. He'd also come up clean online. Son of Harold Montgomery. A thorn in his popular father's side, if gossip around the bar was to be believed. Really it was amazing what people would tell her when they found out she was new in town. Everything she'd heard about Harold said he was an upstanding man, a *good* man, whatever that meant— everything a pastor should be. Philip, on the other hand... If she had to guess, she'd say he had a case of daddy envy. She debated for no more than a moment before placing a star next to his name. People who lived in a fishbowl tended to break after a while, and there was no more restrictive fishbowl than being a preacher's kid. If Philip had the means and opportunity, she could definitely see him being the contact in this area.

Time would tell. Now that she knew Taylor had been involved with the shelter—*and so had Jack; don't forget Jack*—she just might have a way to become involved there without raising suspicion. Margaret Hawthorne was known for her generosity and compassion in her role as director of Hope Place, but she was also known for guarding the privacy of the shelter and its residents with the ferocity of a bulldog. Maddie would have to move carefully to make that contact.

A glance over the files had her stare catching Vaneqe's in the grainy newsprint. The fifteen-year-old was missing, maybe dead. Maddie was the only one looking for her, the only one with a possible key to finding her—and probably the least qualified to do so. She had no clue what she was doing, no certainty that she was right, only her instincts and a determination that would not let her go. She would find this one; she had to.

She forced herself not to look away from Vaneqe's smiling eyes. "I'm coming. I'm coming." If her voice broke, she certainly wouldn't admit it, and there was no one here to argue.

Her lower back and the barely padded chair both protested as Maddie shifted in the seat. Time for bed. Same as every night, she gathered the papers into a neat pile, giving each one a last once-over in hopes her subconscious would make connections she hadn't, then turned out the light and walked into the bedroom. Changed her clothes. Brushed her teeth. When she lay down, her backpack went next to her pillow, and Vaneqe's picture went on the floor beside her mattress, the first thing she'd see when she rose in the morning. It was the last thing she saw before she closed her eyes and waited for sleep to come and, with it, the nightmares.

But hours later, it wasn't her hunt that refused to let her rest. Nor the nightmares. It was the look in a certain pair of eagle-sharp eyes and the feel of a steel-hard body against her back.

Leave it to the jackass to keep her awake.

Chapter Three

Two days. Two damn days, and he'd gone from being pissed off at Con to being pissed off at himself, all because a blonde-haired firecracker had gotten under his skin. He couldn't stop thinking about her, not at work, not at home, and certainly not in his lonely bed the past two nights. She was constantly at the back of his mind. He didn't get it. She was a woman. He'd known hundreds of women, slept with his fair share. Why did this one get to him in a way he couldn't seem to escape?

It didn't help that he'd been the jackass she'd called him Wednesday night. He'd walked in angry, and his short fuse had found its spark the minute Maddie gave him her first sarcastic look. If it wasn't for the raging hard-on he'd sported as he walked out of the bar—and every time he'd thought of her since—he'd chalk it up to mutual dislike and be done with it. There might be dislike, but it sure as hell wasn't mutual; he just wasn't sure what to do about it. Walk away? Forget they'd ever met and hope to God they could start fresh next time? Considering how much time he spent at the bar, the latter really was the only realistic option.

As evidenced by the fact that he was walking in Halftime's front doors at this very moment. Normally he spent most of Friday night here with Con, but he and Jess had a thing they had to attend and Jack had been in full avoidance mode. But missing Friday night poker was pushing avoidance too far. Besides, she was probably already done for the night and on her way home anyway.

And if she wasn't? He might as well get their second meeting over with before his cowardice garnered notice.

The sound of the wooden planks of the dance floor under his boots was a bit like coming home. He crossed the room to where Tommy Ray already had the poker table set up by the TV wall.

"Jack, missed you tonight. Everything all right?"

See? Nothing got by his friends. "Just some work stuff to do." Sort of. Jack avoided more conversation by gathering chairs for the players already in attendance: Troy, his red hair slicked back into a stubby ponytail, gauges on full display; Harold Montgomery, fire-and-brimstone pastor and damn fine poker player; Evelyn Maynard, the no-nonsense county commissioner who took no prisoners in politics or play. Jack spotted John finishing up the cleaning behind the bar. With Jack and Tommy Ray, that equaled six for tonight's game. Maddie was nowhere in sight. Jack stuffed down his disappointment and settled into a chair to begin doling out chips.

"And how are you, Jack?" Harold asked as he took the nearest seat. The man's expressive eyes were kind, though Jack had seen them go steely with displeasure, especially where his son was concerned. Philip had fallen pretty far from the family tree.

"I'm good; you?"

Harold accepted his chips with a nod. "Good as well. Any news on that little girl?"

Jack's heart squeezed at the mention of Vaneqe. The teenager had disappeared from Hope Place several weeks ago, and despite his best efforts, Jack had been unable to locate her. The police were convinced she'd run away. Jack knew better. Vaneqe would never have left her younger brother behind. "No, no news."

The pastor shook his head. "I'm sorry to hear that. I'll be praying for her."

Jack didn't doubt it. Many of the good people of First Baptist Church said the same, but their actions said something different. Harold practiced what he preached, including modeling Jesus, which was how he'd found himself at the Halftime for poker every week. Nothing like sitting down with the "sinners" to keep you humble and realistic in a job that often put its owner on a pedestal just by sheer title.

Tommy Ray interrupted with drinks—Sam Adams for Jack, a Sprite for Harold—and talk turned to the game. Jack had often wondered how Harold justified gambling to his congregation. Southern Baptists didn't smoke, drink, dance, or gamble, at least the ones he'd known. Considering their little group didn't play for money, Jack figured it didn't count. Harold seemed to think so too.

An hour later Jack's enthusiasm for the game had sunk as low as his stack of chips. A hundred in the hole and wishing he'd gotten more sleep this week than he had, he tapped his finger impatiently on the green felt. "Give me another card and hold the sarcasm, Troy."

"But you've been so much fun to rag tonight."

And didn't he know it. "It won't be near as fun when I stuff that rag up your ass; you hear me?" Chuckles circled the table.

"Lima Charlie, my friend."

"What'll be 'loud and clear' is my reaction if I don't get my card in three…two…"

Troy smirked, and the card off the top of the deck landed in front of Jack just as the word *one* left his lips. Jack exchanged the new card for a face card he no longer needed. Most of the players sitting around the table followed suit, exchanging one or two cards for something in their hand. Much to Jack's amusement, Troy took three cards. The bouncer gave him a dirty look when he sniggered.

Tommy Ray folded with a colorful curse. "I'll go get some snacks while you guys finish up. Any requests?"

"For you to stop calling me 'guy'?" Evelyn calmly threw two chips into the center pile, but none of them were fooled. The older woman wore her gender as a badge of pride—especially when she beat the rest of them. Tommy Ray grumbled an answer on the way to the kitchen.

"Don't forget the hot sauce," Evelyn called after his retreating back.

"What d'ya say, John?" Troy asked.

"I say read 'em and weep." He laid out an ace-high flush.

Damn it.

Harold shook his head. "The Lord giveth, and the Lord taketh away."

"Mostly he's taking away tonight," Jack said, throwing his cards down with disgust. John's chuckle as he collected the pile of chips from the middle of the table qualified more for the devil than the Lord, though.

A heavy growl rumbled in Jack's stomach. He stood, his muscles aching as he stretched. "I'll go help Tommy Ray."

Catcalls followed him across the barroom to Halftime's kitchen. Jack pushed one hand behind his hip—the opposite one to Harold's chair—and shot a bird back at his tormenters.

"Tommy Ray, you might be short one bouncer tomorrow ni—"

Maddie glanced up at him from the opposite end of the kitchen. She was standing at the back counter, a piece of celery in hand. Something about the way her tongue cleaned the drop of ranch dressing from her lower lip made his jeans tighter than they had been ten seconds ago.

"Maddie." Jesus, how could this be happening again? It was like a punch to the gut, this hard arousal that hit every time he saw her. But it wasn't just the need to fist her hair and fuck her mouth with his tongue that gathered in his belly. It was anticipation. He liked the challenge. This woman's pissy tongue and prickly hide were just as much of an aphrodisiac as her beautiful body.

Maddie cocked one perfectly arched eyebrow in his direction. "Jackass."

His breath stuttered in his lungs, which just proved his point, damn it. He'd thought to get his equilibrium back, to meet her again on equal ground. He was beginning to see how flimsy—and overrated—that equilibrium was.

"She's got your number, don't she?" Tommy Ray laughed, his belly shaking over his belt as he stood at the fryer.

Okay, I deserved that. He wouldn't even defend himself. It wouldn't be any use anyway; she wasn't gonna give an inch. The knowledge shot a tingle through his balls that propelled him forward. He held her dark brown stare as he moved deeper into the kitchen, noting the slight smirk tilting her full lips, the only real clue to the amusement he knew she felt. He couldn't read it in her eyes, her expression, just that tiny curve. This was a woman who held her cards very close to her chest. Unfortunately for her, Jack was very good at reading tells.

Tommy Ray and the snacks were bypassed in favor of Maddie's small basket of wings and fries.

"I figured you were gone by now."

Maddie lifted the celery. "Late dinner." She took a bite, white teeth gleaming against green flesh, then set the rest of the stalk down and picked up a french fry.

Jack reached for a wing coated in Tommy Ray's signature barbecue sauce.

"Mine," Maddie snapped, smacking his hand away.

43

Tommy Ray roared, reminding Jack that he had an audience. He ignored it, grinning down at the little imp. She might not admit it, but amusement danced in her shadowed eyes. The question was, why? Why was she so buttoned-down that even a genuine laugh was a rare occurrence? In his experience no one was that closed off without a damn good reason. Finding that reason just became his mission.

"I'm sorry," he told her.

"You ought to be. That's my dinner."

While she spoke, he sneaked a wing from the basket. Holding it up, he told her, "Not about that." The wing was in his mouth before she could snatch it back. He chewed and swallowed, savoring the meat as much as he did her fuming. Each finger was sucked clean of sauce before he continued. "I meant for the other night. I was in a pissy mood, and I took it out on you. I'm sorry."

"You come in here and tell me you're sorry and steal my food all in the same breath?"

He shrugged, barely suppressing a grin. Maddie responded with a frown and a wily finger pulling her basket of wings away from him.

Yeah, not gonna give an inch.

"Who got you in a pissy mood?" she asked before taking a big bite of wing.

"My business partner." Licking her lips really was unfair in this little competition they were having.

"Well, remind me not to piss you off directly then."

He couldn't tear his gaze away from her mouth, which was why her response didn't register for a moment in his desire-hazed brain. When it did, he shook his head. "Considering how this relationship is starting off," he said, words full of faux sadness, "I can pretty much guarantee that will happen at some point in the future."

"Good." She grinned—a full one this time—stuffed the last french fry in her mouth, and took the basket to the sink.

"Course, I can't promise not to do the same."

"Then quitting's my only option," she said over her shoulder, the words lilting around her still-curved mouth.

No way in hell. When Jack snapped around to catch Tommy Ray's reaction, the man chuckled. "Uh-uh." He piled baskets of food on a massive tray, his expression indulgent. "You're the first bartender I haven't wanted to kill besides John. You're not going anywhere, missy."

Jack could relate. He no longer wanted his hands around Maddie's neck; he wanted them on her body, and he wasn't about to miss the chance to make that happen.

Something soft sneaked into Maddie's eyes as she looked at Tommy Ray, there and gone again, returning to their usual unreadable state. "It's a necessity. If I have to come in to work every day and see his obnoxious face"—she nodded in Jack's direction—"I'm going to start pouring drinks over heads. Or breaking a lot more than noses."

"I guess I'll just have to compensate Tommy Ray for any business he loses."

She narrowed her eyes at him. He stared right back, barely withholding his amusement. Two could play at that game. Except he'd realized sometime in the last few minutes that it wasn't just a game anymore. He hadn't been this challenged and excited—and yes, horny—in months, and he refused to give that up. He wasn't going to leave her alone. He was going to wear her down and enjoy every minute of doing it.

"Well, that doesn't leave me much choice, does it?" she asked.

"Nope."

She started to wash her dishes, refusing to respond. Jack dragged a stool close to the sink and took a seat. It was time for Maddie to realize exactly what she was up against.

They played Mexican standoff until she finished in the sink. When she turned off the water and reached for a towel to dry her hands, Jack was right there.

She stared at the towel in his hands, water dripping from her fingers onto the floor. Without waiting for her to decide, he reached out and grasped one hand between his. Maddie startled, stepped back, but though she pulled, he refused to release her hand. As he rubbed the towel over each finger, her palm, the back of her hand, he watched her eyes dilate, her breathing quicken until he wondered if—and kind of hoped—she might pop the single shiny button holding her vest closed. Her surprise kept her compliant as he switched hands, drying the other one

46

and enjoying the look of hunger barely shimmering across her face.

The moment didn't last, though. As if finally realizing what was happening, Maddie snatched her hand back. "Don't."

"Why not?"

She didn't answer. The stubborn press of her lips holding back the words made him want to kiss her, to break through that ironclad control until all the reasons for her withdrawal, all the secrets she held, spilled out. Maddie was a woman with a lot of secrets, secrets that kept her apart from life. He'd simply have to peel them away one by one until nothing was left between them but skin and sweat and sex. And God, he couldn't wait for the sex.

He leaned forward, deliberately invading her space, warming her skin with his breath. "Maddie—"

Swiping her hands on her jeans as if Jack had somehow contaminated her with his touch, Maddie turned away from him. "I'm headed out, Tommy Ray."

The older man grunted a reply as he lifted the tray of food for the poker gang. "Drive safe."

"I'll walk you to your car," Jack told her.

"No." She kept walking. A leather backpack, worn with use, waited near the back door. Maddie slung it onto her shoulder without a backward glance.

Jack followed her out the door. "It's not optional, so stop arguing—if you ever stop arguing."

"I don't."

"Is that supposed to scare me off?" he asked. The hot Georgia night immediately beaded sweat on his brow. He swiped at it, ignoring her ignoring him. "I'm the kind of guy who loves a challenge, you know."

That's when she did stop and turn around. The look on her face said she knew that pesky character trait already—and it didn't make her happy.

Too damn bad.

He grinned. Maddie walked away without comment. When he saw the motorcycle she was approaching, he held back a groan. *First the boots, now a motorcycle. This woman just hits every one of my buttons, doesn't she?*

"Nice bike."

Maddie climbed on.

"Did you fix her up yourself?"

She leaned forward to turn the key. Her position showcased that delicious ass. She revved the engine while he swallowed his tongue.

"Maddie—"

When she pushed the kickstand up, he knew he was losing her. "Maddie, you didn't say you forgive me."

She threw him a look over her shoulder, the shadows hiding her eyes. They didn't hide her smirk, however. "I'll let you know."

And then she was gone.

Chapter Four

Maddie stared at Jack on his regular bar stool the next night and wondered what little worm had burrowed down into his brain. *Third night; third time's the charm, maybe?*

God, she hoped not. The strain of avoiding him was wearing her down. So was the strain of failing, like last night. He'd touched her like she mattered, like it mattered that he do some small kindness for her. She'd cursed her inability to move and to forget a million times since, but it didn't stop the memory from looping in her head. She felt branded in a way she couldn't explain, and the thought swirled panic and excitement in her belly in almost equal measure.

So now I'm a sadistic bitch and *a harlot. Great. David would be proud.*

Not that it mattered. Wanting Jack was a far cry from actually sleeping with him. She had no doubt she could resist the latter, even if the former kept jumping her bones at the most inopportune moments. Like now.

She had to get this obsession with him out of her head.

Seated next to Jack was a man that could've been his bookend, they looked so alike. The easy way the two men talked and laughed told her they'd known each other a long time. His brother, maybe? A

49

pang of envy hit her at the thought. She'd never had a sibling. Her parents—

No, she couldn't go there; she couldn't go to any of the places she'd been visiting with far too much frequency lately. Squaring her shoulders, she let her mask settle onto her face as she crossed the room. Not a moment too soon, either, because Jack's gaze met hers long before she reached the bar. The impact was like a missile hitting its mark, battering at her walls, doing its best to crumble any barrier it encountered. She held the look through sheer will until John's greeting pulled her away.

"Maddie." John gave her a nod, already wadding up his apron.

"It's busier than I expected tonight." Saturday nights were always busy, no matter the bar, but somehow she hadn't realized the Halftime could hold this many people. Surely there was a fire ordinance they were breaking.

John moved to gather his stuff from beneath the bar top. "It is. You sure you can cover things all right?"

"I have done this before, you know." She'd tended bar for years—she hadn't lied when she'd told Tommy Ray that. Her first job after…her first job behind a bar had been Arkansas. She'd tried waitressing, but the money flowed with the liquor, so she'd wheedled her way into a friendship with the gruff bartender at that hole-in-the-wall that held a much lower place on the sliding scale of class than the Halftime. The old man had known his stuff, though, and taught her well. No, she wasn't worried about covering anything tonight. Except Jack.

John tossed her a carefree grin that made her feel a hundred years old. "I have no doubts. And the girls will help when you get slammed."

"Sure, sure." She waved him along. "Now get to class. You've got finals coming up." She remembered well how tough summer semesters were, so much crammed into a few short, sweltering weeks.

"Yes, ma'am."

Maddie rolled her eyes and took his place, grabbing her customary dry towel and looping it on her belt. She studiously ignored the tall, dark, and brooding presence at the other end of the bar. Or rather, two presences, though Jack's friend was a little less broody and a lot more...something. Friendly, maybe? It was his aura, or maybe it was just the comparison to Jack's that made him seem more approachable.

The man was also drop-dead gorgeous, no doubt about that, but Jack... She sucked in a breath and pulled her gaze away before the two men noticed her surreptitious glances.

Jack was just so damn big. What, did they grow 'em for their muscles around here? Really, it was ridiculous. And unfair. He could use his size against her—she knew that far more than most—and still she had that stupid feminine melty reaction to those broad shoulders encased in a skintight black T-shirt. The heavy muscles along his chest and arms were showcased perfectly, her tightening thighs told her. Ridiculous.

And Jack's eyes. She peeked again. Those dark eyes were fixed on her once more, but...

A shiver hit her spine.

Something had changed. She didn't know what, but that look was nothing like the way he'd looked at her before. Last night he'd been overwhelming, but now? She swore, watching him watch her, that she felt him listing all the ways he could take her down like a gazelle in the Sahara. This time holding his gaze was impossible.

She'd avoid the man all night if she could, but the two empty beer glasses sitting on the bar finally had her heading in that direction. Sure as shit Jack would report her to Tommy Ray just to get a rise out of her. Not that she planned to give him great customer service. The thought of exactly what she would give him brought a smirk to her lips.

She kept her attention on Jack's friend as she approached.

The man's eyes were light gray but just as intent as Jack's brown ones. She gave him the easy, slightly flirtatious smile she practiced on every male customer. "Need a refill?"

"Hey. Yeah, that would be great." He extended his glass toward her. "Conlan James."

"Maddie." She picked up Jack's glass without asking.

"Hey, Maddie."

Lord, even his voice made her shiver, and not in the way it should. The awareness in his eyes said he knew it too. This man knew far too much, it seemed. She had to convince him he didn't. "Jack."

She turned, but before she could manage a step, Jack was reaching for her. Maddie caught the motion from the corner of her eye and shifted instinctively to face him. "Did you need something else?"

He raised the hand to rub at the back of his neck instead, a sheepish smile the icing on the cake of his good looks. Conlan turned toward his friend, seeming to likewise wonder what Jack was getting at.

"I...I needed you to stay. Talk to us. You know..."

"Oh my God, he's speechless. What did you dose him with?" she asked Con. "By now he's usually jumping down my throat."

"Am not. At least..." Jack seemed to think about that a minute, then mumbled a grudging, "I said I was sorry. I just..."

Maddie raised an inquiring brow, clamping down on the sudden urge to smile. She'd never seen such a tough guy look so embarrassed. Apparently Conlan hadn't either, because he was currently hiding a grin behind a big hand.

"Okay, I needed to prove I could play nice and make friends."

She already knew that. Everybody in this place loved him, especially the women, but he deserved to be taken down a peg or two; his ego was way too big as it was. "I can see that," she told him. "Good boy."

Conlan howled. The man was practically rolling in his seat, he laughed so hard. Maddie let a chuckle peek through.

And that's what you get for telling me to "stay," Jack.

"She— You—" Conlan's laughter left no room to form words.

Jack shot a sour glance Conlan's way and, when his friend wasn't looking, shoved him off his bar stool. Conlan kept on laughing. Jack turned the look on Maddie. She covered her glee with a what-did-I-do? expression.

Conlan finally managed to crawl, still laughing, back onto his stool. He wiped tears from his eyes. "She has a sharp tongue. I like her."

Just for that, he earned her brightest bartender smile.

"Watch it," Jack said. "Her elbows are even sharper."

The comment set off another round of laughter. Jack just watched, silent, but she thought she detected a spark of amusement in his eyes. Yep, there it was, in between the flecks of amber. The sight birthed a strange ache behind her breastbone. When Jack shifted and their eyes met, held, the ache grew stronger.

She gestured with the glasses she held. "I'll just get your drinks." Jack's silence filled her ears, louder than Conlan's laughter and even the noise of the bar.

The chaos of a crowded Friday night was the perfect excuse to stay busy, but avoiding Jack was impossible. He spent the next few hours in that spot at the end of the bar, even when Con, as Conlan insisted she call him, abandoned him for a round of pool. She had to admit, Jack had a charm that drew people, got them talking, and, added to his looks, it

54

made every woman in his vicinity swoon. She spent as much time as she could far away from that end of the bar. When midnight hit, she tagged one of the waitresses, Brandy, to take over for a desperately needed break, timing her escape at a moment when Jack was deep in conversation with Con and one of the locals about the building of a new superstore on the outskirts of town.

The dance floor had cleared out a bit as people stopped to eat, drink, talk. If she wanted to get to the break room, that was the only feasible path, so she set out to dodge the obstacle course of moving couples. Her feet throbbed in time with each step, telling her exactly how long of a night it had been. All she could think about was getting to the back and getting off them for the next half hour. She'd made it about three-quarters of the way across when a firm grip circled her biceps and pulled backward.

Her heart slammed into her throat. Between one moment and the next she went into fight mode, but as she turned around, Jack crowded into her, leaving no room to throw a punch. The hard feel of his chest against hers told her it wouldn't have mattered anyway, but the adrenaline dump was already there, her heart already racing. It pissed her off. A jab to Jack's ribs left her feeling slightly better.

"Ow!"

"Don't sneak up on me," she told him.

"Then don't sneak away from me," he shot back. He took both arms into his possession, keeping her close when she would have backed up. "You are not getting away from me that easily."

The current song ended with a hoot and holler from the crowd. When the strains of Rascal Flatt's "Stand" filtered through the speakers, Jack smiled. "Dance with me."

"Jack, I'm on break. I've been on my feet for six hours. I want to sit down." He'd been on his ass all night. And being this close to him was killing any perspective she might hope to have.

"Dance with me, Maddie."

"No."

Jack didn't respond. His intense eyes bored into her as if he could strip away her protests with nothing more than a look, delve into her psyche and find the approach that would get her to comply. She forced herself to be still, to wait him out, not give in to the need to flee, hide, anything but let this man get a centimeter deeper into her than he already had.

The lights over the dance floor dimmed. "Jack—"

"Just for a minute. Please."

She blinked.

Jack's hand left her arm, his fingers rising to brush across the heat of her cheek. Maddie's breath froze, her protest caught somewhere in her closed throat. Jack skimmed rough fingertips along her jaw, over to her ear, then into her hair, pushing back a strand that had somehow escaped. Amber streaks of fire lit in his eyes.

And still she stood there.

What the hell am I doing?

Jack's hand slid down to her shoulder, her arm, her elbow, the caress setting the tiny hairs along her forearm on end. She couldn't decide if that was good or bad. Jack didn't seem to notice, either what he was doing or her reaction. She glanced down to watch, to wait for the moment when his fingers slid from her skin, but instead they hooked into hers, tugging them lightly. The giddy feeling his touch sparked in her gut made her want to throw up, but when she looked at Jack, that same surprise was reflected in his face.

God, she couldn't do this. She had to leave, had to stop this before Jack realized exactly how damaged she was, how much she held back. Not knowing what to say, she yanked her fingers free and tried to turn away, but Jack was already there, his arm around her waist, his hand clasping hers. His feet moved, one step, two, and it was move or fall. The natural way she fell into rhythm with him had her heart slamming against her breastbone.

"Jack, I can't—"

He tucked his head down near hers to whisper in her ear. "Shhh. We do much better when we don't talk."

How true that was.

The cocoon of his body surrounding her shouldn't have felt good. She should be panicking instead of savoring the tangy scent of citrus and beer that filled her nose. Jack smelled good, felt good. Her body said this *was good*, even if her mind was recalling all the times a man surrounding her had been a nightmare. Apparently her body wasn't listening. It was reveling in the feel of Jack's solid chest flattening her breasts, the rock-hard plain of his stomach beneath her hands. The palm heating the hollow of her lower back said she was safe, protected; the one at her nape said he'd guide her wherever she needed to go.

It had never been like this before. It shouldn't be like this now. She had to put some distance between them.

"You really are a jackass, aren't you?"

Jack's laugh rumbled far too enticingly through his chest. The vibrations set off that unfamiliar ache once more. "You've just got to get to know me, that's all. I'm really charmin', just like everyone says."

"That's not all they say." She'd heard more about his adventures with the women in town than she'd ever cared to know.

Jack turned them, his thick thigh moving between hers, his erection brushing her hip. Maddie flinched automatically, but Jack's warm breath on her skin drew her in. She was too busy fighting the pull to be afraid.

"I know what all they say, Maddie," he whispered in her ear, "and believe me, it's all true. Every last word."

He tilted her chin up, and something soft and impossibly tender brushed the corner of her mouth. Jack's lips. *God.* For one beat of her heart, she closed her eyes and let herself fall into the feeling, relish human contact that wasn't joined to gut-wrenching fear or heart-hardening rage. And then the steps of the dance moved them into the path of another couple. The man's back hit Maddie's, pressing her flush against Jack.

Her vision went black. It was no longer Jack holding her, close but careful. It wasn't his hands gripping her arms. It wasn't his breath whispering across her skin as he bent over her. No, it was a hard, cruel grip, pain aching right down to the bone, the harsh whisper of cruel words in her ears. A tiny whimper, one she knew she must hold back at all costs, escaped.

"Maddie." Jack stopped moving, right there on the dance floor. "Maddie?"

She jerked back, his touch all at once hot, unbearable.

"You okay? You look—"

She could imagine how she looked. She never wanted anyone to see that look, ever. Ever. She closed her eyes, hiding, giving herself the time she needed to blank everything out.

And then she looked back at him. "I'm fine."

Jack shook his head, reached out to her. "Maddie—"

"I'm okay, really." She cleared her throat and turned away. "I just…I need to go."

She made it a few feet before Jack's voice stopped her. "Maddie."

She didn't turn around. "What?"

"You didn't answer me last night."

About what? And then she remembered his parting shot, and hers, out there in the parking lot. Turning her head, not quite to look at him but almost, she whispered under the straining music. "I forgive you."

And though he couldn't possibly have heard her, he said, "Then go out with me."

She couldn't answer. She walked away, and this time he let her go. But his stare seared her the whole way back to the break room, a brand she wasn't sure she could ever get rid of.

Chapter Five

Maddie's alarm went off at noon on Monday. After talking herself out of throwing it against the wall, she stumbled into the kitchen, dumped her backpack by the table, turned on the coffee, and slumped into a chair, bleary-eyed, until it was finished brewing. Her half-asleep brain screamed at her to get up, get moving, cleaning, cooking, anything to appear productive. Anything to avoid punishment. She closed her eyes instead and sat, soaking in the warmth of the quiet apartment. Only when the coffeepot beeped its readiness did she allow herself to move.

Coffee. Creamer, the flavored kind so she didn't need sugar. Spoon to stir. She felt herself coming online as the rich scent hit her nose, then her tongue. She looped her bag on her arm and cuddled the coffee cup like a sacred offering to her senses as she walked into the too-bright living room and sat on the couch. Half the cup was gone before she noticed she was sitting on a particularly prominent lump. Shifting to the opposite end of the couch helped a little. Darn rental furniture.

Her phone beeped at her as she turned it on. Thank God for Zylo and his false identification or she wouldn't have access to Wi-Fi. The forger had set her up with everything she needed for utilities, housing, even work. She didn't like using the documents more than she had to—too much of a trail to follow—but for reliable Internet access, she'd

61

do it. Driving to the library a couple of times a day wasn't feasible, and she couldn't track David's movements without it. Fortunately he was frequently in the news.

The phone beeped again and buzzed in her hand, a signal that she'd received a text. Her pulse sped up. Only two people had this number: Zylo and Tommy Ray. If it wasn't one of them, she might kill her spamming service provider for giving her a heart attack.

She tapped the text icon. Zylo's name came up.

Meet @ library ASAP.

Damn it. She didn't want to meet at the library; she'd just gotten up. But Z wouldn't contact her if it wasn't important. The text was time-stamped at nine this morning. She wanted to ask questions, find out what was going on, but the less she communicated with him, the better. She took the time to shoot him an *okay*, then hurried into the bedroom to dress. Her coffee went with her.

All the way to the library, the fact that Zylo had made contact niggled at the back of her brain. She could be walking into an ambush. It was impossible to know with certainty that a person had betrayed her until that person made their move, no matter how much she speculated; she'd learned that. The easiest thing was to limit contact. Fewer people equaled fewer opportunities for people to deceive her, to be bought out by David if the man tracked her down. It had happened before, but speculating about it was a one-way street to driving herself crazy. She put her head down and revved the motorcycle, ignoring the prayer that whispered in the back of her mind for everything to be okay.

The small Freeman Library was quiet on Monday afternoons. Maddie nodded at the blue-haired checkout lady who squinted at her from behind thick glasses, and wandered over to the reference section. At the back, out of sight, a carrel of desks offered the opportunity for quiet study. Maddie couldn't imagine too many students taking advantage of the spot, but she did, sitting in the last nook on the row and taking out her phone. How did people manage to appear busy before the advent of cell phones?

Ten minutes later when the chair next to hers was pulled out, Maddie refused to look up. What sounded like a heavy stack of books thudded onto the desk, and then a slim young man, one she knew looked more like a surfer than a scholar, settled into the chair. Just the thought of his spiky hair, streaked with pink, had her holding back a smile.

"What the hell, Z?" They all had letters, the underground ones. She'd actually joked that he was the last, the end of the line. She certainly hoped not.

"Sorry, Maddie. I had a few more books to pick up."

"To read or to copy?"

He chuckled. "Good one."

Maddie imagined his pale green eyes flashing with amusement. The kid—he had to be almost a decade younger than she was—always seemed to be amused. His thin lips wore a smirk like they'd been created for it.

"What do you need, Z?"

Zylo shifted on his hard wooden chair. "Jeez, no wonder no one sits here. A little padding wouldn't kill them."

"Z…"

"All right, all right. No sense of humor."

That happened when someone was trying to kill you.

"David is coming to town next week to speak at a law convention in Atlanta."

Maddie's heartbeat thudded in her throat. "I could've found that out on the Internet, Z." And not been scared to death all the way over here.

"Word on the street is, his buddy's coming with him. Got some business to take care of. Something big."

Shit. Was it Vaneqe? Were they bringing her back here? If they even had her. Maddie could be on a wild-goose chase, putting herself in harm's way for nothing—even if her instincts said otherwise.

"What's the something big?"

Zylo snorted. "Do your own dirty work, girl."

Maddie ignored the sarcasm. If Z really felt that way, he'd never have contacted her. Apparently interest in other people was as foreign to him as it was to her.

"Okay." She slid her phone into her back pocket. "Have a nice day."

"Wait—" Z grabbed her forearm when she started to stand. She had his wrist in a lock faster than he could draw a breath. "Ow, damn it! I'm sorry. Let go, Madelyn."

She tightened her grip as she leaned in close. "Don't ever call me that again, got it? It's Madison, not Madelyn." Not ever again.

"Got it."

She loosened her hold, and Zylo turned to stare up at her. "I'm sorry, *Maddie*. Don't be so touchy." He glanced at her hand, still wrapped around his wrist.

"You first." But she let go.

"I got the message." He massaged his wrist. "I want to know what you've found out."

That had all her senses zinging to alert. "Why?"

"Why? For God's sake, Maddie, I live here. This is my town. If someone's helping that bastard, they're incredibly good, because I know everyone in the underground and I don't know them. I'll do anything I can to shut 'em down."

She narrowed her eyes, searching his face—for what exactly, she wasn't sure, but she needed to know whatever it was. The fierce green fire staring steadily back at her, enduring the scrutiny without flinching, convinced her he was telling the truth—or he was a very good actor, but it didn't matter either way. She had nothing to tell him.

"I haven't found out anything definitive yet. Whoever it is covers their tracks well, assuming there is someone. David could just as easily be using a roving band of cutthroats."

65

"Cutthroats? You've seen one too many pirate movies."

"Yeah, well, what else you gonna do at three o'clock in the morning?"

Z shuddered. "Not that." His glance softened. "Thanks, Maddie."

"Thank you." Any help she could get, she'd take. "Gotta run."

Zylo watched her walk away but didn't tell her good-bye.

Fierce late August heat slapped her as she exited the library. By the time she made it back to the apartment, she knew she had to move forward. Z's information had put an exclamation point on what she needed to do. She'd gotten good information at the Halftime, despite the distraction that was named Jack, but she needed more. She needed direct contact with the people who knew Vaneqe best, who could give her details about the kidnapping that might click with the evidence Maddie had gathered on her end. It was going to be a slow process, earning the trust of the director so she could get into Hope Place itself, then earning the trust of the residents, but she could do it. She needed to do it today, before David discovered she'd brought the fight right to his backyard.

At home she retrieved the contact information for the shelter from the kitchen table, then returned to the living room with a glass of icy water. Between sips she stared at the phone and tried to ignore the rumble of nerves that masqueraded as hunger in her belly. There was so much riding on this one call. She couldn't screw it up.

The phone's low beeps as she tapped each digit into the keypad reminded her of the countdown to a bomb exploding. Maddie ignored the ominous feel and the death grip she had on the phone and instead counted off the rings as they came through the line.

One.

Two.

Three.

Four.

Maybe the office staff was out to a late lunch. Maybe they were closed on Mondays. She pulled the phone away from her ear, finger hovering over End Call.

The ringing was replaced by the hollow sound of air as the call was answered. Maddie pulled the suddenly hundred-pound phone back to her ear.

"Hope Place. This is Margaret."

The woman's voice held a faint, familiar Southern accent. Maddie's reply stuck in her throat, pounding out the rhythm of her heart.

"Hello?"

Maddie finally managed to untangle her tongue. "Umm, hello. My name is Maddie Baker."

"Good morning. How might I help you, Maddie?"

A grimace twisted Maddie's lips as the woman's politeness twisted her heart. Thank God Margaret was on the other end of a phone line instead of in the room. Surely the word *liar* was written in red across Maddie's forehead.

It's not like you aren't actually going to volunteer; you are. That's not lying.

And even if it was, Maddie couldn't afford to care. Vaneqe couldn't afford for her to care. She cleared her dry-as-dust throat with a quick sip of water, slid on her happy-bartender persona, and forged ahead. "Actually, I was hoping to help you. I wanted to see if you have positions open for volunteers."

"We certainly do. Was there something specific you had in mind?"

"No, ma'am. I heard about you through a coworker, Taylor Curtis."

"You work at the Halftime, then."

Maddie rolled the woman's tone around in her mind. No disapproval. *This might actually work.* "Yes."

"Well, there's always something that needs doin' around here and never enough hands to do it, so an extra pair is surely welcome. Why don't you come in to the office Wednesday around three and we can see about fixin' you up?"

Her muscles went lax in relief. Maddie caught her glass before it fell and resettled it firmly on her thigh. "Would one be possible? I have the early shift Wednesday night."

"Sure, hon. Just let me get some information."

Her earlier flush returned. *Here we go.* Carefully she answered each of Marge's questions, for a background check, she presumed. She'd paid Zylo dearly to pass it. Her forged history had done fine so far; hopefully it would do equally well now.

Seemingly unaware of her anxiety, Marge gave her directions to offices across town. They wouldn't be anywhere near the shelter itself, of course, in order to keep the women who took refuge there safe. Visiting the actual shelter would require a lot more hoops than a background check, none of which had to do with official information. Maddie knew from experience. She also knew she could meet every challenge. She had to.

Margaret's good-bye was firm but friendly, her accent still in evidence. Maddie hung up and blew out the breath she'd been holding.

Okay.

At least they hadn't turned her down. Step one complete. As she gathered her laundry to carry the two blocks to the Freeman City Laundromat, she prayed the steps to follow fell into place as easily.

Chapter Six

"Jack."

Margaret's voice triggered the same gentle flow of comfort that he imagined warm cookies and cold milk did. He hadn't grown up with a mama that provided those things, which was why he was grateful that Margaret Hawthorne was the director of Hope Place. He leaned back in his cushioned desk chair, a smile tugging at his lips. "Hey, Marge. How's today going?"

"Like someone set fire to my feet and forgot to tell me where the fire extinguisher was."

"So, normal, huh?"

Marge blew a loud raspberry through the phone, but he could hear the amusement underlying it. The woman loved every minute of the chaos the shelter provided, whether she'd admit it aloud or not. And to prove his point, a cacophony of shrieks and running footsteps and bangs came through the line. Marge yelled after the kids, her reprimand sounding more indulgent than threatening.

He laughed. Marge ruled with a will of iron, but the children found ways to get around her. It didn't help that they knew she was equally a sucker for a pout or a smile on their faces.

Of course, so was he. An afternoon spent wrestling with some of the younger boys at the shelter had become the most worthwhile part of his weekends lately. Especially one particular little boy, the one who was no longer speaking to him.

When the noise wound down, Jack cleared his throat. "Did you have a reason for calling, darlin'?"

He expected a snappy comeback to his teasing, but Marge turned serious. "I had a talk with Charlie today."

Jack put a steel clamp around his hopes. "And?"

"And…he said no."

His heart wrenched. Hard.

"He's just a kid, Jack. Give him time. Heck, follow the stubborn thing out into the woods. Once he sees you—"

"No." Jack would come out to the shelter on Saturday like he always did, but he would respect the boy's refusal to see him. Still, it was a punch to the gut every time. Jack took it like the soldier he'd been for so long. "He has to come around on his own."

"He will. You know he will."

"Maybe. I've disappointed him." Charlie'd had far too much of that in his young life. "Disappointed myself too."

"You've done the best you could." Margaret's voice took on the growl of a mama lion. "If anyone could find Vaneqe, it's you. We can't give up yet, on her or Charlie."

"I won't." He'd search for Charlie's sister until he found her; he didn't care how long it took. Which might be a while considering he had literally nothing to go on.

Charlie and Vaneqe Wilson had been at Hope Place three months when Vaneqe disappeared, just long enough to worm their way into his heart. Into everyone's hearts, actually, which was why none of them bought the story the police had settled on: a homeless black teen abandoning her younger brother to run off to freedom. Charlie had been plugged into the system, and both kids seemed to have been forgotten about. Even Jack's contacts on the force hadn't been able to get the case jump-started.

It had been almost four weeks now, and he knew better than most that four weeks could be a death sentence on the streets. He was doing what he could on his own, but he simply didn't have enough pieces to put them together. It truly was as if the girl had walked out the door and vanished into thin air.

The helplessness of the thought burned. Jack didn't do helpless well.

Marge was still talking. "It would help if I can get him into school, get his days occupied, but the counselor will only agree to admit him if he goes into a lower grade. She says he's too far behind."

Jack grunted. "School just started. What about a tutor?"

"He won't work with any of us. Just sits there and stares until we let him go. I'm at my wit's end, Jack."

Marge's frustration gave his name a hard edge, but Jack didn't take it personally. He was frustrated too. He tried to help all the children and their mothers who came through Hope Place. They needed more than his hacking skills and his ability to fight;

they needed someone to care. But Charlie? There was just something special about Charlie, something that reminded Jack of the ten-year-old boy he'd been back before he met Conlan and their friend Lee and realized there was more out there for him than the foster system he'd been shoved into after his mother's death. He wanted to give Charlie that same gift, but first he had to give the boy back his sister.

His office door opened, and Conlan strolled in, two large cardboard cups in hand, the scent of coffee immediately filtering through the air. Jack covered the receiver.

"Just a minute, 'kay?"

Con smirked as he handed over one of the cups. "What, do I look like I've got nothing better to do than twiddle my thumbs while I wait on you?"

Jack lifted his coffee. "You look more like a lackey."

Con snorted but sat in one of the two chairs waiting in front of Jack's desk.

"Sorry, Marge." Jack caught the handset between his ear and shoulder and used both hands to take the lid off his coffee. "Con just came in."

"No worries. Give that boy a hug for me." He heard papers shuffling on the other end of the line as he palmed the handset once more and carefully sipped his steamy drink. "I shouldn't keep you, but I did have another reason for calling." More shuffling. "Ah, there it is. There's a new volunteer I need you to work up."

Hope Place might appreciate more than his hacking skills, but sometimes hacking was exactly what they needed. He ran background checks on volunteers, tracked deadbeat fathers, whatever Margaret and the women needed. Even a few things Atlanta PD would lock him up for. They'd have to catch him first, of course.

"Sure thing. What's the name?"

"Maddie Baker."

The coffee he'd just sipped hit his windpipe. "Who?"

Margaret's voice filtered through the epic coughing fit that followed, asking if he was all right.

"Uh"—*cough*—"sure. Just a"—*cough*—"minute."

He covered the phone, coughed some more. Con watched, laughing.

"Don't help or anything, dumb-ass," Jack choked out.

Another laugh. "Okay."

Jack uncovered the phone. "Sorry about that," he said, voice raspy. "So, Maddie…" What was her last name again?

"Madison Baker. She called this morning to ask about volunteer positions. Seems like a nice girl, but you know no one comes in here unless you've vetted them first."

He didn't respond to the nice-girl comment. Maddie was nice when she wanted to be. When she was riled? She fought dirty, and her tongue was caustic, to put it mildly. Too bad that trait just made her hotter in his estimation.

He didn't figure Marge needed to know that.

Marge gave him Maddie's information, and he wrote it down automatically, his thoughts on how she'd felt against him last night. Shifting in his seat didn't help as shit got tight behind his zipper. His libido had gone totally off the rails from what he could tell. Remembering a dance with a woman—or any other fully clothed activity—had never earned so much as a twitch from his dick, but Maddie did. Of course, everything about Maddie made him hard.

He glanced at his straining pants. Yeah, completely off the rails.

Still, his conscience wouldn't let him do anything less than a thorough investigation, no matter the candidate. He wouldn't risk Hope Place for a woman he'd known a week, no matter how much she drew him. And his curiosity had absolutely nothing to do with it. Nothing.

He shifted again, cleared his throat. A glance up caught an uncomfortably speculative look on Con's face, half-hidden by his coffee cup.

"I'll look into it and let you know, Marge."

"Thank you." Marge hesitated. "I guess you'll call before you come on Saturday."

So she could warn Charlie. The boy would disappear into the woods and not reappear until Jack left. Again. "Yeah."

"See you then."

Jack signed off.

"Maddie? Your Maddie? That's quite a coincidence, isn't it?"

Glancing up, Jack met his friend's intense gaze. When he wanted to, Con could bore into someone's psyche with those steel-gray eyes of his. Unfortunately he wanted to right now, and Jack was equally determined not to allow it. His psyche was fucked up enough without sharing it.

He ignored the question, instead nodding toward the coffee Con had brought him. "Don't think you can come in here and butter me up, you traitor. I'm still not ready to forgive you for Saturday night."

Of course, that hadn't kept him from drinking said bribe. He took another quick sip.

"Oh come on. All I did was laugh. You, on the other hand, threw me off my chair."

The reminder brought a satisfied smile to Jack's lips. "That's the second time you've landed on my shit list."

"You're still throwing last week in my face?" Con's empty cup sailed through the air, barely missing Jack's head. "You needed a night off. It was supposed to make you feel better, not get your panties in a twist. Besides, all I did was insist."

"You sicced Lori on me. She led me to the elevator by my ear!"

"And I got it on video too," Con said, his smug smile tempting Jack to punch him. Their receptionist was a bulldog. All Con had to do was mention what he wanted and wait—camera at the ready, apparently. "What'll ya give me not to show it at this year's Christmas party?"

"The back end of my fist?"

Con cowered playfully in his seat, waving limp hands in front of him. "Please, no! I'm shaking in my boots."

"You're not wearing boots, ass hat." Jack threw a pen at Con's head, just to reciprocate. Con caught it neatly on the downslide. Jack muttered not so nice words at his friend as he turned to his computer. "Did you bring the time sheets?"

The loud slap of files on his desk was his only answer. Jack eyed the stack with resignation.

"So, Maddie?"

Jack valiantly refrained from rolling his eyes. Lori wasn't the only bulldog in this office. He reached for the files. "She's volunteering at Hope Place. Marge wants a workup, that's all." He flipped the top file open, pretending extreme interest in the uninteresting printout on top.

"Uh-huh." Con twirled the pen Jack had thrown at him around his fingers. "And how do you feel about that?"

"Who are you, Oprah?" Feelings. Jack glared at his friend. Con returned the favor with a bland stare.

"You know, before you introduced us, you told me she was trouble. You didn't tell me she was beautiful."

Con's idea of gorgeous and Jack's ran along the same lines, as evidenced by the fact that Jess, Con's wife, was a petite, curvy beauty just like Maddie. Jack loved Jess like a sister, but Maddie... *She's the sexiest thing I've seen in my entire life. She's got my boxers so twisted I can't think about anything else, and it's driving me insane.*

He'd keep that to himself. He'd keep it all to himself. "She's pissy."

77

"She gets to you." The words were speculative. "That's why you didn't mention it, because she gets under your skin."

That's putting it mildly.

"She's perfect for you, isn't she? You like her. You like her a lot."

He glared at Con, gloating at him across his desk. No one should gloat in another man's office. "Sometimes I hate you."

Con shot him a big grin. "I know. Now what're you waiting for?" He nodded toward Jack's computer. "You know you want to know."

"Do you think Jess would be as agreeable if she'd known you ran a background check on her before you slept together?"

"See! I knew you planned to sleep with her."

Grumbling the whole time—because really, he wasn't a good enough liar to deny that one—Jack turned to his computer, pulled up a search program, entered Maddie's name, and set it to run.

An hour later, payroll only half-done, the computer beeped. Jack leaned over to check the results and frowned.

Con didn't glance up from the spreadsheet he was filling in. "What's it say?"

"I'm getting nothin'."

Con snorted. "Well, that doesn't surprise me in the least, if you're as grouchy with women as you are with me lately."

"What?" Jack shook his head. "Not sex, you idiot. This search, it's coming up empty. Well, not empty." Any other basic search probably would've passed inspection just fine. Jack's program, however, had a few special modifications. All of Maddie's basic information stacked up, but there was no history behind it. No name changes, address changes, school records, or any records at all beyond five years ago. For all intents and purposes, Maddie only existed on baseline, current official records.

Con dropped the paperwork onto the desk and came around to look at the screen. He scanned the short list of information. "Well, I'll be damned."

Jack too. His instincts were screaming that something wasn't right.

"So…" Con straightened. "Maybe a different spelling?"

"With the same social security number?" Con knew better than that. "You know what this reminds me of, don't you?"

"Zylo."

They both said it at the same time. Zylo was a local forger, one Jack had trusted more times than he'd like when they had a case that needed special attention. Jack had served his country all over the world, worked with and supported law enforcement every day, but he wasn't above breaking those same laws if it was the right thing to do. The system wasn't perfect. Women in danger fell through the cracks. He saw it over and over again; hell, he'd lived it until he was ten years old and that same system finally took charge of his little orphaned ass. If he had to hide a woman—or her children—from her abuser, he'd do it by any means necessary, including hacking into whatever he had to hack or hiring Zylo's magic hands.

Hands that created profiles for the women they needed to hide that looked very much like this. A standard background check would verify the current information, including lack of an arrest record. Jack's software delved deeper for this very reason.

Had Zylo created a fake identity for Maddie?

His mind drifted back to those moments on the dance floor. Every time he'd touched her, she tensed, as if she couldn't trust the pleasure, couldn't get used to someone handling her body. It wasn't shyness, though—the woman didn't appear to have a shy bone in her body. He remembered the wonder in her eyes the other night when she'd watched his fingertips drifting over her skin. That little whimper that had torn his heart out. The way she pushed him—and everyone else—away with false charm or, in his case, blatant dismissal, when he could see the longing in her eyes, read it in her body. There was obviously something there he hadn't yet gained access to. Could this be it?

Con's mind seemed to be running the same pathways. "You need to get closer."

Jack nodded. There were a couple of other avenues he could explore, but the fastest and easiest way to find out what he needed to know was from the source. That decision had nothing to do with the way his body went haywire when this particular target was in close proximity, either.

Get real.

"You're already interested in her; I can tell, no matter how much you deny it," Con said and repeated his earlier words. "You obviously want to know."

And Jack did. He was practically jumping out of his chair, he wanted to know so badly. "If she did use Z, there's likely a good reason."

It fit; it all fit.

"Can you trust yourself to take this further?"

The question burned. Jack let a snort answer for him.

"I'm serious, Jack. The whole world turns on its fucking head when feelings get involved." And Con would know. He'd twisted himself into knots over Jess before the two finally came together.

Jack met Con's concerned gaze. "I can do this."

Con nodded his agreement and moved back to his seat, no further words necessary. As they continued work on the time sheets, that tiny whimper Jack had heard Maddie utter rang in his ears. He'd hated that sound. It had made him want to crawl inside her and never leave, except maybe to kill the bastard who'd made her feel that way. And that wasn't just his libido talking. The question was, could he get Maddie to talk? He'd never had to work hard for a woman to come to him, open up to him. Maddie was proving a whole other breed of female in a lot of ways, sheer cussedness for one. Somehow he didn't think just asking outright was gonna work in this scenario.

Chapter Seven

Jack bypassed his usual bar stool Monday night. He bypassed the whole bar, in fact, instead waiting till closing time was half an hour away before sneaking in the back door. A quick glance into the main room showed Maddie chatting with a couple of older women as she cleaned behind the bar. Perfect.

The hall was clear as he made his way down to the break room, which was also clear. The back side of the break room held a wall of lockers, all closed, several with small padlocks to keep the contents secure. He started at the top left and worked his way right.

Five minutes, five locks, no backpack. If the damn locks weren't so old, he'd be done by now. Assuming the bag was here. It should be here. The woman never seemed to be without it unless she was bartending; no way had she left it at home. Dropping to the bottom row, Jack went to the leftmost locker and started again. The second lock on the row opened to reveal Maddie's bag sitting pretty in the shallow metal space.

Ignoring the guilt that roared through him, Jack retrieved the backpack, carefully closed the door, leaving the lock unhooked but in a position to appear closed unless one examined it closely, and stepped into the employee restroom. Maddie's bag was neat and tidy, everything in its place. Her wallet had a few twenties, some coins, and all the appropriate cards:

driver's license, car insurance, library card, a couple of discount cards, the kind the store scanned when you made a purchase but that didn't contain names. No health insurance cards. He filed his pang of concern in the same place he'd filed his guilt and kept searching.

Brush, makeup, cell phone charger, two thumb drives. He was tempted to take them, check them out, but not unless he had to—and based on the cards he'd seen already, he didn't have to. It wasn't that they didn't look legit; it was that they looked new. All of them. Even the bills he found—water, electricity, heat; who carried those carefully bundled in their purse?—were crisp and fresh, with dates ranging in the past few months. Papers carried around that long didn't look like they were fresh from the printer.

When he'd emptied the contents, he took a closer look at the liner. One rough area appeared to have been opened and resewn, if carefully enough that a casual glance wouldn't catch it. No time to open it now. Instead he felt carefully along the bottom of the bag adjacent to the patch. At first the bottom seemed solid, the kind of semirigid lining many backpacks had to keep them steady and upright when set on the ground. As he fingered the surface, however, he found lines. Seams. And tracing those seams showed rectangular areas about the size of dollar bills.

Maddie had stacks of cash sewn into the lining of her bag. A lot of it, if what he was feeling was correct.

The front of the backpack, like most, had two puffy pockets for incidentals, in Maddie's case lip balm in a couple of different flavors—*don't think about how they'd taste; if she catches you, you'll never find out*—a package of tissues, an extra hair clip. Between the front pockets and the central holding area, though, he could feel a few items in the lining. Probably anyone sticking their hand in the pocket wouldn't notice, maybe chalk it up to something rolling around on the inside of the bag, but the inside was empty right now. Careful examination revealed a couple of cylinder-like objects, maybe old-time film canisters, and what felt like four or five more flash drives.

So the ones lying free inside the bag were probably decoys, dummy drives. Someone found them, assumed they had whatever information they were looking for, took them, and missed the real gold mine in the lining.

This was Maddie's go bag, her escape pack, but escape from what? Looking down at the brown leather in his hands, he realized he couldn't imagine Maddie being afraid of anything or anyone. She was so full of spunk, so full of guts, that he couldn't figure fear into the equation of who she was. It didn't fit.

This bag said differently, and the answer to what she was running from was hidden in the lining of this pack.

Maddie, sweetheart, what have you gotten yourself into?

If he didn't get her bag back in the locker, he'd find out soon enough, and not in a way that would get her to trust him. And he did want her to

84

trust him; he realized that now more than ever. Yes, she'd appeared volatile the first time they met, but knowing her now, he could look back and see the deliberate control she'd used, control he'd missed because he'd been blinded by fear for her. He looked at her and saw not a spy or criminal, but a woman in need. He just prayed to God his instincts were leading him in the right direction. If something else was leading him, he'd be screwed before that something else ever got inside Maddie's sweet body.

Getting everything back in Maddie's bag and into the locker took less than a minute. He walked back toward the main room while he pulled his phone from his pocket, knowing what he had to do. Debating it anyway.

He pulled up Zylo's number.

The sound of fear escaping Maddie's lips on the dance floor echoed in his head.

He gritted his teeth. At the far end of the bar, Maddie loaded Brandy's tray with drinks. A slim strip of bare, creamy skin peeked from beneath the tails of her shirt every time she lifted her arms.

He looked down at his phone. Back up.

Fuck it. He keyed in a quick text to Z. Hit Send.

Without waiting for a reply, he slipped outside to the parking lot, implemented the second part of his plan, and was in the kitchen with Tommy Ray, snacking on wings, before the bar closed. Glimpses of Maddie through the kitchen window stirred emotions he couldn't afford to put a name to now. Focusing on the job he'd been given was best, at least until he could get Maddie alone and talking, which he hoped to do shortly.

An hour later, cleanup done and bar shut up tight, Tommy Ray led the way through the Halftime's back door. "The bastard tried to tell me his daddy would pick up the tab. Can you believe that? As if I don't know Harold well enough to know he ain't gonna pick up anything Philip leaves behind."

"Uh-huh." Jack searched the shadows. His and Tommy Ray's trucks waited in the parking lot, but Jack had eyes only for the two most important things: Maddie and her bike.

Tommy Ray secured the back door, waited for the alarm to beep, then turned around. "I'm no idiot, I told hi— Maddie!"

She knelt in the gravel next to her motorcycle. It rested on its side, dust coating it. Maddie had dropped her backpack to the ground and was running her hands over the rear tire, spinning it, probably making certain nothing was puncture or twisted. And even though he'd been careful to ensure the damn thing was fine, the pained look on her face rubbed his conscience raw. He shoved the guilt aside and walked over to her, Tommy Ray keeping pace.

"Problem, Maddie?" Tommy Ray asked.

Maddie straightened, bringing the bike with her. A sharp flick of her booted toe settled the kickstand back onto firm ground. "Somebody knocked it over. In too much of a hurry to get outta here, I guess." Again she ran her fingers over the bike, starting at the handlebars and working her way down, checking it the way she would a child who'd fallen.

Jack forced his attention back up to her face. He was here to gather intel, not wonder what those fingers would feel like on his skin, and definitely not to feel bad for mistreating Maddie's pet motorcycle.

Maddie straddled the bike, and Jack's breathing sped up. Jesus, what that position did for her ass. Curses circled like vultures in his head.

He watched her elbow shift as she turned the key, her other arm move forward to press the Start button.

Nothing.

"Everything okay?" Jack asked.

"Sure." She repeated the process once, twice. Still nothing. Maddie climbed off the motorcycle and opened a saddlebag, rummaging until she surfaced with a flashlight.

"Maddie." Tommy Ray kept the parking area well lit, but that didn't mean he was comfortable leaving a woman here to fix a broken vehicle. "Let me give you a ride home. We can call a mechanic in the morning."

Jack caught the twist of Maddie's lips as she turned to face them. Did she not have the money for a mechanic or just not want someone touching her bike? Well, the money in her pack sort of answered that question, though he knew it was probably hidden for a much different purpose than motorcycle repairs. Not that she would need repairs anyway.

"No, thanks," Maddie told her boss. She pushed those sexy bangs out of her eyes with the hand not holding her light. "I got it. I'm sure something's rattled loose with the fall. Just a glitch. I'll have it fixed up here shortly."

"Still, we'll help you—"

"I got it, Tommy Ray," Jack assured him. "You go on home to Martha."

Maddie looked ready to protest, but Tommy Ray's cheeks stretched into a wide grin that said he knew what Jack was up to. Jack sincerely hoped not.

"All right, then." Tommy Ray turned to Maddie, whose eyes were so wide Jack could see the whites, even in the dark. "You okay having Jack wait with you? I'd rather you not be back here on your own, but Martha's been hurtin', what with her arthritis and all, and I—"

"No one needs to stay. I'm fine. You go on." She didn't look at Jack, but he felt her need for him to leave. Unfortunately for her, he had more important needs to fill.

He clapped Tommy Ray on the back. "We got it," he told his friend. "I'll text you when we leave, let you know everything's fine."

Maddie was already shaking her head, once again bent over the bike. "Suit yourself, Jack." A faint "ass" followed close behind.

Since her back was turned, he didn't bother to refrain from rolling his eyes. *I thought we were past this, Maddie.*

Tommy Ray chuckled and threw Jack a good-luck wink before he walked over to his old Ford sitting in the farthest corner of the lot. Jack divided his attention between the truck's exit and Maddie's bowed head. When the rumble of the aging engine finally faded, that soft middle-of-the-night silence kicked in.

Maddie inspected the bike. Jack inspected her. He couldn't help it, mission or no. The length of her spine and that delectable ass begged him to look. He traced down her jeans-covered legs with his gaze, all the way to those too-sexy-for-her-own-good boots. The damn things had made her just tall enough that her nose met the hollow under his shoulder on the dance floor. He fought back a groan at the memory.

Work, remember? Marge? Charlie? Find out who the fuck this woman is.

"Sure you don't need any help?" he asked.

Maddie snorted, her head still down near the engine. One hand reached into the saddlebag to grab a ratty towel, then disappeared again. So much effort put into ignoring him. It wouldn't take much to break through that wall, uncover her secrets. Or rather, more of her secrets. Just the idea was enough to twist his gut.

Focus, dickhead.

Several steps took him to the head of the bike, where he could watch Maddie's fingers deftly fiddling with the spark plugs, checking to see if each one was clean, their wires secure. "You definitely know your stuff. How long've you had her?"

"Awhile."

The bike was a mutt with so many parts replaced on its sporty frame that it was no longer one recognizable model. "You rebuild her?"

Maddie's grunt could've been agreement or not; he couldn't tell. That she loved the thing was obvious, though, in the way she touched it, the condition the bike was in. The polished chrome along the handlebars shone even in the questionable lights of the parking lot. He locked away his guilt at sabotaging her baby and instead ran his fingers along the smooth surface, ignoring the way Maddie's gaze followed the move, the way her spine stiffened in protest. "She's in good condition."

Maddie moved on to the fuse box, but a peek of a smile curved the corner of her lips that he could see. "Gotta be. What's the use in having a bike that won't work?"

He snorted. "Now, a lot of us Southerners would take offense at that. Just owning a good bike is enough. Like trucks. Doesn't matter if they run as long as you've got one."

"And you can sit it in your yard and plant flowers in the bed?"

"Exactly. Same with washing machines, tractor tires…" He definitely heard a laugh, despite her attempt to muffle it. Good. "You should know that; you're a Southerner, aren't you?" Her accent was soft enough not to be Northern. Not Georgia, maybe, but nearby…

"Not really."

Liar. "Where'd you come from then?"

"Florida."

Jack forced back a growl. He was rapidly coming to hate that blank voice, the damn emotionless tone she adopted when she had something to hide. It made him want to rile her up—or fuck her till she screamed. Anything to get to the core of who she was. The woman wasn't just hiding her name and her past; she was hiding her emotions. What would it take to pry loose her restraint?

"Really? When?"

"Moved up a few years back."

"What, you don't like the beach?"

"I don't swim."

"No?" She wasn't from Florida; he'd bet his truck on it. Maybe somewhere up north if she was deflecting, but that accent... No, it didn't compute. "Did you bartend there too?"

He knew the moment she discovered the loose fuse for the starter. A satisfied grunt came from her lips, and then she stood, wiping her hands on the rag. "Why do you want to know, Jack?"

God, the way she snapped out his name... That should not get him hot, but it did. He shifted from one foot to the other. "Because you're worth knowing, *Maddie*."

She turned off the flashlight. "No, I'm really not."

The light had barely settled into the saddlebag before he was beside her, his skin tingling with the heat of her nearness. "Now that's where you're wrong," he whispered. Darkness wrapped his words in intimacy. "I want to get to know you very well. I want you, Maddie."

"Jack." With a sigh Maddie stepped back, the space between them a buffer zone he was already tensing to cross. "You can't want me."

He glanced down at the obvious bulge between his legs, then met her gaze with a wink. "My dick begs to differ."

A startled laugh escaped her full lips. Jack stood transfixed, watching her head fall back, her mouth fall open, the play of pleasure across her face. It erased the shadows, the secrets, and left her unguarded. Honest. Happy.

He had to taste it. Taste her.

So he did.

One minute she was four feet away, and the next he had her in his arms. The feel of her against him, warm, giving flesh meshing perfectly with his…even the shallow dip at the small of her back fit his hand exactly. Need flooded him, overwhelming everything else, and he cupped the back of her neck, bringing her mouth to meet his in a move as old as the earth and just as powerful. A pained moan escaped him as the soft curve of her mouth settled on his.

Maddie gasped—in shock or surprise, he didn't know. Didn't care. Jack took whatever advantage he could get. He traced her lips with the tip of his tongue, opened them, and ducked inside. The taste of her, of beer and honey and woman, exploded on his tongue. He needed more. He tilted her head until their open mouths dovetailed like they'd been doing this forever.

Maddie's hands slapped into the hollows below his collarbone. Instinctively he tightened his grip, hardened his lips in denial, taking, devouring, thrusting his tongue into the burning heat of her mouth in an unmistakable rhythm.

Her hands fisted his shirt. Pushed.

Jack broke the kiss. "Maddie, please. For God's sake…" She wanted it; he knew she did. He could feel it in the needy points of her breasts, the brush of her pelvis across his steel-hard erection, tilted toward him even as her hands insisted on distance. Whether she recognized it or not, she did want him—and he thought he'd die if he didn't have at least this one small taste of her.

They hung in silence for long moments, the sound of their rough breathing the only relief. Finally Maddie opened her mouth to speak. Jack could see the rejection in her eyes. His stomach dropped into his well-worn combat boots. Goddamn, he'd blown it, pushed too hard too fast.

Maddie closed her eyes. Jack braced himself for whatever she threw at him.

But it wasn't a slap Maddie gave him. Instead, tentative strokes of heat seared his skin as she trailed shaking fingers up each side of his neck. She drove them into his hair to grip the base of his skull. Pulled. Their mouths met, opened once more, and heat damn near hot enough to incinerate them both exploded in his gut when Maddie drew his tongue into her mouth, sucking lightly, tasting his hunger, sharing her own. He moved against her, unable to control the drive to grind his painful erection into the supple give of her belly, hard to so, so soft. He needed her surrender more than he needed to know what she was hiding, and that was dangerous. He knew it but he couldn't stop, especially when she was arching into him, moaning, wanting him just as much as he wanted her. He couldn't stop. He couldn't—

Maddie ripped herself away, her agonized cry slicing the air between them. Jack took an instinctive step forward, reached to pull her against him once more. The sight of her skittering backward, fear edging out the desire in her eyes, stopped him cold.

"Maddie?"

The hand she brought to her lips shook almost as much as her voice. "No—"

"Maddie."

God. She curled in, arms crossed to protect herself, to stem the shaking he could see even in the dark. But it was her eyes that hit him hardest. They were wide, empty of any recognition, only the darkest terror he'd ever witnessed.

That look was harder to take than the hardest of blows. He couldn't do it; he wasn't that strong. He had to have her safe, had to ease that gut-wrenching pain. He gathered her to him, ignoring her protests, ignoring the fight she put up, and simply held her, trying somehow, in some small way, to keep whatever was hurting her at bay for just a little longer.

A knee to the inside of his thigh, right up next to his tender groin, loosened his grip just long enough for her to slip out of his arms.

"Maddie, damn it!"

But she was already out of reach. Ten feet away, backed against the dingy wall of the Halftime, Maddie crouched, hands up, claws out. Wincing, he took a single step toward her.

"Stop! I mean it, Jack."

He stopped. "Maddie, it's okay—"

"It's not okay!"

The high note of hysteria in her voice convinced him to stay where he was. He wouldn't put it past her to have a knife in those sexy boots—and know how to use it. He put his hands up, the universal signal for *I'm harmless*.

Maddie knew better. She pointed a shaky finger at his chest. "Don't…don't touch me again."

"Sweethea—"

"Don't!"

"Okay, okay."

She gasped in a ragged breath. The haze of tears in her eyes twisted him into knots. "No." She dug into her hip pocket and pulled out her key. "I'm going home. Move away from the bike."

He didn't have to; if he was any other guy, he could've blocked her escape and gotten his answers any way he wanted, no restraint needed. But he wasn't any other guy, and he'd seen the look on Maddie's face too often to try to push past it—in the faces of women at the shelter, in his mother's face. The look of fear. The look of self-disgust.

Hands still up, he stepped aside, allowing Maddie the access she wanted. He couldn't, however, allow her to leave without making one thing clear. As she straddled her bike and inserted the key, he told her, "Running won't make it go away, Maddie." He knew that far better than most.

The roar of the bike's engine tried to drown out her reply, but Jack caught it anyway. "It's worked fine so far."

Chapter Eight

He gave her some space. Not much, but the ache in his thigh convinced him that giving her time to calm down was for the best. Unfortunately that made him more impatient with everything and everyone else, which was how he found himself climbing the stairs to Zylo's apartment late Tuesday night. Darkness barely covered the dilapidated state of the building and made the numerous obstacles— rotting boards, overgrown vegetation poking through the slats, empty cans and bottles and trash—that much more hazardous. Jack ran the maze like a veteran hurdler. Nothing was keeping him from answers, not any longer. Twenty-four hours was long enough.

Zylo, despite his punk-rock name and hair to match, had an eye for detail that most people wouldn't credit after seeing the outside of his place. Jack knew him well enough to know every bit of junk was placed there with as much precision as Z used for the careful loop of a cursive letter. Zylo left nothing to chance, which made it all the more confusing that he hadn't responded to Jack's message the night before.

The top step led to a patio and a crooked screen door that gave vague protection to a weathered, cracked wooden door behind it. Jack ignored the flimsiness of both structures and knocked hard, a sharp let-me-in rhythm, on the paneling to one side of the door.

No answer. No movement. Jack's heart thumped hard, just once, that well-remembered signal that trouble was on the way. He knocked again.

Nothing.

The rusted hinges of the screen didn't squeak. Easing it open, Jack reached for the doorknob.

The door jerked inward. A ghostly white hand clutched Jack's shirt, yanked, and sent him stumbling inside. A slam signaled the closing of his exit.

"Z, damn it!"

The hand that had forced him through the door released him just as abruptly. Jack watched Zylo run it through the shock of pink and white spikes that covered his head. "What do you want, Jack?"

"Well hello to you too."

"Shut up." Zylo turned to walk through a massive steel door that led into the heart of the apartment, where a bank of computers threw their harsh green glow across stacks of files, pens, laminating equipment, paperwork supplies, all in perfectly aligned rows. Z's inner sanctum was as neat as his work. Jack's face staring at Zylo's front door was frozen on one screen.

"What the hell, Z? Why haven't you answered my calls?"

"And texts, don't forget texts. You nag like an old woman, Jack." Z dropped his skinny frame into a rolling desk chair, his light eyes accusing. "Did it not occur to you that I don't want to get involved? No answer should've clued you in to that, dude."

"You don't even know what I'm asking."

"There's only one thing you'd be asking me about because I've only done one job in your area in the past two months."

So the kid did know Maddie, or knew of her. Jack looked into Z's eyes, and what he saw there wasn't encouraging. In his early twenties, Z had been in the business for closer to a decade than not. He dealt with criminals and competition and cops the same way he usually dealt with Jack—a piss-off attitude and unbreakable discretion, not to mention a totally pristine record. Not even a parking ticket. Went a long way toward convincing customers their business was safe from leakage. Yeah, Zylo had plenty of experience with this, so what was it about Maddie that had the guy chewing his stud-pierced lip like an addict with a really bad case of the munchies?

"I'm here now," Jack said. "Why don't you explain it to me in person?"

Z groaned.

Jack narrowed his eyes. "Look, I know you helped her. I saw it."

"And you're not dead? 'Cause seriously, dude, she'd as soon bust your balls as give you the time of day."

Z knew her better than he wanted to let on. "Yeah, I like her too."

Z grinned at him.

"Look, I'm here now, not with the cops, so why not spill it? Just tell me what's going on."

"I don't know what's going on, not for certain."

"But you know what happened to her, don't you? You know what she's running from."

"Yeah, I do, and trust me, Jack; you don't want to know."

Jack went still. "Know what?"

"Uh-uh. No way." Z stood and began steadily pacing across the small room. "Maddy knows and I know, and that's one person too many as it is. Besides, she'll kill me if she finds out I told you. I'd rather stay alive."

"We all have that worry around Maddie, at least those of us who piss her off on a regular basis."

Z grinned. He obviously knew exactly what Jack was talking about.

"Look, Jack, I appreciate your business, I really do. I hope after all these years that we're friends. But I can't do this for you."

He thought it over, his brain running scenarios, matching pieces, coming to possible conclusions. "You're not in love with her, are you? Is that why you won't give her up?"

"If I was, you'd be looking at the front end of a Sig, not my ugly mug." Zylo finally went still, staring at Jack as if trying to figure out what made him tick. Jack wanted to ask Z to share it with him if he figured it out. He didn't. And as interesting as this conversation was, it wasn't getting him the answers he needed.

"Look, Jack, Maddie's a client, but she's…in a lot of hot water. My goal is to help her avoid that, because finding her means bringing me to the attention of all the wrong people. So you can forget it. I'm not telling you anything."

He didn't believe that either. Zylo could be self-serving, but he cared who he helped. Jack leaned his hip against the edge of Z's desk. "I just need her name." Not the one Z had given her; the one that was actually hers.

"You don't want it, Jack; you really don't."

"Yes, I do." Now more than ever.

Z's shoulders slumped, his entire body hunching in. "I'm sorry. I won't give it to you."

"Okay." Jack straightened.

When he turned toward the door, Zylo cleared his throat. "If..."

Jack glanced over his shoulder.

Z shifted from one foot to the other. The silence between them pulsed with the secrets Z kept and Jack's determination to discover them.

"If she ran"—Z's pale eyes were full to the brim with cool green fire—"then it's the best decision she ever made. Think about that before you go hunting."

Jack held the kid's gaze a few seconds longer, then nodded once more. "Be safe, Z."

"Watch your back, Jack."

On the way back down the steps, Jack pulled out the photo he'd pocketed from the file on Z's desk. The picture they'd used for Maddie's driver's license. Z might not give him answers, but this would.

The office was empty when he got back. Jack fired up his computer system. A quick scan and the facial recognition software he'd developed was running Maddie's image through every database he could access—and a few he wasn't supposed to but did anyway. The match that came up wasn't in a database, however. It was on the Internet. He clicked the link.

A picture of Maddie standing with an older couple filled his screen. Her hair was darker, a rich chestnut brown, cut short around her face, but there was no mistaking those lips, those eyes—eyes clear and so damn innocent as she peeked shyly at the camera. God, she looked young. Soft. Not like the woman who punched out drunks and stood toe-to-toe with him when he got angry. What had happened to her?

The picture accompanied a news story in the *Tennessean*, Nashville's biggest newspaper. Jack clicked for the full story.

"Dr. Thomas Brewer's Daughter to Wed."

The headline hit him like an F5 tornado, leaving just as much chaos in its wake.

Madelyn Brewer.

Brewer, not Baker. Clever. The Madelyn fit, somehow. He filed the name away.

The Brewers were elite members of Nashville society, or had been ten years ago. So was her fiancé, David Reed. That name Jack knew. The man was a world-famous criminal lawyer who spent half the year in New York and the other half in his birthplace, a lush estate outside Nashville, Tennessee. If some high-profile psycho was on trial for murder, Reed was more than likely defending him—and getting him off.

The bastard was a shark, pure and simple. How the hell had Maddie ended up engaged to him?

Jack skimmed the article, ignoring the throb of his pulse in his temples. Prominent family, loving parents. The comfortable way Maddie leaned against her dad in the picture, the happiness on her face, backed that part of the story up. "Fairy-tale romance"? That he wasn't so sure about. He guessed Reed would go after whatever he wanted with a vengeance, even a decade ago. People were different in their private lives and public ones, sure, but—

Stop making excuses for her and get on with this.

The story said she was getting married; it didn't say she was married. She could've backed out at the last minute. Please God, let her have backed out...

She hadn't backed out.

The "related story" section led him forward. Jack clicked and felt a punch to his heart as a picture of Maddie in an expensive lace wedding gown filled the screen next. The picture had been taken in front of a historic mansion he recognized as the Belle Meade Plantation in Nashville. Barely out of her teens, Maddie smiled for the camera, excitement glowing on her face. Reed stood in the background, off to one side, his expression that of a man admiring his prize. If Jack had won Maddie, he would look exactly that way. But this man had only won her for a short time; they weren't together anymore.

Of course they weren't together anymore.

Jack clicked the next news story, his fears confirmed as the gossip column detailed a night out on the town for Reed without his bride of barely six months. The story was accompanied by a photo of the couple at a prominent Nashville restaurant. Maddie was looking up at a waiter while her husband stared at her. She was smiling, but the smile didn't reach her eyes. She'd been unbearably beautiful, even then, but the empty mask he was coming to know so well had already been creeping in. And the expression on Reed's face... Jack's stomach turned.

A glance to the bottom of the page showed related stories, all of which dealt with Reed's prominent courtroom escapades. No more social events. Jack clicked on each one, but got nothing but business. A Google search for Maddie's and Reed's names and the word *divorce* brought up nothing. Newspapers and public records exhausted, Jack turned to what he did best. Court records were a fairly easy hack. And fruitless. No divorce records in the state of Tennessee.

That turn in his stomach got harder.

She couldn't be married. But records didn't lie unless someone paid for them to. Maddie wasn't paying for a divorce decree; she was paying for a new identity altogether. Why?

And why did the news leave him feeling like somehow had hollowed out his insides and replaced them with a boulder the size of his truck?

The phone was in his hand and ringing before he fully realized he'd dialed.

Con's disgruntled voice came across the line. "Hey, man, it's three o'clock in the morning. What the fuck?"

Jess's sleepy voice filtered through the phone, not so much words as a questioning tone. Jack cursed. He'd forgotten about time, about everything as he'd gone through the details of Maddie's past.

"Sorry, Con."

Something in those two short words must've clued Con in to trouble, because he didn't take the time to bust Jack's balls further before he asked, "You need me?"

Did he? He wasn't weak, but he knew the value of a team. He and Con and their best friend, Lee, had been a team since the sixth grade, and even after Lee's death, Jack had continued to rely on his friend. He didn't really need anything right now except to be with Maddie, and that was impossible; Con's voice was the next best thing.

"No. No," he said again, rubbing a thumb and fingertip over his gritty eyes. This was ridiculous. He hadn't even known Maddie existed a week ago; he shouldn't be blasted by what he'd learned in the past few hours. "No, man, it can wait. I'm sorry."

Jack could hear him moving around, probably leaving his cozy bed and his warm, willing wife to listen to Jack freak out.

"Listen, seriously, it can wait till morning. Come by when you get to the office?"

"Just shut the fuck up and give me a minute."

The words were mild for all that Con was cursing him. Jack managed a tired smile and shut the fuck up.

Con came back on the line a minute later. "What's up?"

Jack filled him in. The tomblike atmosphere of the empty office weighed down on him as he spoke, threatening to crush him.

"So your woman is married and on the run."

A harsh growl threatened to choke him. "She's not my woman."

Con's grunt said he begged to differ. "It's okay to be angry. I get it. You care about her. But—"

"No, I don't. It's just lust; it has to be. We've only known each other a week."

"And half the people you ask will say loving someone that soon is a fairy tale. The other half will say it happened to them. The point is, it doesn't matter what anyone else says; it matters what your gut tells you. It did for me."

"My gut isn't telling me anything except that it wants to turn inside out."

"Exactly. She matters to you. Stop trying to deny it and start trying to figure out why she left the security of a rich husband and a loving family to live under the radar the way she has the past however many years."

Because her husband was an asshole? Jack didn't know. He couldn't think beyond the gnashing of teeth in the back of his mind every time he thought about Maddie belonging to another man.

"What about Reed's background?" Con asked.

"He's a pretty prominent public figure, Con. I wouldn't think there'd be many places to hide secrets that couldn't be found."

"Brit Holbrooke did."

Jack clenched his teeth at the reminder. Jess's stalker had been from an old-money Atlanta family. He'd hidden at least one murder and a long history of violence easily. A big name could hide a lot of things.

Was Maddie running from Reed? Something Reed was involved in?

He stared at the blurred image of Maddie's face in her wedding photo, staring out at him from the computer screen, and something in him, something he'd been aware of since the moment he saw her behind the bar at the Halftime and hadn't wanted to acknowledge, swelled inside him, clamoring for attention, demanding he give it despite his attempts to push it into the background. Yes, he wanted Maddie, with a deep, burning need he had never experienced before. Why? Because that need wasn't just for her body. If he could, he'd capture her soul. He was beginning to fear that what he really wanted was her everything.

Was it too soon? Yes. Did his heart give a shit? No. The question was, what was he going to do about it, about all of it?

"Jack?"

He wasn't ready to talk about this, even with Con. He needed to think. A lot. "I've got some digging to do."

"I'll come in and help."

"No, it's okay." Jack needed the quiet. "Give me a few hours. Go back to sleep. Jess needs you."

Con went silent for a moment. "Sure. But I'll be in first thing. Whatever you need me to do."

"Good. That's good. In the morning."

After disconnecting, he pulled up his e-mail and opened a new message. Marge's e-mail address went into the To box, Maddie's fake name in the Subject. He stared for a long time, trying to find the words he needed. Her past wasn't as straightforward as most candidates, but neither did he see any harm in her volunteering. There was nothing for Maddie to gain from Hope Place, nothing to steal, only places to give. He could offer that to her while he figured out his next move. His gut told him there was zero doubt that Maddie could be trusted at Hope Place; the question was how to tell Marge that without revealing more than he should know. Finally, knowing Marge trusted him, he tapped to move the cursor to the body of the e-mail and added two words: *She's safe*.

The rest would come; he'd make sure of it. His mission was no longer for Marge; it was for himself. When he was through, Maddie wouldn't have any secrets left. That he could guarantee.

Chapter Nine

Maddie squirmed on the hard plastic chair and stared at the clipboard of paperwork in front of her. This was worse than going to the doctor, but she knew from experience how important information was in their business. Hope Women's and Children's Shelter had too many people to protect, people who had already been victimized, hurt, abused, and making them safe was the number one priority.

Maybe this had been a bad idea.

Margaret had called this morning to confirm the time and location for the interview. It had taken more nerve than Maddie would've expected to dress in her newest, yet still faded, jeans and a T-shirt and make her way across town to the office. Now here she sat, trying to remember what she was supposed to write, the history she and Z had created. She could face down angry drunks and handle a bar for two hundred people single-handedly and not let a line form, but put her in a women's shelter and every bit of composure she'd earned over the past four years went to pot. It wasn't fear, really; it was the memories. Memories that were bad enough when they revisited her as nightmares.

She focused on the paperwork in her lap, refusing to let the memories win. She had to get her story straight.

Contact information.

Work history.

Past volunteer experience. *Does being a shelter resident count?*

She choked back a slightly hysterical giggle and put pen to paper. Once the words started appearing, they flowed out as automatically as she'd trained them to. Even if they hadn't, she had to push forward. David had to be stopped. She needed proof, and the process was like pulling off a label: first you peeled the corner, then a bit more so that the piece got wider, then the fat middle, until you worked your way back to the final crucial corner. The linchpin, so to speak. The Halftime had been the first corner, then Hope Place. David was the linchpin, and she hoped, prayed Vaneqe would be that big fat middle she could rescue along the way.

If not, it would probably be because the girl was already dead. The thought squeezed Maddie's lungs in a vise.

"Ms. Baker?"

Maddie hesitated, at the "Miss" or the "Baker," she wasn't sure. The fraction-of-a-second delay cost her a lot in composure. The mask she relied on was slipping, had been since she'd come to Freeman, though she refused to think about why. Instead she glanced up to find an older woman standing at the doorway leading to the inner offices, her hair an odd shade of red Maddie knew had to come from a box. Faded blue eyes still held the sharp gaze of a hawk, though, and she was suddenly certain that getting anything by this woman was not going to be easy.

Gripping the clipboard tight, Maddie got up, her feet automatically taking her across the room to meet the woman who watched, hand extended.

"Margaret Hawthorne, the director here at Hope Place. It's a pleasure to meet you."

Maddie nodded, clasping the warm hand briefly. "And you," she said.

Mrs. Hawthorne confiscated the paperwork, then led Maddie down the hall to a small office, her steps brisk.

"So you want to volunteer with us?" She ushered Maddie into a comfy chair in front of a small, inexpensive desk.

"Yes, Mrs. Hawthorne."

The formality was waved away. "Marge, please." And then quiet consumed the office as every line on her paperwork was carefully read.

Maddie hadn't realized she was holding her breath until Marge looked up at her. "So, tell me about yourself."

Ah. Okay, not as easy as it sounded. The plastic chair squeaked as she squirmed. "Well, I recently moved here from Florida."

Marge shook her head. "No, I already know what you put on the application." She glanced down, scanning the paper. "Recently moved, bartending experience, basic computer skills." Eyes that seemed to see far too much met Maddie's. "I want to know about you. Tell me about Maddie—who are *you?*"

I couldn't tell you even if I knew.

A bittersweet laugh escaped. "Good question."

"Isn't it, though?"

And that was it; Marge didn't say anything else. The woman was good at getting people to talk, obviously. The pressure to fill the silence built with every second. "I…" Who did she want to be? "I'm…tough."

Marge hummed. "You've had to be, have you?"

"Yes."

The woman nodded.

"I'm… I want to help."

"You're a bartender. Makes sense that your gift would be service."

Maddie didn't know about a gift. She knew necessity. It had been necessity that started her bartending career.

"Why do you drive a motorcycle?"

A lot of practical reasons. She was probably at the point where she could buy a used car, but… She smiled. "Because I like it. I like tinkering with it, being able to fix it myself, but mostly I just love riding it."

"That's what I'm looking for," Marge said, returning her smile.

"What?"

"Emotion."

Well, then Maddie was screwed.

"Does that scare you, Maddie?"

Hell yeah. "I'm an inherently private person."

"Most people are. I don't usually require you to spill your guts, so you're safe there. I'm just looking for something to connect to."

Maddie could do that, at least. "Marge…the truth is"—she barely held back a laugh at her chosen wording—"I'm just…*me*. I tend bar, ride a motorcycle. I can do most things that require common sense and basic intelligence and a working body. I don't have a lot of technical skills, but I do have some practical ones I can share. That's it. I want to help, so put me to work."

Marge watched her for a long while, and Maddie had to stiffen her spine to avoid the need to cower away from that X-ray vision. Finally Marge leaned forward, plunked her elbows on the desk, and broke the silence. "Maddie, do you realize how many of the women who come to us have nothing more than housekeeping or child-rearing skills, if that? They don't know how to buy, much less fix, a car, or any vehicle, for that matter. They often have no practical job skills, whether it's waitressing or bartending or something more complicated. They don't even know the first steps to getting the skills they need. That's what we're here for." Her frank look pinned Maddie into her seat. "Don't sell yourself short."

God, this woman was something else. Someone powerful. Not the way the people in Maddie's past had been powerful; Marge possessed something money and social standing couldn't buy: truth and passion.

It took a moment to clear the lump from her throat, but Maddie finally managed. "Okay."

Marge nodded. "Okay." She stood, leaving the clipboard on the desk as she rounded it. "So…follow me."

Releasing a silent sigh—of relief or something else, Maddie had no freaking clue—she followed Marge across the hall to what looked like a break room. A table in one corner, legs spindly and seeming ready to give up their strength at any moment, was piled with papers and phone books and a phone that looked about ten years old. Maddie knew just how hard funds were to come by, even harder than volunteers, so the cramped conditions and aging equipment didn't surprise. her. What did was the paper lying on the table.

A flyer featuring a missing girl. A familiar missing girl. Vaneqe.

She barely had a second to hide her shock before Marge picked up the flyer and handed it to Maddie. Sadness deepened the lines etched around the older woman's faded eyes and tightening mouth. "This is Vaneqe. She and her brother were with us at the shelter for a short time."

The moment felt hushed, breathless. Maddie had to force herself to speak. "And she's not still there. What happened?"

"I wish I knew. One day she just…disappeared." Marge laid the flyer back on the table, visibly squaring her shoulders. "Charlie is still with us. Not for much longer, but the child screams if we even suggest taking him somewhere else. It's as if he believes he has to be there for her to walk back in the door."

God.

"I convinced the social worker it was in his best interests to let him stay a little longer." A sigh escaped her. "We'll see."

"The police haven't found anything?"

"Nothing."

That one word held a wealth of emotion: resignation, pain, fear, hope. Maddie was intimately familiar with them all, except she'd learned to shove them aside. Otherwise they would swallow her whole.

"What can I do?"

Marge gave her determination a tired smile. "I need you to make some calls. All the shelters in this region know me. We work together frequently, especially in cases like this." Marge's tone told Maddie exactly how frequent that was. "Whatever detective work the police did didn't turn up anything. I've hired a friend to help search—"

Alarm zinged up her spine. "Um, isn't that...unusual?"

"Yes, but he had experience with this type of case, and Charlie is...well, Charlie is special to him. But he can't do everything. I want to see if any of the directors can give us some leads—someone to talk to, unusual activity, anything. It's a long shot"—Marge shrugged—"but it's what we can do."

"Got it." It was more than a long shot, Maddie knew, because though directors might be willing, most residents didn't want to talk to strangers, but whatever Maddie had to do to get herself involved, she would. Settling at the table, she asked, "Who do I call first?"

The look Marge gave her was almost fond. She grabbed a paper from a nearby stack and handed it over. A list of shelter contacts. "Thank you."

Maddie let her smile answer as she picked up the phone and began to dial. Who knew, maybe someone did know something. She just hoped they figured it out before it was too late for Vaneqe—if it wasn't already.

* * *

Maddie wasn't at work by the time Jack managed to get to the Halftime Wednesday night. She wasn't there Thursday night either—and Jack was going insane. So he did something he probably shouldn't and went to her house. The answers he needed couldn't be found in newspaper facts and public records; they could only be found in Maddie, in the truth of who she really was, not who she claimed to be. He had to see her; he couldn't wait another twenty-four hours.

He'd memorized the address from her driver's license. The street was familiar, one he passed every time he went to the bar. He might not have grown up in Freeman, but he'd learned its nuances over the months he'd lived near here. Maddie's apartment wasn't in the best part of town, but he couldn't do anything about that. Not yet, anyway.

The flimsy screen door didn't even latch. The thin metal slapped lightly against its jamb as he stepped up to the door. Jack ignored a screen for the second time in twenty-four hours and knocked on the siding instead.

Light footsteps approach from inside. The walls had to be incredibly thin. He stared into the peephole—at least the place had one good feature—and waited for Maddie to open the door.

She would open the door.

She opened the door.

"What the hell are you doing here, Jack?"

It was such a classic Maddie reaction, he had to smile. "Coming to see you?" He put some extra *duh* into his tone.

The light behind her silhouetted her curves, especially the one where her hand settled. That cocked hip matched her cocked brow, visible even in shadow. The look she gave him couldn't have been more appalled if she'd stepped in dog shit. "Really? This is my home, Jack."

"That's kinda why I'm here." He shrugged one shoulder, his heart rate stepping up a notch as Maddie's gaze followed the move, darkening with an appreciation she'd probably never admit to. "You weren't at work."

"Oh my God. You are officially nuts." But she didn't tell him to leave.

Jack made sure his smile was all gleaming white teeth. "Maybe."

"Well, you can just go away. I don't feel like shoveling shit tonight."

Like she did every other night, she meant. Maddie was a pro at chatting up customers; she had to be to make a living as a bartender. No, it was him she didn't want to chat with. She wanted distance between them, breathing space to get comfortable, relax. All the more reason to make sure she didn't get it. Muscles tensing, he eased toward the unlatched side of the screen. Maddie stiffened as if she expected him to spring at her.

Smart girl.

Instead he leaned forward until his nose almost touched the screen. "I think you are very good at shoveling shit, darlin'."

"And I think you're delusional."

"Can I come in?"

"I think you just proved my point."

"Maybe." He straightened. "Maddie, I obviously pushed too hard too fast the other night. Let me make it up to you."

She tilted her head, examining him. For sincerity, maybe? She could just as easily be looking for spots for a kill shot. "There's nothing to make up for. Good night, Jack."

The door was almost closed when he spoke again. "There's ice cream involved."

The door stopped. Jack held his breath. Hopefully the information he'd gotten from John would pay off.

"The Tasty Cream?"

Methinks I've found the lady's weakness. "The Tasty Cream."

The door opened. Maddie squinted into the darkness as if trying to read the truth of his words. He refused to let the irony sour his mood. He was finally talking to her; he had a mission; nothing else would get in his way tonight.

"Wait here," she finally said.

He opened his mouth to protest, but she left the door open. He waited, watching through the screen as she turned to walk back into the apartment. The dim light that had silhouetted her body came from a small lamp on a side table next to a ratty old couch. A rectangular coffee table, one of those old '80s ones with a glass center, occupied the space between the couch and the front window, but that was the extent of the living room furniture, all of which, judging from its condition, probably came with the dilapidated apartment.

He raised his voice to be heard as the distance between them grew. "Nice place."

"Thanks. Your opinion is important to me." The words were thrown over her shoulder as she moved toward what looked like the kitchen. She returned seconds later, boots in hand. The woman never went anywhere without boots. It was definitely one of the things he loved about her.

Liked. Cared about. Damn it.

The trail of his thoughts started a distinct ache in his chest, one he didn't want to inspect. The one in his groin was much safer—and growing by the second as she crossed the room. Her backpack was scooped from the floor and tossed onto her shoulder, her keys were fished from a pocket in her skintight cutoff jeans, and then she was moving through the door and turning her back to him so she could secure the lock. She turned, pocketing her keys. Before she'd taken two steps past the screen door, he was reaching for her hand.

Maddie jerked back hard. "What is it with you always touching me?"

You need to get used to me touching you. I intend to do it a lot.

"It's instinct." The truth. He hadn't even thought about it; his natural inclination had been to take her hand. What was so horrible about that?

Maddie crossed her arms over her chest, plumping the mounds under her thin cotton tee in a way he had a hard time believing wasn't intentional. One glance into her eyes told him she hadn't a clue how much the move made him want to stop talking so damn much and put their mouths to better use.

Yeah, not endearing. He'd keep that to himself.

"You didn't answer my question."

Because he'd lost track of the conversation. Breasts—hers, anyway—did that to him. "What question?"

Maddie inched backward. Jack inched forward.

"Why are you always touching me?"

He snorted. "Because I need to? Because I want to so damn much I just can't breathe? I don't know why. Does it matter?"

"Yes." Maddie ducked her head, her bangs hanging forward to cast a shadow over her eyes. "I think you just don't like someone saying no to you."

"I don't like you saying no to me, but I can be patient. We'll get past it."

He couldn't miss her eye roll. "You really are an arrogant jackass."

He laughed. "I think you like me more than you want to let on." He reached for her again.

A low growl left Maddie's lips. She smacked his hand away.

Jack's laugh got deeper as he shook out the sting in his hand. "Sorry, wildcat. You make it too hard to resist."

Moving to cross the road toward his truck, Maddie shot a rude gesture his way. He had her hand in a secure grip before she could drop it back to her side.

"You do realize this constitutes a date," he said.

Maddie tugged against his hold. "I don't date customers."

"Fine, you've given me the obligatory rebuttal. Can we go eat ice cream now?"

Her fingers relaxed into his hold, but she stopped walking. When he looked at her, she was looking at their hands. What was she thinking? Was she enjoying the feel of them together as much as he was?

Maddie didn't say. When she looked up, it was with a determined glint in her eye. "I want caramel and pecans."

She said *pecans* the Southern way, with a soft *e*. The right way.

"I think we can accommodate that request."

Maddie took the last few steps to his truck. "You promise?"

He suppressed a smile. "Promise."

Chapter Ten

She didn't trust the man or his promise. But she was so damn tired of doing the right thing. Of always being careful, wary, afraid. She couldn't get past those sexy puppy-dog eyes—or his words as they echoed in her head:

Why are you always touching me?

Because I need to? Because I want to so damn much I just can't breathe?

That wasn't need; it was a compulsion, one she related to all too well. Sometime in the past few days, that same breathlessness had taken her over. It was why she'd avoided him as much as she could, only it wasn't working. Nothing was. She couldn't get the kiss they'd shared, the way he'd touched her—the way she'd responded—out of her head. She should turn around, go back inside, and stop this right now. But she couldn't. She didn't want to, and for once, she was going to do what she wanted. Just once.

She glanced at Jack. Satisfaction gave his rugged good looks an edge that had her swallowing hard. If he noticed, he didn't acknowledge it, simply opened the passenger side of his truck and gestured her in.

Jack's 4x4 was massive. Midnight blue, it gleamed with chrome and wax and that extra something masculine that Jack himself had. She was surprised the truck didn't sport those monster-truck tires like the other backwoods boys, just for the added

123

kick. As they came alongside the passenger door—and the running board that hit her knees—Maddie snorted up at the thing.

"Most men with a truck this size are said to be compensating, you know."

Shifting to one side, Jack plunged a hand into his pocket to deposit his keys. The move pulled the jeans material tight across a bulging crotch she could see clearly in the light filtering from the truck. "Don't worry," he told her as he glanced down, a wolfish smile tugging at his lips. "The advertising speaks for itself."

Maddie forced a roll of her eyes. "Really, Jack?"

"I've never had any complaints, wildcat." Without another word he grasped Maddie around the waist and lifted her into the passenger seat.

A highly undignified squeal escaped before Maddie could clamp her mouth shut. By that time Jack had the door slammed closed and was circling the vehicle, his deep laugh ringing in her ears.

She really did hate him. She did; she declared it firmly with a mental stomp of her foot. Her mind responded with the memory of those massive hands on her waist, his warm breath on her neck, his strength placing her precisely where he wanted her.

Jack wasn't the only one laughing; her body was joining in.

The he-man was climbing into the driver's seat like there wasn't a ten-foot drop outside his door. "Jack—"

"I love the way you say my name"—he leaned over to pull the seat belt across her body—"especially when you're irritated." That knowing laugh of his made her want to kick him—hard. When she tried, a warm hand clamped down on her knee. The look on his face didn't even change.

"You are infuriating!"

"Yeah, tell me something I haven't heard since I was born."

And that was it, the last straw. A laugh spilled out despite her best intentions to hold it back.

Jack grinned. "Come on, wildcat. Can't you just relax and come have some ice cream with me?"

His arrogance combined with that sweet pleading did funny things to her insides. "There is something seriously wrong with you," she told him, relaxing against the door.

He cranked the truck. "You know I'm just right."

He was. That was the problem.

Thirty seconds later he had turned the truck around and headed toward Main Street. True to his word, he took them straight to the local Tasty Cream, an old-fashioned drive-through that, from what she'd seen, was the teen haunt in Freeman on the weekends. The typical Southern sixteen-year-old's pastime. Maddie felt a strange sense of déjà vu, as if she and Jack were teenagers heading out for a Saturday night make-out session. Which was ridiculous. They weren't teens, and they sure as hell weren't making out. That didn't keep outlandish

125

scenarios from popping into her stupid brain, however.

She held her breath as Jack tucked the hood of the truck under the lighted archway that covered the individual parking spots. The front end filled the entire space, practically touching the waiting drive-through menus on either side. Of course, Jack made the shot without a scrape to the navy paint that gleamed in the shop's neon lighting.

"Vanilla or chocolate?" he asked.

She gave him a sideways look. "Chocolate, of course." Hadn't he ever heard of chocolate turtles? What else would she eat with caramel and pecans?

Jack didn't respond. When Maddie turned his way, she found those amber flecks in his eyes glinting in the light.

"What?"

"I just wouldn't have pegged you for chocolate," he said. The window whirred as Jack lowered it. "Vanilla, yes. In your own way, you're very straitlaced. Strawberry, maybe, just to prove you don't conform to what anyone else thinks you should do. Chocolate? I don't know."

What the hell? The guy was analyzing her ice cream choices?

But Jack was already pressing the button to order. "One sundae with chocolate ice cream, caramel, and pecans." He glanced back at her, eyebrow quirked, and she nodded her acceptance. "And one large chocolate waffle cone, please."

The speaker squawked, the server giving Jack his total, and then he turned back to her. "So…" Jack shifted in his seat, one knee taking over half the space between the two of them.

"So…"

Silence sizzled in the truck cab. Maddie stared at Jack's knee and waited, her breath tight. It had been far too long since she'd been completely alone with a man in a small space, too long since she'd felt the kind of awareness that sparked in her belly every time Jack entered a room. In all honestly, she'd never felt that. As the silence stretched between them and her nerves drew tight, she wondered why she'd ever want to. "Jack—"

A sound like a gunshot echoed against the opposite side of the truck. Maddie jumped. Her head hit the window behind her. "Ow! Damn it."

Jack was there in a second, wrapping a hand around the back of her head and rubbing the sore spot. "Careful," he warned. Before she could open her mouth to blast him for that useless piece of advice, he turned away.

"Sundae and an ice cream cone," a perky voice said. Maddie leaned to one side and watched as a teenage girl, her black hair in a perky ponytail, passed their treats through the window. She must've knocked on the truck's door. Giving Maddie a heart attack—not to mention a concussion—meant she definitely wasn't getting a tip. Maddie glared as the girl accepted Jack's money and skated, on actual roller skates, back to the restaurant.

"Stop throwing killer looks at the poor carhop and eat your ice cream."

Maddie turned to Jack, coming face-to-face with the small white boat-shaped bowl that held her precious treat. She let her first bite soften her up.

Jack's gaze went dark as she licked the spoon.

"Stop! Just stop that. Jack, we can't—"

"Why can't we? If you could answer that question with anything resembling logic, I might agree with you, but we're both consenting adults." He eyed her carefully, an imp of mischief lurking, his ice cream cone held just below his mouth as if forgotten. It made her want to nip those sexy lips and find out if they were already cold. "You are, aren't you? Just how old are you?"

She sighed heavily. "Thirty-one."

It wasn't until the words left her mouth that she realized lying hadn't even occurred to her.

"Good. We're safe then."

No, no we're not. She was trying to protect him as much as she was herself, if only the big lug would listen to her. She opened her mouth, to say what, she wasn't sure, but Jack cut her off.

"Give me one good reason that we can't see each other, Maddie."

"Because I don't want to see you."

"Okay, let me rephrase that: give me one good reason I can actually believe." He took a bite of waffle cone.

"I—" *Have no idea.* She couldn't convince him she didn't want him; her body wouldn't let her. "Jack—" She couldn't tell him the truth; that would put them all in danger. "Because—"

Oh hell.

Jack reached for her, running his fingers along her cheek and down her neck—her suddenly hot neck. When she swallowed, he grinned. God, the man's grin made her pulse race.

"So, did you have ice cream for your thirtieth birthday?"

Maddie hesitated. "Why?"

He shrugged. When his shoulder nudged hers, Maddie realized he was much closer than he'd been a minute ago. "Thirty's a big milestone. How'd you celebrate?"

"I didn't."

"You're kidding! Why not?"

Now it was her turn to shrug. She took a big bite of her sundae, making sure to include at least one pecan. "Just didn't," she mumbled around the cold treat.

What city had she been in when she turned thirty? Albuquerque? Seattle? Maybe El Paso. It had all just blurred together after a little while, and since she'd had no one to share the day with, her birthday had been just like any other day. Lonely.

"Well, we'll have to change that this year."

No, we won't.

But she didn't say it aloud. It wouldn't help; she knew that now, so she kept silent. Words would never convince Jack to back off.

"No boyfriend when you were thirty, then, if you didn't celebrate. Anybody since then? Before?"

"Jack."

He sighed, the breath puffing the ends of her hair in their customary clip. "Just answer, Maddie. Why does everything have to be so hard with you?"

Why indeed? Maddie relaxed slowly back against the seat. The edge of weariness in his voice softened her where his irritation hadn't, though she refused to actually voice her capitulation. "Nobody since." Would the truth turn him off? It was worth a try. She clutched her spoon, watching as a single drop gathered on the underside and then dripped down. She didn't stop it, afraid to take another bite, afraid she'd choke. "I was…um…in a long-term relationship before." *The longest kind.* "But nothing the past few years."

"Family?"

She fought to keep her body from tensing back up. "Parents."

"Are you still in touch?"

Sadness added to the lump in her throat. "No." *Turn the tables, Maddie. Make him talk.* "What about you?"

"Just my mama and me growing up. She died when I was ten." Unlike her, Jack showed his sadness plainly, his words going soft with emotion. "My stepdad—second stepdad—was a bastard. He killed her." Jack swiped a bite off his half-eaten cone as he stared into space. "I met Con not long after that, if you could call it meeting. I was busy fighting the school bully when he joined in—thankfully on my side. Con's dad, Ben, practically raised me." He chuckled at what must have been pleasant memories.

"He did pretty well seein' as how he had us hell-on-wheels boys to tackle."

"So you've known Conlan a long time." That must be nice, having someone who shared so much of his life and was still there for him. The closest thing to having a sibling.

"Yeah, twenty-three years." He nudged her side with a gentle elbow. "I'm just a little bit older than you."

"How old?"

"Thirty-four." He finished off the rest of his cone in one massive bite.

Not that much older, then. David had been…
Don't think about David.

"Have you ever been married?" she asked. Anything to redirect her thoughts.

"Nope. You?"

Maddie fought not to choke. "No."

Jack had turned to the rolled-down window to settle his trash on the waiting tray, but he nodded. He was in his midthirties. Was he one of those guys that preferred to continually play the field? He was certainly beautiful enough. "Why haven't you found anyone?"

His first answer had been flip; this one he took his time with. "I didn't have a great example of marriage growing up. More like no example, really. Mama kept whatever man she could get to pay the bills. When one of them finally beat her to death…" He shook his head. "The risk assessment said, 'Hell no, marriage isn't for you.'"

Why was it that Southern men called their mothers *mama*? The word made her want to cry, as did his description of his childhood. Her heavy swallow seemed to stick halfway down her throat.

"But…maybe I've seen different lately."

Tension tightened deep in her gut. "I need to go. It's been a long day," she said, wadding up her napkin. She stuck the white ball inside the paper bowl and passed it to Jack. Silently he took the trash, set it outside, and cranked up the truck. They were quiet on the drive back to her place.

Jack parked in the same spot across the road from the apartment. She had her hand on the door latch before he turned the truck off. He had his hand on her arm.

"Why are you always running away from me?" he asked.

Because I don't trust myself around you. She could finally admit, way down deep, that it had nothing to do with Jack and everything to do with protecting herself. "Jack— Because…this isn't a good idea."

"Why not? Give me one good reason why we shouldn't be friends."

She turned to him, to look into his face as she finally spoke the truth. "You don't want to be just friends."

He wanted so much more from her than friendship—and what was she supposed to say to that? That she was leaving as soon as she discovered what had happened to Vaneqe? That she wasn't who he thought she was? That Madison Baker wasn't her real name and even her hair color was a lie?

132

Apparently saying anything wasn't on Jack's mind. His hands found her waist, and she was dragged without warning onto his lap. How he managed to turn sideways and get them between the steering wheel and the back of the seat was lost on her as his lips met hers and a bomb full of pleasure exploded in her core.

Somehow her knees were parted, straddling him, her pelvis brushing his, her breasts against his chest, her mouth open to Jack's. His lips were sweet, his tongue like melted sugar as it slid along hers. The clasp of his hand on her nape should've set alarms screaming in her head, but there was that stupid feminine melty thing again, turning her soft at the feel of him guiding her, holding her to him like he could never get enough of her taste. She knew the feeling. Closing her lips around his tongue, she sucked lightly. Jack moaned against her mouth. When she did it again, he bucked beneath her.

He shouldn't be the only one who got to explore. Maddie brought her hands to Jack's hard jawline. Beneath her fingertips, the scrub of his heavy stubble set her nerves alight. His cheeks were rough, his ears soft, the thick silk of his hair just the right length to capture her fingers. She was lost in the feel of him, the scent of him, the taste—God, he tasted so good. Instinctively her hips curled, grinding her pubic bone against the rock-hard evidence of his arousal. Jack growled, the sound a clear command, and her body complied. She did it again. This time the rough vibration that escaped him sounded like her name.

Jack squeezed her closer, the desperate pound of his heart clear against her breast.

Maddie's heart started to race, fear and need mixing, rising.

Jack tilted her backward. Her spine hit the seat. His weight came down on top of her.

Maddie screamed.

From one moment to the next, desire died. All she knew, all she could comprehend was the fight to get away, to get him off her, to breathe. She couldn't speak beyond panicked cries that scraped her throat raw. Her fear soared higher and higher and higher until she was certain her heart would burst.

"Maddie!"

Her legs were trapped. Her hand struck something hard, the sharp pain resonating up her arm. Maddie fought harder.

"Maddie, damn it, stop!"

Jack heaved backward, taking Maddie with him.

"Maddie!" More swearing. Cursing. Maddie didn't care what he was saying; all she cared about was getting out of this truck and getting away. But there was no moving Jack. He simply held her in place like he would a too-rowdy puppy until all the fight left her quivering muscles and she sagged reluctantly against him. Tiny shivers shook her frame, over and over, and she thought for a moment she might throw up her ice cream.

"No, you don't, wildcat," Jack said. "Just breathe. Breathe."

I can't! But her body obeyed as if he was her master. She hated him for that, but the nausea subsided all the same. The gentle circles he rubbed along her back and arms sent warmth through her chilled skin.

"Shh, it's all right. It's just me. Just Jack. Easy, darlin'."

Jack crooned to her. She stared hard over his shoulder at the darkened field outside the window. Her breathing was ragged, torn, loud and terrible in her ears, but Jack didn't seem to notice. He just kept talking, rocking her, slow and soothing, and gradually his arms and legs became a cave of comfort instead of a dangerous cage. Memories receded, and she went limp against him. Jack stilled.

"Maddie."

"What?" she croaked through her tight throat.

"Talk to me."

"No."

"Tell me."

"I don't—" She closed her eyes against the demand, but it wouldn't go away. And maybe it shouldn't. This was the second time she'd freaked in his arms, and he wanted to know why.

The words were a long time coming. "I was raped."

She could literally feel the wave of emotion move through his body as his muscles tightened beneath her. She tensed too, fixing her stare on the flashing red light she could just barely see over on Holmes Street, beyond the field. It was a few minutes before Jack broke the silence.

"When?"

"Four years ago."

They sat that way, in the quiet, Jack's breath teasing her bare neck, as Jack digested what she'd told him. As Maddie admitted, deep down where no one else could see, that she wanted this man, despite the fear, despite the pain she knew would come, and the risk to her safety. She wanted him, but that didn't mean she could go through with sex. Every time she was in his arms, she panicked. Making love to Jack was just another dream David had taken from her, another part of her life destroyed by her sadistic husband.

She closed her eyes, settled her forehead against Jack's shoulder. David would always be there, in the back of her mind, in her body's responses. She could never truly get away from him.

"Who was it?" Jack asked.

Maddie scraped away the mud of her thoughts. "What?"

"Who raped you?"

No, she wasn't answering that. She couldn't. She stayed silent, waiting, but so did Jack, his hands soothing the knots in her back again, his breathing strong and even. After a while it became clear they weren't going anywhere if he didn't get the answers he wanted.

"It was a stranger."

Jack shook his head, his five o'clock shadow scraping the delicate skin of her throat. "I don't think so."

His obvious disbelief wounded her more than she'd like. "Believe what you want," she snapped, tensing, trying to pull away. Of course, he was right— it wasn't the full truth, although it was as honest as she could get. The man who had raped her had been a stranger. A stranger in a familiar body.

"Be still." Despite his words, Jack acted as if he hadn't even noticed her attempts to get off him.

"Let go."

Jack eased his hold just enough that Maddie could sit back, see his face. His incredibly earnest face. "Maddie, you're not gonna convince me you didn't know your attacker. Statistically it's unlikely. But even more, you wouldn't be here with me, wouldn't have gone so easily if you had that kind of baggage regarding strangers."

"You're not a stranger," she whispered, the words barely escaping into the dark between them.

He breathed in deep, his chest pressing against her now soft nipples. "I would never hurt you."

But he already had. He made her want things she shouldn't want, made her comfortable with things that shouldn't be comfortable.

He was dangerous. And she wanted him all the more.

"I need to go in."

It was a moment before Jack finally spoke. "All right," he said. "Right after you kiss me."

"No."

His hand came up to cup her cheek. Maddie flinched. "Yes. I can't walk away knowing the last

137

thing you felt with me was fear, not when I can make it better. I won't hold you down, I'll stay just like this"—he held his hands out to the side, at least as much as he could in the close confines of the truck—"but I need you to kiss me. Please."

He was not a man afraid to say *please*; she'd noticed that about him. One simple word shouldn't soften her as much as it did.

"It's just a kiss, Maddie. Only a kiss."

"No, it's not. It's—" But she couldn't tell him it was so much more than that, that despite the fear and the memories and the anger, it felt like he was taking over her soul. She couldn't give him any more power over her than he already had. It was dangerous, destructive, this need for him.

It was also undeniable.

Without words, without argument or explanation, she brought her lips to his and kissed him. Eyes open, staring into his. Even when his mouth took over, when his hand cupped her neck and pulled her closer, she kept her gaze locked with Jack's. Jack. Not David. Not—

She started to shake. Broke away.

Jack kissed her this time. As she watched, his eyelids slid down, and a single tear escaped. For her. He cried for her. The salty taste tinged the sweetness of their kiss. Maddie ignored it and kissed him back.

Chapter Eleven

He let Maddie go inside alone, but he couldn't make himself leave. He'd held her, shaking, in his arms, and had to keep his own rage and horror hidden as he worked to gain her trust, her friendship. He needed to be holding her still, but Maddie had been at the end of her rope. Giving her peace had been what she needed.

But he couldn't deny that he'd wanted more. How the hell he wanted so badly to both make hot, sweet, overwhelming love to her and protect her from everything, including himself, he didn't know, but there it was. He sat in his truck on the dark street across from Maddie's apartment and wanted so damn bad to go in there, he ached with it. All over, not just between his tension-filled thighs.

Around one o'clock, the distinct crack of a door opening echoed across the street. Jack's tension ratcheted up another notch. Through his open window he could hear the drag of the wood along carpet. Heart thumping, he watched as the patch of darkness that was Maddie's entryway went gray, then faintly yellow. Maddie stood in the doorway, her curves hidden by what looked like an oversize T-shirt. Could she not sleep either, or was she just pissed that he was still out here? He watched, waiting, but she didn't move.

He was out of the truck and crossing the road before he could talk himself out of it.

Her eyes glittered in the darkness, and this close he could see the faint trembling of her body. "What's wrong, wildcat?"

The sound she made was somewhere between a laugh and a snort. "You're not seriously gonna keep calling me that, are you?"

"Of course I am." *Wildcat* was the perfect endearment for her; that it riled her up only added to its rightness. "Now tell me what's wrong."

"You, that what's wrong! Sticking your nose in things, dragging up memories that should've died a long time ago." She slapped the screen door, rattling the rickety thing in its frame. "Why can't you leave me alone?" And just like that, the fight went out of her. She leaned forward until her head rested on the corner of the door, weariness dragging at her shoulders. Were nightmares keeping her awake? He knew all about nightmares. Ten years on active duty and five more seeing the worst humanity had to offer—and what that worst did to women and children—didn't make for easy sleep, and that didn't include the nights he woke up with his mama's lifeless, bloody face flashing before his eyes.

Yes, he knew all about nightmares. The question was, could he help Maddie fix hers? Would she let him? Could she, after all she'd been through?

Leaning his head close, only the screen door between them, he whispered, "Let me in, Maddie. Let me help you." Just to get through the night. If it was all she'd give him, he'd take it; he'd take anything he could get.

140

For the longest time she was silent, and his heart sank into his boots like a rock. But finally, *finally* her hand went to the thin screen and pushed it open. He swung the door wide, but still she didn't move.

"I know what you want, Jack."

"Well, I haven't exactly made it a secret."

A faint smile tugged her full lips up. She tilted her head until her gaze met his. "I don't think I can give it to you."

"*It* isn't all I want, Maddie." He reached up, caution pounding in his head, and ran a finger down the flushed curve of her cheek. "Besides, there's nothing you have to give. There's plenty to share: warmth, comfort. None of that requires you to go any farther than you want to."

"You really expect me to believe that?"

"You don't have to believe it. Let me show you."

She stared at him a few seconds more, and then she turned to go inside. Jack followed.

Maddie didn't turn on any other lights. She crossed the living room in the dark, her steps taking her to a short hall. She walked down it, the hem of her shirt lightly tapping the backs of her thighs with each step. Jack watched, practically hypnotized, until she entered a doorway on the left.

This room was dark too, though a cracked door that probably led to a bathroom allowed the dull shine of a night-light in. It was just enough to keep from stubbing his toes on the mattress Maddie collapsed onto. The bed lay on the floor, no bed frame, rumpled covers bearing evidence of how restless Maddie had been. Without speaking she crawled on hands and knees to the opposite side. Jack swallowed hard at the faintest peek of panties as her shirt rode up, but gave his dick a stern reprimand before he slid off his shoes and socks and went to his knees on the edge of the bed.

The catch of Maddie's breath was clear in the quiet. "What now?"

In response Jack stretched out on top of the covers, keeping strictly to his side. The full-size mattress didn't quite accommodate his body; his feet hung off the end. He raised his head, grabbed one of several thick pillows leaning against the wall in lieu of a headboard, and tucked it underneath. Quiet rustling followed as Maddie settled in as well, and then silence except the gentle hush of their breathing.

She'd never sleep with this much tension pent up inside her. "Why don't you tell me where it is?"

Maddie shifted to face him. "Where what is?"

Jack was glad the darkness hid his amusement. "The weapon."

"What weapon?"

Jack turned on his side as well. "Wildcat, I seriously doubt you ever *don't* have a weapon on you—those sexy boots are perfect for more than giving me a hard-on—but given that I'm in your house, in your bed, I'm doubly certain you have at least one weapon somewhere." His laugh went a little strained. "And I've seen enough to know you don't have it on ya."

A light *click* rent the air, the sound of a folded knife locking into place, and Maddie chuckled. "Well, I do now."

Jack felt every muscle in his body go tight, and not with fear. "Darlin', you have no idea how much that turns me on. Might ought to put it away."

"There is something seriously wrong with you."

"I know, but you like me anyway, doncha?"

Maddie's response was muffled in the pillow, but he could've sworn it sounded like "God knows why."

Their shared laughter broke the tension, and he listened as Maddie rustled around, searching for the perfect spot. He was here, in bed with the woman who had taken over most of his waking moments in the past days, and quite a few sleeping ones too. A married woman. He should feel guilty about that— sleeping with another man's wife. He didn't; all he felt at the thought was rage. Maddie wouldn't tell him, but her rapist had to be Reed. Yes, it could've happened after she left the man, but why leave without returning to her parents? Why not flee to them for safety instead of dropping off the grid? When had Maddie learned to sleep with a weapon?

When her home, her bed had become unsafe.

Even now she didn't completely relax. The knife hadn't been unlocked. Just thinking about the fear it would take to make her this way tore at his heart, and made him more determined than ever to protect her, whether she wanted him to or not. Whether she hated his guts or not, which she might when she discovered she wasn't the only one with secrets.

Long hours later, Jack surfaced from a doze to the creeping fingers of dawn sneaking below the curtains and the sound of whimpering beside him. Maddie, her legs twisted in the blanket, jerked in her sleep. Her hands were fisted, her back arched as if she fought to free herself of restraints. Jack cursed softly, the abrupt awakening and the knowledge that Maddie was fighting for her life, if only in her dreams, churning his stomach until he had to fight the need to throw up. He'd seen soldiers reliving their worst moments in their sleep, but never a woman, especially one he cared about. Con had told him about Jess's nightmares, her struggle to heal after the attack she'd endured last year, but he couldn't have imagined how much that ripped Con up inside until this moment.

Easing closer ever so slowly, he crooned nonsense and endearments, letting his heat and gentle tone seep into her subconscious. Gradually she settled back onto the mattress, though her cries didn't stop. After a weapons check—he wasn't taking the chance of Maddie stabbing him instead of whoever haunted her dreams—he dared to slide an arm under her neck, one over her hip, and tug her closer to his body. Despite the late summer heat he swore he could already feel building outside, her skin was clammy, and she shivered in reaction as she made contact with his warmth. Her deep breath spoke of relief, though, her exhale seeming to empty her soul as she snuggled into his chest. The whimpers disappeared, and the steady rise and fall of her chest assured him she'd returned to sleep.

She was so delicate in his arms. It caught him off guard. Yes, she was small, but she was always fighting, either the world or herself. The fragile frame of her echoed the vulnerability he knew was inside. Fingers that could fist for a punch now lay open, limp, relaxed in sleep. The need to protect that weakness, allow her to be weak when she should be and strong when she had to be, was an urge he could not ignore. He lifted a heavy thigh over both of hers and used it to pull her hips against his early morning erection, surrounding her completely.

"Jack," she whispered, the sound ragged, then settled once more.

"It's all right, wildcat," he whispered back. He rubbed his nose along the top of her head, breathing in the sweet scent of her, the tiny hint of alcohol from long hours at the bar. "You're safe. I'll show you. You can trust me, Maddie; I swear it."

A promise he needed to keep. And sometime in the long hours of the night, he'd come to a decision: he had to tell her the truth about his job, about what he knew; he couldn't risk lies of omission driving a wedge between them, ruining whatever this was he—no, *they*; he was certain of it—felt.

Maddie would try to run. His instincts screamed it. But the bonds he'd built tonight, the ones that allowed her to sleep wrapped in the warmth of his body, wouldn't let her get far. And even if she did, he would move mountains to find her, to convince her to take a chance on him. To make her safe. No matter what it took.

Chapter Twelve

David Benjamin Reed V lowered himself into the elegantly carved French chair held out by his butler, Jacobs, and unfolded a snowy-white linen napkin, settling it in a perfect diamond over his lap, point directly between his knees. A plate of delicate poached eggs, fluffy biscuits, and lightly crisp bacon awaited him. He sighed in contentment. Breakfast was the most important meal of the day, and every morning, his was prepared with precision and attention to detail. He accepted nothing less.

Sipping the finest coffee money could buy—Ethiopian, not Columbian; the roast was darker and richer—he enjoyed the pleasant ache of his muscles after last night's session. His thighs burned, his forearms ached, but he had proven quite thoroughly that Carson did his job well. The girl was indeed ready for their buyer. And David was ready to face a day of ruthless power brokering with his mind clear and hunger, for the most part, appeased.

Only when the final morsel of bacon was consumed did he allow himself to lean into the back of his chair, coffee cup in hand, and close his eyes. He absorbed the silence, the solid quiet of his family mansion, his home since birth and that of six generations of Reeds past. His ancestors had avoided the plundering and destruction the War Between the States brought to so much of the South by playing both sides, a talent passed down the line all the way to

147

David. A talent he would pass to his son when he had one. When he chose the right woman to mother his legitimate offspring. He would not repeat the mistakes of the past.

There was still time. And until then, there were the lovely playthings, like the one that awaited him in the basement.

The gentle tap of footsteps approaching from the hall brought a frown to his face. "Yes, Jacobs."

David opened his eyes to meet his emotionless butler's gaze. The man's bland brown eyes and bland brown skin occasionally stirred something in David, a primordial hunger to see if he could generate emotion, reaction, in his longtime employee. A hunger to feel not just feminine flesh beneath his whip, but the flesh of those he ruled, like Jacobs. His ancestors had thrived on the backs of these people, learned to control and conquer through those they enslaved. What would he learn if he took his control of Jacobs a step further?

"Sir, Mr. Carson awaits you at your leisure."

Putting aside fantasies of muscled chocolate flesh ripped open and bleeding, he stood, placed his neatly folded napkin next to his empty plate, and proceeded from the room. Jacobs knew better than to follow.

The beginning of September in Nashville was always scorching, the last gasp of summer before October finally held sway. Each stained glass window doing sentinel duty along the sides of the long hall spilled the heat and the sun's brightness over him, preparing him for the cool gloom of the basement.

The keypad beeped as he entered each number of the entry code; then the thick soundproof door popped open, revealing the silence of the stairway to the lowest level of the Reed mansion. David took the steps one at a time, anticipation tightening his genitals and speeding his heart. He had won a dozen landmark cases in as many years, lived like a king, but nothing made him feel as powerful as controlling life and death. Here, in the basement, that control belonged to him alone, and nothing, no one could take it away.

A second keypad and second code protected his secret. Stepping through the heavy door, David inhaled the scent of fear—a comingling of piss and sweat and blood and despair. The scent was muted this morning by the antiseptic Carson's crew had used to clean the room after last night's session, but even the astringent tinge heated David's blood, the scent of fulfillment, of a mission accomplished. As he walked farther into the room, his gaze fell on his current mission, now huddled on a thin mattress along the back wall.

Carson moved to meet him as he approached.

"And how is our flower this morning?" David asked.

"All is in order."

David's partner was a man of few words, but the pleased grin on his face as he looked down at the teenage girl, her café au lait skin gleaming even in the dim light, told David all he needed to know. The girl had been trained thoroughly in the past few weeks—a fact David had proven last night. She took pain like a dream, sucked cock like a desperately nursing baby. But her value lay not in her training. David could have a hundred girls like her trained and sold in a year. Not even her youth and soft beauty could command the price they were getting for her. Only her virgin cunt could command a million dollars. A final doctor's exam this morning, under Carson's watchful eye, had ensured not only that the girl had held up well under last night's demands, but that the precious membrane was indeed still intact. An unhappy buyer could become a vindictive buyer, and David hadn't lasted this long by leaving a trail of vengeance seekers behind him.

A twinge of regret hit as the girl stirred, turning onto her back, only to moan and return to her side, facing the wall. He'd wanted very much to use more than that talented mouth last night. Of course, once this pretty one shipped out today, another would take her place. Until one did, there were girls in the servants' quarters. Tonight, perhaps, he could let his rigid control relax. Perhaps.

"You'll go with her then?" he asked Carson.

The man nodded. "Delivery sometime in the next week. The buyer is currently on a business trip in New York."

"That's cutting it close." The sale was next weekend.

"I'll be driving up with the merchandise in plenty of time."

The girl's new owner won her from the online auction Carson had held after her special attribute was discovered. Luckily the customer lived most of the year in nearby Atlanta. "Make certain he's happy. When he's done with her, we might arrange a trade-in."

Carson remained silent.

Another moan came from the girl as she rolled once more, this time to her opposite side. Beautiful brown tits poked out at them, and the sweet valley of crisp curls between her legs had David's tension rising swiftly. He reached for his belt buckle. "Wake her up. I think she needs a going-away present."

* * *

The scent of man and spice filled Maddie's nose as she stretched awake. It took her a moment to figure out why, to realize that the weight on her legs wasn't just blankets, that the constriction around her chest wasn't just the covers pulling a little too tight. She was in a full-body Jack wrap, and judging by the way he clamped down when she tried to wriggle out, he was content where he was.

Her heart went haywire, thumping so hard it resonated up her throat. She swallowed the feeling down. "Jack."

"Good morning, wildcat."

The words rumbled through his chest. It reminded her of a cat's purr, and the effect was the same: soothing, comforting. Still, she wanted out.

She punched him in the chest. Unfortunately, the Jack wrap didn't allow for much windup. All she got in response was a chuckle.

151

"Is that any way to greet a man you just slept with?"

"Jack."

One hot, firm hand slid the length of her spine, the touch almost as soothing as the rumble of Jack's words. "Relax. I didn't jump you during the night, and I can pretty much promise I won't now."

"Pretty much?"

He grunted in agreement. His hand made the return trip from tailbone to shoulder—and took her nightshirt with it. Maddie stiffened, but before she could sink her teeth into the hard pec in front of her face, Jack crooned in her ear. "It's all right; you're safe." His soft words stirred something, not quite a memory, not quite a dream. "It's all right, Maddie. You didn't think you could sleep with me beside you last night, but we tried it, slow and easy, and you did. Same thing now. Just let me touch you, nothing else." His fingers traced the bumps and ridges of her spinal column. "Nothing else, I promise. Just this."

"I don't—" She had to swallow against the desert-dry state of her throat. "I don't like to be touched."

"I think you like me touching you all too well, which probably scares you just as much as not liking it."

She closed her eyes against the truth of his words. God, why did he have to be right?

"I told you last night, wildcat: you'll get used to it. To me." He wasn't arrogant or condescending; his voice was full of the same tenderness with which he'd treated her the past few hours.

She believed him. She lay quiet, her heart going from bass drum to thump, then down to its normal gentle swoosh as Jack stroked and petted her. They were close enough together to feel his erection even through his jeans, but he didn't move anything but his hand. Instead Maddie found herself fighting her own urge to move, to arch against him like a cat, her skin tingling and sensitive from his attention. Her nipples went hard, her core ached—and she couldn't deny it. She refused to look up at him, though, to see what she hoped she wouldn't see: triumph in his eyes or, even worse, calculation. David used to do that, use her reactions against her. She couldn't bear to know Jack was the same kind of man.

On a loud groan, Jack curved until his breath hit her neck. His open mouth slid down to the dip of her shoulder, and Maddie couldn't hold back her gasp, the tiny push to get closer. Jack sucked her flesh into his mouth, desperation in the almost bite, in the tightening of his arms and leg, before pulling away. "Jesus, you're way too tempting."

He turned onto his back, one arm across his eyes, heart pounding out a rhythm at the side of his throat that told her his need was riding him much harder than she'd realized. She watched, fascinated, her body primed to jump and run the minute his control broke. It never did. His pulse slowed, the rigid line of his erection calmed, and his fists relaxed. He'd promised her he wouldn't push any further than just holding her, and he'd kept his promise.

That knowledge triggered a surge of need she was in no way ready for, but lying there, in the quiet

153

of her bedroom, on a mattress on the floor, she could finally admit to herself that they would have sex at some point. It felt as inevitable as the tide and as terrifying as plunging over the first hill of a roller coaster. In fact, the bass drum was back, and it was absolutely time for Jack to leave.

She shot up off the bed and grabbed a pair of shorts from the floor. "You have five minutes to use the bathroom and go."

She expected him to fight her, but all she got was a grin. He kept his eyes covered. "Yes, wildcat."

Hmph. Hurrying through to the kitchen, she hastily searched to make sure she'd gotten every scrap of research when she'd stowed it in the pantry last night before letting Jack in. She'd barely gotten a good glance in before Jack walked into the kitchen.

"What, no breakfast? No coffee? Is this the thanks I get?"

"Pretty much." She tugged him around and, with a hand in the small of his back, propelled him toward the door.

"Okay, okay." Jack flipped the locks on the front door, pushed open the screen, and turned back to her. "Not even a good-bye kiss?"

She closed the door in his face.

The idiot laughed like a loon all the way across the street to his truck. She could hear him— she bet her neighbors did too—but she also watched, barely peeking through the front curtain until Jack pulled away.

"Stubborn jackass."

It took a twenty-minute shower and half a bar of soap to get Jack's scent out of her pores. Of course, when she walked back out into the bedroom to dress, it assaulted her again. Finally she gave up trying to rid her place of him and decided to get out herself before thoughts of Jack, of what they'd done together and what they would probably do in the future, drove her insane. Hopefully leaving a window cracked would air out her room before she returned, or she'd never sleep tonight.

The heat seared her skin and shriveled her lungs as she drove the bike through town and out to the highway. Automatically she turned toward Hope Place's office, though she wasn't scheduled for another shift until tomorrow. Spinning her wheels while she waited to gain enough trust to go to the shelter was giving her far too much time to think about—and meet up with—Jack. She needed something to do, some way to advance the investigation; she just wasn't sure what.

As she pulled into the parking lot of the strip mall containing the office, Marge stepped out, her arms stacked with files and keys in hand. She glanced up as Maddie cut her engine.

"Well, look who's here." Marge's smile was warm with welcome despite the lines of stress around her eyes.

"Everything okay?"

Maddie swung a leg over her bike and headed to relieve Marge of her files. The older woman locked the office door. "Just the same ol—"

The word cut off as Marge turned and her gaze landed on Maddie's motorcycle. Unsure what had caught the woman's attention, Maddie glanced from Marge to the bike and back again. "Same old…?"

Marge's smile went brilliant. "Actually, not the same old." She eyed Maddie now instead of the bike. "How would you feel about a little road trip?"

Maddie's pulse thumped. "Uh, sure. Where?"

"You'll see." Marge walked toward her car, an older model beige Cadillac occupying a reserved space nearby. "Let's just drop those files in the backseat."

"Do you want me to ride with you?"

"Oh no," Marge told her. "I want you to bring that whiny little motorcycle with you. I've got someone I want you to meet."

They were going to the shelter. Maddie had no doubt about that, just as she knew there must be something seriously upsetting Marge that she would bring Maddie there so quickly. Though she regretted the stress on the woman, she couldn't help but feel elated as well—finally, after a week, she was going to make progress; she knew it.

Her bike did indeed whine as she followed Marge's car onto the highway, then hit the interstate that took them toward Atlanta. Marge exited about five miles later, the sign reading WARREN COVE.

They wandered for another twenty minutes down a rural highway before turning into a quiet neighborhood with alternating '70s split-level homes and brick ranches in need of new roofs. The road twisted and branched off, but eventually they came to a NO OUTLET sign near the end of the street. Marge stopped at a wide gate, the kind used for cattle fields, hung between two tall brick fence posts. Thick trees lined the fence like sentries. With an electronic *click* and *whir*, the gate swung open, and Marge pulled through. The gravel drive cut through the guardian vegetation and into a wide-open field, its end obscured by the balding top of a hill.

They inched along for nearly a quarter mile, but as first Marge's car and then Maddie's bike topped the hill, Maddie got her first glimpse of Hope Women's and Children's Shelter: a sprawling two-story house, older but still in good repair. She could see the fence that had extended from the gate circled the field where the house sat, then cut into a swath of woods thick with late-summer foliage at the back end of the property. She followed Marge to the rear of the house, where a graveled parking area was flanked by a concrete basketball court and a cluster of well-used playground equipment.

Maddie pulled her helmet off, shaking her sweaty hair out in the slight breeze. Her sweaty body, in bike-riding jeans and boots, she could do little about till they went inside, but the relief of the wind on her cheeks helped. By the time she'd hooked her helmet to the handlebar and swung herself off the bike, Marge was out of the Cadillac and walking toward Maddie, her gaze on the woods farther off.

Maddie glanced that way, seeing nothing but an old-fashioned tire swing and tree house she would've loved to play in as a kid. She'd been something of a rebel even then, not going for figure skating and the other more expected sports most kids in her tax bracket had enjoyed. Thank God her parents hadn't cared how she played as long as she was happy. "Everything okay?"

Marge gave her a snappy nod. "Perfect. Come on in and I'll show you around."

She followed the older woman toward the rear entrance to the house. As Maddie walked, she found the knowledge of where she was and the memories of a similar place warring in her head until she had to fight to stay steady. Sisters of Charity had been her home after she'd escaped David's estate. She could still remember her first glimpse of the place, not in a rural field but in inner city Nashville. She'd gone straight there from the hospital, assured by the nurse in the ER that the church would take her in. Four months of her life had been spent in that shelter, four months where she'd relearned what acceptance was, what love was—only to have it destroyed in the end. The memories flooded her, paralyzing her feet, churning in her stomach until she was certain she'd puke.

"Maddie?"

You can do this. You have to do this—for Vaneqe. For yourself. For Amber.

"Sorry." She smiled at Marge, not sure how great the effort was but determined to take this step. "Just a little overheated, I think."

Marge nodded. "Of course. Come inside where it's cool."

Stepping across the threshold was easier than she expected it to be. It was as if the homey atmosphere of the place reached out and enveloped her, pulling her into its warm embrace. Her nerves quieted, the nausea settled, and Maddie breathed a sigh of relief as she took in the cheery yellow kitchen that greeted them.

The room was cluttered but quiet. Obviously the lunch rush hadn't yet started. One side of the room was taken up with two dining tables, the furniture mismatched but clean, while the other side held industrial equipment for cooking, a butcher-block island that stretched half the length of the room, and more cabinets than Maddie thought she could ever figure out what to do with.

"This," Marge said with the air of a queen showing off her kingdom, "is Hope Place, as we call it. HWACS is just too much of a mouthful." She gestured Maddie farther into the room. "Come on in."

Directly ahead, a set of open double doors led to what looked to be the living area. Marge gestured around the kitchen as she walked in that direction. "The house was donated by the children of a prominent Atlanta businesswoman after her death. We are very lucky to have several companies that have taken a generous interest in us as well. Like most nonprofits, we run on a shoestring budget, but with their help we manage without the constant headache of wondering where the next penny will come from."

They walked into the front room—what would have, in a normal family home, been the living room. The huge area was sectioned off with couch and chair groupings for conversational and relaxation areas. The space in front of the fireplace was left open, and at the moment the area was occupied by a couple of women playing with small babies on blankets. Maddie swallowed hard and glanced to the opposite side of the room, where a bank of tables held mismatched computers and office equipment.

Marge's face as she glanced around, almost as if trying to see it through a guest's eyes, was serene. Happy. Sister Sinclair had often looked the same way, like her life had meaning because of the work she did. Maddie's would too, when her quest was done, even if she had to die to complete it. Every girl she could save would be worth it.

"The upstairs has been converted into suites. We have some permanent residents, some who stay just until they get on their feet. We have a community college just over the county line toward Atlanta, so our women have access to training. One of the job-placement firms in the city helps us too."

Maddie took it all in with careful eyes, wondering what living here had been like for Vaneqe. Had she been content? Had she found her footing? Or was the police's assumption that she'd just wanted to escape back to a life of drugs and Lord knew what else correct? Maddie wanted to find out, needed to uncover the truth with a desperation that closed her throat, making a reply to Marge's ongoing commentary impossible.

"But none of this is why I brought you out here."

"It's not?" Maddie knew that; Marge had told her she needed to meet someone, but Maddie had no idea whom.

"No." She jerked her head back into the kitchen, and when her gaze met Maddie's, amusement lit her faded blue eyes. "I need you to keep a lookout on the backyard while I drop off these files."

"You need me to…" She glanced at the kitchen, then back at Marge, a little ache accompanying the crease between her brows. "Watch for what?"

Marge chuckled. "You'll know it when you see it. I'll be right back." And with those cryptic words, she headed toward what looked to be a meeting room across from the nearby staircase.

"Okay." Maddie wandered back into the kitchen, to the windows overlooking the play area and cars. Empty. Whatever she was looking for, it wasn't there yet. She grabbed a chair from one of the tables and settled in to wait for Marge's return.

Chapter Thirteen

She'd been staring at the silent backyard for about fifteen minutes when she saw it: a creeping shadow extending, bit by bit, from the woods in front of the tree house. First the shape of a head, then shoulders, then a long thin body. By the time the feet appeared, the figure had crouched, there at the edge of the field, waiting as if afraid someone would jump them. Maddie took a little closer look and thought it was a boy. The head full of kinky black curls might've gone either way at this distance.

Without warning the small figure darted across the empty space between the woods and the house. Bare, dirt-smudged legs raced to cover the distance, equally dirty arms pumping. The boy reached the basketball area, crouched as low as he could get without crawling, and approached Marge's car on the opposite side from Maddie. She caught a view of him as he rounded the front of the Cadillac, and then the child disappeared between her bike and Marge's car.

Rough palms rubbed across her eyes didn't alleviate her dread. A child. Marge had wanted her to watch for a child. And if Maddie didn't very much miss her guess, this wasn't just any child, but the child she'd steeled herself against meeting since she'd ridden into Georgia two and a half weeks ago: Vaneqe's brother. She didn't know his name—the papers hadn't printed it—had never seen pictures, but she had no doubt that's who he was.

Children were her weakness. She'd known it before going into her marriage, and David had discovered it far too well after the wedding. She'd been studying for a degree in early childhood education at the time, had planned a career around nurturing kids, wanted desperately to have children of her own. It was the only thing she and David had in common, she'd soon discovered, if for different reasons. David wanted an heir, a successor to the twisted legacy of his family. Maddie had wanted to love and care for a child the way her parents had loved and cared for her. That dream had died when David's abuse began.

Over the past four years she had made it a point to be as far away from children as physically possible. Sure, she had seen them across the room in a restaurant, on the playground as she drove by, even standing in line at whatever grocery store was local at the time. But she had not been alone with a child in all that time, for a very good reason. She tried to forget exactly what that reason was as she tensed to rise from her chair.

Her brain continued to replay that first sight of him, the bowed brown head, curls tangled with leaves and grass as if he'd lain on the ground to look up at the sun. Spindly arms and legs gave him the thin look of a kid at the end of a growth spurt, as if he hadn't had time to fill out his skin yet. Now she could barely see the play of his fingers over the bike seat, tank, handlebars. He touched it all with interest,

163

poking, prodding, twisting. Maddie hated anyone touching her motorcycle—it was hers, the first thing that had really been hers after she'd left everything behind—but as she watched, all she saw was this boy's tiny body broken, lifeless, the skin no longer smudged but bruised and torn. A sob caught in her throat, the image was so strong, but she forced the tears away. "This isn't Amber," she whispered, more in her mind than aloud. "It isn't Amber—and it won't happen here. I won't let it."

Even as quiet as she was, the boy heard something. His head lifted, dark brown eyes peeping over the bike to meet hers through the glass. Staring her down. When he stood, defiance sat on his shoulders.

Like Vaneqe, the boy was a beauty. The same high cheekbones, full lips, distinctly stubborn chin. That chin gave her hope when she worried over Vaneqe in the dead of night. She had no doubt this urchin with bare feet and messy hair shared that trait also.

The boy went back to exploring the bike. Marge had known, that sneaky woman. She'd known the boy would be drawn to the motorcycle. But why bring Maddie out here? Why did Marge need him drawn out of the woods?

Whatever the reason, Maddie wasn't about to be a coward now. She stood, ran sweaty hands down her jeans, and went to meet the best clue she could hope to find.

The creak of the door opening earned her no more than another wary glance. She stepped onto the back patio and closed the door. "Hello."

The boy threw her assessing looks but refused to speak. He kept himself on the opposite side of her bike, but his little elfin face, so wary and needy at the same time, drew her forward even as her heart shrieked for her to retreat.

"You like my bike?"

A spark lit his eyes. "Not yours. No way."

"Way, I swear." A couple more steps brought her to the edge of the patio area. She sat on the concrete, crisscrossing her legs. "She doesn't look like much, but she runs great."

"She?" The disgust on his face had Maddie holding back a laugh. "Motorcycles aren't girls; they're boys."

"Really? Well, I'm pretty sure she told me she was a girl when I bought her." She tilted up one leg, hugging the knee to her chest. "I don't think I heard her wrong."

The boy seemed to be about ten years old, but his eyes were far older, without the hint of wonder many kids that age still possessed. That Amber had still possessed despite their circumstances. Right now those eyes looked at her like she was certifiable. He snorted through his nose. "Motorcycles don't talk either. They're machines, not people."

"Just because she's a machine doesn't mean she can't talk. Mine's been talking to me since I bought her. She makes noises too. She purrs when she's happy and growls when she's mad."

"Most people just yell when they're mad."

She had a feeling he'd seen more of that than a child should in his life. "Well, I don't usually yell, but I do stomp my foot sometimes. A girl has to have some way to get out her mad."

Laughter escaped, though he obviously didn't want it to. The sound tugged at her heart, and she melted. Her arms ached to hold him. Her tear ducts picked that moment to sting. Her chest squeezed at the thought of scaring him—and at the thought of caring.

She cleared the lump from her throat. "So…are you gonna tell me your name?" she asked.

He seemed to consider it for a moment, then shook his head. "Don't think so. You're a stranger."

The back door opened, and Marge stepped out. "Hey, Charlie. This is Maddie."

Charlie. Maddie had the sudden completely contradictory wish to go back, to not know his name. What she didn't know couldn't be used against her, or them.

"Maddie," Charlie repeated, his gaze dropping back to her motorcycle. "Can you gimme a ride?"

Maddie opened her mouth, not sure how she should respond, but Marge's laugh beat her to it. "I don't think so, squirt. I think you have tutoring right now."

Charlie's face went blank, the spark of rebellion in his eyes the only clue that he had no intention of doing what Marge was asking of him.

"Of course," Marge continued, ignoring the mutiny, "Maddie will be here for a little while. Maybe she could help you with your work *and then* give you a ride."

No. Marge, the supreme manipulator. God, Maddie would have to remember this later—after she refused. This was obviously an issue for Charlie, and she understood, she really did, but just the thought of hugging him, holding him close and protecting him while they rode, cut like a knife to her gut. She couldn't do it. She just couldn't.

Charlie narrowed his eyes at Maddie. "Would you do that?"

All it took was one look from those suspicious brown eyes, the same eyes that stared out at her from Vaneqe's picture every night, and she felt the refusal in her heart crumble into a million pieces. She glanced at Marge, who stared back with a slight smile that said she knew Maddie would give in eventually.

Damn it.

Maddie mentally threw up her hands. What was she really fighting, anyway? She needed to find out what Charlie knew. She just hadn't expected it to be this hard, to dig up this many agonizing memories. Besides, she'd never been good at protecting herself. She'd picked up the pieces and moved on before, and she could again, if it meant those eyes went bright with laughter like they had a few minutes ago.

"Sure."

Charlie nodded as if he'd expected nothing less. When Marge stepped aside, he squared his shoulders and headed into the kitchen. Maddie followed his lead, a smile tugging at her lips when she realized they both acted like they were headed for their execution, though probably for very different reasons.

Marge's hand on her arm held her back. The older woman waited until the door closed behind Charlie before narrowing her eyes at Maddie. "You."

Charlie wasn't the only one with a good blank face. "Yes?"

"You didn't tell me you were so good with children."

Uh-uh. "I'm not."

A thoughtful smile curved the edges of Marge's thin lips. "Remember Vaneqe?"

Maddie waited, knowing anything she said would reveal far more than she wanted it to.

Marge waved toward the back door. "That boy is her younger brother. He hasn't voluntarily done anything since she disappeared except eat and dress. He's as stubborn as they come, and if I was a betting woman, I would've said even a motorcycle couldn't change that. It didn't. You did."

"No—"

"Yes."

Maddie dropped her gaze to the ground, rubbing a hand across her forehead to hide the fear of where this was going. "Even if you're right…"

"I am." Marge took her hand, pulling it and Maddie's attention back to her. "He's not in school because they won't take him, not till he's caught up, not unless we hold him back a grade. He doesn't need that on top of everything else going on with him right now. But he won't work for us. He will for you, though."

"He will for the bike."

"He will for you," Marge said again. "You…you've intrigued him—and you own the bike. So what do you say?"

Feeling like she was making a deal with the devil, Maddie sighed. "I'll do it."

"Good." With a brisk pat, Marge moved past her into the house. "He needs at least three days a week."

Maddie raised her eyes to the blazing sun, now at its highest point, said a quick prayer, and followed Marge through the door.

* * *

"I think I know why Z was so cagey."

Con raised an eyebrow as he wandered into Jack's home office. "Well, I figured you had an important reason for calling me out here instead of coming to town."

"Other than that Lori would cut off my balls if I showed up at the office and pissed off any more employees?"

"That too."

Jack shrugged. He'd been in a sorry-ass mood the past couple of days. Maddie wasn't at work. He'd gone by her house, but the bike was nowhere in sight. He'd worried that she'd skipped town until Tommy Ray told him she had the weekend off but was scheduled for work tonight. In the meantime, Jack couldn't go to bed without dreaming about lying beside her, and between not seeing her, not sleeping for shit, and being so damn frustrated he'd developed a permanent case of blue balls, he wasn't in the mood to put up with people. He was better off at home, far away from everyone, focused on the hunt and nothing more.

And hunt he had.

Turning toward the bank of computers lining the wall above his desk, Jack began pulling up files. When each screen was full, he picked up his phone, hit Speaker, and dialed.

"Who are we calling?"

"Gabe Williams."

Gabe had been under Jack's command in the marines. Now home in the Texas hill country outside of Dallas, he was a police detective with just the expertise Jack needed.

"Williams."

"Gabe, it's Jack Quinn. Got a minute?"

"More than a minute for you, Boss."

Jack couldn't help but grin. Gabe rivaled him physically, an inch shorter but with heavier muscles, but the man insisted on treating Jack as if he was still Gabe's superior. The detective didn't know as much about cybersecurity but could run circles around Jack's investigative instincts. In fact he'd tried to hire Gabe away from the small-town police department he now worked for, but Gabe had refused. No amount of money and no authority would separate him from his home and his twin ever again, he'd said. Jack didn't know Sam, but he knew the two men were close, and he'd understood Gabe's refusal.

But this wasn't about the past; it was about the present, and Jack needed to get to it. "I've got a situation here I need your input on. You still involved with that narcotics task force?"

"Yeah." The gravel in Gabe's voice came straight through the line. "We're stalled out at the moment. You got something going down your way?"

"What the hell?" Con whispered.

"Gabe, you know my partner, Conlan James." It wasn't a question, just a courtesy. "He needs to hear this too."

"Sounds like he hasn't heard much yet."

"No shit," Con muttered.

Gabe chuckled. "He thinks it's better if he springs it on you all at once."

Jack frowned, mostly because both men knew him far too well. "If you two are done…"

"All right, Boss, whatcha got?"

"What can you tell me about Carson Alexander?"

A low whistle came through the phone line. "That he's one sick fuck. Alexander has his fingers in a lot of pies. Drugs, prostitution, you name it. The narcotics unit I'm with has picked up a couple low-level players who've pointed fingers in his direction, but they never made it to trial. That's not his real name, by the way, but it's the closest they've come. Aliases seem to be his specialty."

And Z probably knew that, since fake identities were his. Jack grunted. "What else?"

171

"There was an investigation in Dallas last year, one of Alexander's sex clubs, eXstacy. A BDSM club they believed was using underage workers. Doesn't matter how closemouthed you try to be, word gets out. The investigators and their families began receiving death threats, having little so-called accidents. They could never tie anything to Alexander or his associates, but he was responsible, no doubt about it. He has a reputation as a vindictive son of a bitch that protects both his possessions and his privacy obsessively."

Con leaned closer to the phone in interest. "So he's a one-man organized crime syndicate they can't get enough dirt on to bag."

"Exactly."

At JCL they worked with a lot of women whose abusers were able to bend the law, skirt it for their own purposes. Jess's attacker last year had worked the system quite effectively with his family's name and social standing, contacts. But this was a whole different scale. Jack looked at Con, wondering if the heart-pounding fear he'd felt when he first discovered the truth showed in his eyes.

Con stared back, a frown drawing his brows together.

"Alexander has ties to Maddie's husband."

"Shit." Con closed his eyes. Yeah, he understood exactly where Jack was.

"Who's Maddie?" Gabe asked.

"A…friend of mine," Jack told him. "A very close friend. Her…husband is David Reed."

Gabe wisely bypassed the first statement. "The lawyer?"

"The one and only."

"Slimy motherfucker."

A grunt signaled Jack's agreement. He rubbed the base of his skull, wishing he could get rid of the vise gripping his head.

Con's eyes narrowed. "And he ties in to Alexander how?"

"I'll show you. Gabe, files coming your way now." Jack went to each screen, clicked, and each file was sent through an encrypting program to Gabe's e-mail. As he worked, he explained. "Each of these businesses belongs to HMA Industries. Run by Alex Carrington."

"Never heard of him." Gabe's distracted tone said he was racing through the intel Jack sent as he listened.

"Neither has the IRS, the SSA, or anyone else I could hack. At least, they have no records of him. So I dug further. Alex Carrington is, I believe, Carson Alexander."

"Just another alias? How do you know?" Con asked.

"Because if you follow the profits, eventually they each feed into one of Alexander's known businesses."

Jack pulled up a new set of files. "So, we have Alexander at the bottom end. Back to the top. HMA, owner of these fine companies and run by Alexander via an alias, is a shell corporation. It in turn is owned by a series of companies—I've sent you a breakdown,

Gabe—whose CEOs I finally traced back to an Arlington Investments. The primary shareholder for Arlington is David Reed."

"How the hell did you find all this?" Conlan murmured, gaze tracing the lines on the various screens.

"Days of nothing else to do but go crazy," Jack answered.

"Now that is fucking interesting," Gabe said through the speaker.

"And also fucking secret," Jack told him. He knew he could trust Gabe, but this was Maddie's life, and whatever was going on between them, he wouldn't put her in any more danger than she already was. "Reed's wife is on the run, and I'm willing to bet it isn't all about her husband's abuse. She's gone completely off the grid. This has to be about Reed's connection to Alexander. She knows something about their business."

Con stood to pace the room, swearing under his breath.

"How did you find her?" Gabe asked.

"She got into an altercation at my favorite bar." Jack chuckled at the memory despite the heaviness sitting like a lump in his gut. "Let's just say she drew my attention."

Gabe's response was a noncommittal *humph*.

"And you think this is why Zylo's laying low?" Con asked.

Jack nodded. "He didn't know who Maddie was until after he'd agreed to help her. Maybe he didn't know about the connection between Reed and Alexander at the time, either. Who knows?"

"He does, now."

Gabe was silent, listening to them or working things out in his head, Jack wasn't sure. "What about your girl?" he finally asked. "What evidence does she have?"

"Whatever it is, she isn't telling," Con said.

Jack sighed, knowing what he had to do, knowing what it might cost him. "She will."

"Jack—"

"She will, Con. She grew up in Nashville, lived there all her life, even while she was married." His throat got tight on the word, but he coughed it away. "She's spent the past four years out West, from what I've managed to track, a little time in New England. She wouldn't be back here, so close to Reed's home turf, without a reason. I have to find out what that reason is."

Con shook his head, his eyes dark with sympathy. "You can't. You've already lied—"

"I didn't lie!"

"You didn't tell her everything either. When she finds out who you are, what you are, and that you used your position to uncover so much about her— she won't trust you, Jack."

A growl filled his chest, his head. "She will. I know she will. I can make her understand. I can help her."

"She's not gonna believe anyone can help her. She hasn't gone to the cops; she isn't using her real name. She doesn't know you, not really, and you're about to prove just how little she really does know. The information you've uncovered puts her in serious danger. Jack—"

He was on his feet, every muscle tight with strain, before he even realized it. "I know, Con. Okay? I know. There are a million reasons why she won't think she can trust me, and a million more why she should. But...she will." He stared into his friend's eyes, wanting to believe it, wanting Con to see how much it had to be true. "When she is safe...when this is all over, she'll know me inside and out, and she'll know no one can protect her like I can."

"What are you saying? Are you in love with her?"

No, he wasn't ready to admit to love. Con was the one who'd jumped into the deep end within a couple of weeks of knowing Jess. Of course, the man had been fascinated with her for months beforehand. Jack didn't have the benefit of months of observation; he hadn't even had two weeks, and though the minute he'd laid eyes on Maddie had been like a round kick to the gut, he wouldn't call it love. "I just need to do this."

Con's slow nod both accepted the admission and told Jack his friend had his back.

"Jack."

They both turned to the phone. Jesus, Jack had totally forgotten about Gabe. "Yeah?"

Thankfully Gabe bypassed what he'd heard in favor of the practical. "Whatever she knows, we need to know it."

"We?"

Gabe shrugged, the rustle of fabric coming through the speaker. "I've got the time, and you need someone with history on Alexander. Besides, if this gets as big as I think it might, you'll need all the hands you can get."

Jack wasn't going to argue with that. "How soon can you be here?"

"I'll check with Sam and then let you know."

"Will do. In the meantime, I'll talk to Maddie."

"What about evidence? I know we're a little in the dark here," Con said, "but is there anything we can do that might give us a head start?"

Jack looked back over the notes he'd compiled. "There are three locations in the Atlanta area linked to Alexander's network. I want men on them 24-7. If he comes into town, if anything suspicious comes up, I want to know."

Con already had his phone out, typing away. "I agree. I'll get Nicolas, T. C., and Zach on it. We'll set up rotating shifts starting tonight."

"Good." Jack signed off with Gabe, shut down his computer network, and turned to his best friend. "Now I've got a girl to convince."

Con's grin was nearly back to normal. "That's a show I don't want to miss."

Chapter Fourteen

Maddie had just returned from a trip to the stockroom for more whiskey Monday night when she noticed a young woman, about her height but with long mahogany-brown hair, lingering near the bar. The woman's brown eyes met hers for just a moment, shy and uncertain, before glancing over her shoulder toward the door.

Waiting for someone, then. Who in hell would bring this shy little thing into a honky-tonk? Even worse, why weren't they there to meet her?

Moving through the swinging door into the work area, Maddie set the bottles on the back counter and turned toward the woman. "Hey, can I help you?"

"Sure." She chose a bar stool, giving Maddie a warm smile. "Just a Coke, please."

"Coming right up."

Bart settled onto a stool a few seats down. "Maddie, tea?" he called. She nodded in his direction and went to fix the two drinks.

Now that she'd claimed her space, the woman seemed more comfortable, looking around, smiling at people, nodding her head to the music. Maddie took Bart his Long Island Iced Tea, noting the way his gaze lingered on the wedding ring on the woman's finger. "Meeting Philip tonight?" she asked.

Bart shook his head. "Family dinner," he told her, grimacing as he reached for his drink. "Afraid

178

I'm bach-ing it tonight." He chuckled, tipped his drink at Maddie in thanks, and pulled out his phone. Maddie walked the Coke down the bar.

The woman's smile reached her eyes, Maddie noticed. She took a quick sip of her drink and stuck out a hand. "Perfect. I'm Jess James."

"Maddie." She shook the woman's hand, fighting back a grin. "Jess James?"

"I know; I know. I'm lucky I wasn't born with Emily or Eve for a middle name or I'd be Jess E. James, and wouldn't that be lovely." Her laugh was warm. "What can I say? I loved my husband enough that I accepted a lifetime of jokes rather than not carrying his last name."

Something about the comment clicked in Maddie's mind. "Do you mean Con?" Whose last name was James and who, she had a strong feeling, would complement the curvy brunette perfectly.

"Yeah, that's him. I take it you've met during one of his boys' night outs with Jack."

His name started nerves fluttering in Maddie's stomach. She hadn't seen Jack in three days, since that morning she'd kicked him out of her apartment, and every day, every hour seemed to stretch longer and longer. She'd be lying if she said she wasn't keeping one eye on the door even now, waiting for him to walk in. She should've gone to see him, called Tommy Ray to get his phone number, anything but wait this long. She just…didn't. It was almost as if she'd needed to wait for the invasion of her boundaries to heal, to get her equilibrium back before reaching out. Thursday night had been too much too fast. Now?

A flush rose in her cheeks. Now…yeah, giddy as a freakin' schoolgirl.

Jess was checking out the nooks and crannies of the bar, the dance floor, the pool tables. "Ever since Jack built his house and he and Con moved their little get-togethers here, I've wanted to see this place. Wife's curiosity, I guess," she said with a wry smile. "I kind of see why they would come here." She lifted her drink to salute Maddie. "Excellent service. Plenty to see—although it really seems more like a great pickup spot than a man cave."

Maddie shook her head. "It can be, but you've got no worries there. I haven't been here long, but Con definitely doesn't come in to pick up girls." She couldn't resist leaning closer to Jess. "I'll let you in on a little secret."

Anticipation lit Jess's eyes as she mimicked Maddie's position. "What?"

"Jack's the ogler, not Con."

Jess giggled. "Caught him lookin', did you?"

Satisfaction at having one-upped him—even if he didn't know about it—filled Maddie's words. "Oh yeah."

"Ha! I cannot wait to rag him about that." She took a drink, her eyes twinkling with delight. "By the way, you didn't have to reassure me about my husband. I know he is definitely a one-woman man. But I appreciate it."

"Anytime," Maddie said, her hands going automatically to her dry towel and a glass. She swiped droplets of water from the mug without thought. Her attention was more on the sudden junior-high urge that filled her, the need to find out all she could about Jack, to uncover as many of his secrets as he had hers. This woman knew him in ways Maddie never would. "I'm amazed Jack and Con are still so close. They've been friends a long time, Jack said."

Maddie nodded. "A long time. Since middle school."

"I don't think I remember a handful of the kids I knew then. I'm certainly not still friends with any of them." Or anyone, for that matter, but that was for other reasons entirely.

"They're more like brothers than friends, really. They act like brothers too. Lord, when they get going..." A wry smile tilted Jess's lips before she took another sip. "Of course, it's a good thing they're more like family. They might get on each other's nerves, but when you run a business together, you can't just dump your partner on a whim."

For some reason she didn't understand, Maddie's heart thumped into her throat. "I didn't know they worked together." Of course, until Friday night she'd been too busy trying to get away from Jack to delve into his everyday life. His past was one thing, but his present? Details were a bad idea when she was trying to avoid caring too much.

"Oh yeah. JCL is their baby."

"JCL?"

"JCL Security. They started the company when they got out of the marines. What else do you do when you've been trained in fighting and intelligence, right?"

The thump got harder, joined now by a roaring sound that filled her ears like cotton. "So, not securities as in money, then. Security as in…"

"Protecting people. Finding the bad guys. Saving the day," Jess joked.

Finding the bad guys. She remembered the way Jack had watched her that first night, the look that'd said he had an eye on her because she was a troublemaker. She'd assumed it was his military experience she was seeing, not his current position. Security, securities. She could see how Taylor would make the mistake, but Maddie should've trusted her instincts, damn it.

Those giddy schoolgirl feelings turned in her stomach, hardening into a lump of something she had no desire to identify. She tried swallowing. The feeling got worse.

There were a billion other jobs in the world that Jack could have. She hadn't considered that bodyguard or investigator could be one of them. Because she hadn't wanted to know. She hadn't wanted to get too close, and now that she was… She thought about the knowing look in his eyes, the ease with which he'd accepted her story after their ice cream date. The way he'd assumed she carried a weapon, even to bed. The puzzle pieces fell into place, and the lump in her stomach got so big she hunched over before she could stop herself.

What had Jack found out about her?

Luckily her towel dropped from her hand at that moment. She bent fully to retrieve it, hiding her face, her eyes, giving herself time to school her expression. For a moment everything blurred, spun, the implications hitting her all at once, too many and too fast to fathom. All she knew was one thing: Jack had been interested in her from the beginning. How much of that was genuine, and how much of it depended on David's fortune and willingness to shell it out freely when it came to finding her?

Tossing the cloth into a dirty hamper, she straightened, asking casually, "So…you're meeting Con and Jack here…tonight?"

"Anytime now. Con called me a little bit ago. They have some more business to go over from today, but things have been busy and I didn't want to spend another evening without Con."

Maddie murmured her agreement, hoping her skin wasn't as green as it felt. Her mind raced, searching for a solution, estimating how much *anytime now* was in minutes, seconds. And all the while, Jess's friendly gaze stared back at her. Was that gaze as deceptive as Jack's might be?

Elena signaled her from the end of the bar, and she excused herself to fill the order—and try to figure out what the hell to do.

She knew the minute Jack walked through the door. Her back was turned, her hands busy with Elena's beers, but she felt his presence in the tingle up her spine, the sudden heat in her body. The ramped-up panic fluttering in her throat. She took a deep breath, forcing herself to wait. To think. To hand off Elena's order. Only then did she turn.

Jack strode across the room, his gaze boring through her, determination in every muscle, every movement, every breath escaping his flared nostrils. He knew. She didn't know how, but he did—her every instinct screamed it. And she couldn't resist that scream any longer.

Her gaze dropped to the half door that was her escape, then rose to meet Jack's again. A warning blazed in his eyes, one word forming silently on his lips: *don't*. He was halfway across the room now and closing fast.

Maddie hit the door running.

She made it to the break room before he rammed into her from behind.

Their combined force slammed the door open and around. It slapped the wall and reversed, flying back their way, but by then Maddie was on the other side of the room and Jack was waiting just inside. He caught the door on its backswing and closed it gently, snicking the lock into place. His stare never broke from hers.

The calculation in his eyes was terrifying. This was the real Jack, the marine, the bodyguard, the...whatever he was. Smoke practically came out of his ears, he was thinking so hard, calculating, finding the best path to manipulate her. That hurt more than everything else, that he would manipulate her. That he could manage to distance himself in a way she couldn't, even in her terrified state. She wanted to close her eyes, give in to the pain, but she didn't dare, not if she wanted out of here.

She braced herself, prepared for anything, but the softness of Jack's voice as it whispered on the air between them wasn't what she'd expected.

"Where are you going, Maddie?"

"I'm leaving."

"No, wildcat, you're not."

The regret seemed so genuine she almost fell for it. "Yes, I am."

Jack shook his head. "I can't let you leave, Maddie. I can't."

Fear thickened her tongue, and tears burned her eyes. She didn't want to fear him, didn't want to care enough that it hurt that she did. Still the agony tore through her. Maddie grabbed on to it, molded it, fashioned her own determination from the dregs of her emotions. Jack didn't matter. Her pain didn't matter. All that mattered was survival. She was Vaneqe's only hope.

So she went for her knife.

Jack was on her before her hand closed around the hilt, buried on the inside of her boot. Maddie felt his hand clamp around her wrist, felt his weight surging forward. Instinctively she brought her fist up, aiming straight for his groin. Jack shifted, and the strike glanced off his inner thigh. Maddie tried to open her hand, go for a grab on the tender skin, but the command left her brain too late. Jack had reversed his hold on her knife hand, whirled her around, and had her back to his chest. One arm whipped around for a headlock. The hand holding hers tightened, pulled, twisted, until the pressure on her torqued wrist forced her fingers to open and she dropped the knife.

"No, damn it!"

Maddie struggled in his hold, but Jack refused to let go. He held her hard against him, his touch firm but not bruising. The bend of his elbow was centered over her windpipe, protecting her from injury; his arm wasn't squeezing in on the sides of her neck to induce a blackout. She didn't want to notice, to think he might care if he hurt her, but she couldn't ignore the fact that he wasn't snapping her neck. Was it good or bad that he didn't want her dead?

They fought in silence, only the sound of their panting breaths breaking through. No matter how hard she pushed, pulled, twisted, no matter how much she squirmed and fought to get away, she managed nothing. Jack was an immovable force, his strength and skill countering everything she tried. Her panting turned to grunts, then wet little cries as the reality of where she was, who had her, what it meant burrowed down into her soul. She couldn't take Jack's betrayal. She'd endured so much and walked away without even a whimper, but this— No, this might actually kill her, whether Jack physically did it or not.

The fight died out of her bit by bit. Her muscles went slack as a sob shook her. Jack's grip on her hand eased, his touch sliding up her arm slowly, carefully. He moved to her stomach, his hand mapping the convulsions as she cried. She never cried. She tried to stop herself, yelled and cursed in her mind, but her body wasn't listening.

Jack was, though. He wrapped that arm around her belly, cradled her against him, spine to chest, and rocked, crooning softly in her ear until the storm finally lessened, only the occasional shudder shaking her in his arms.

"Shhh, wildcat. It's all right."

Her elbow connected with his ribs, but other than a slight grunt, he didn't respond.

It took two tries to get the words through her clogged throat. "Let me go."

"I can't do that." His breath brushed across her ear, raising goose bumps. "I won't do that until I know you aren't going to run. Nothing is solved by running."

She squirmed against him. "I think we've already had this conversation, and yes, running does solve some things."

"It hasn't solved your problems with David."

A prickly sensation, the awareness of a target on her back, crept over her. "You don't know anything about David." He couldn't. No one who hadn't lived with the man knew what he was truly like. The things he did.

"I know you're still married to him."

A sickly little laugh escaped. "Is that what's bothering you, Jack?"

"I don't give a shit if you're married."

"So what do you give a shit about? The million dollars? Is that what you want?"

"What million?"

She wasn't that stupid. "The million David's offering for my return. Alive, of course; the payout's considerably less if I'm dead, I think. Deprives him of the pleasure."

There was no mistaking his jerk of surprise. "Jesus. I'm surprised we're not crawling with bounty hunters for that kind of cash."

"Maybe they just haven't tracked me this far yet."

"Maybe not." His hand rubbed gently up and down her rib cage. "Then again, very few are as good at tracking as me."

Maddie shivered. Jack squeezed her closer, almost in reassurance, before loosening his hold. "I don't care about the money. I haven't been contacted by Reed. I don't care about using you or turning you in. I care about the fact that he's the bastard that raped you."

Her breath froze in her lungs.

"It wasn't that hard to figure out, Maddie." Jack tucked his head down next to hers, his mouth at her ear, his breath warm and real on her goosefleshed skin. "I don't know everything that happened, but I know the rape can't be all of it. He did something bad enough to make you run, disappear instead of stand and fight, and here you are all these years later, still running. It's time to stop."

"I can't." No matter how much she wanted to.

"You can. I can help you."

"Jack—"

His forehead settled on her shoulder. "Tell me, Maddie. Let me help."

She wanted to believe he could, needed to believe it—and her weakness made her angry. "'I can help you'? I can't even trust you, Jack." She lifted her feet, shook her body, trying to get herself free. Jack grunted but held on tight. The pressure, the confinement poured gasoline on the fire of her pain. She bucked and kicked, desperate for release. Desperate to escape. "Give me one good reason why I should for a single minute even think about telling you one. Damn. Thing!"

Jack had her flipped around before the last word faded from their ears. His hands on her arms gripped hard, shaking her. Fierce eyes stared down at her. "Because I said you could," he told her, shaking her again. "And because of this."

His mouth met hers, her back met the wall, and Maddie could do nothing but surrender to the hunger that hit her like a tidal wave, burying everything else in its wake. His taste overwhelmed her, consumed her—hot and masculine and just as hungry as she was. Her world narrowed to his lips and tongue and teeth, his heat, his touch. She twisted, jerked, struggling against his hold, but it only increased the friction between them, forced her breasts, her lips and pelvis and thighs harder against his. The rigid length of his erection branded her belly. She wasn't even sure any longer if she was still trying to get escape or get closer. Either way, she couldn't stop. Wouldn't stop. This had been coming for far too long, and if she was going to have one good thing in this sorry life before she ran again, it would be Jack.

But she wouldn't make it easy. She nipped, bit. Clawed at Jack's arms and back, desperate to get closer, to feel everything he could give her and demand a thousand times more. Nothing else existed.

Nothing else mattered—thought, danger, hurt. Just Jack, his brutal kiss, his bruising touch. It was all she'd ever wanted and more.

More.

Even through their clothes, the heat of him burned her. The muted sensation wasn't enough. In desperation she gripped his shirt and tore at the buttons, popping them, ripping the fabric until his shirt sagged back off his shoulders, baring him to her. White-hot need seared her when her hands hit his naked skin. A strangled groan passed from Jack's mouth to hers, vibrating on her tongue. Hands as impatient as hers lifted the hem of her shirt. Cool air hit her overheated skin, a chill Jack massaged away with rough hands. She arched into his touch, mindless, hungry for more, and Jack gave it. He traveled the soft plain of her belly and the ridges of her ribs, making his way with single-minded intent toward his destination. The clasp of her bra.

She spared a fleeting thought for the fact that they were in Halftime's break room, a flimsy lock all that separated them from possible embarrassment. But if that embarrassment was the price to pay for experiencing his hands on her breasts, she would endure it. She would have begged him to hurry if she wasn't too busy just trying to breathe. And kiss. And get closer. And—

A keening cry passed from her lips to his when Jack popped open her bra and dug inside, coming skin to skin with her hardened nipple. They writhed together, pelvises grinding, legs tangling, breath mingling, but all Maddie could focus on was that taut nub, Jack rubbing it, pinching it, rolling it between his thumb and finger until her spine bowed and she couldn't hold back a desperate plea.

"Jack, please!" She was sobbing. Squirming. Arching into his touch like a wild thing. God, she needed this, needed him. Now.

Jack swore against her mouth, a word that both shocked and inflamed her. He fumbled at the button of her jeans, then yanked the zipper down, diving into the hot, steamy bath he had created. She could feel his fingers sliding in her cream, knew she should be embarrassed at her total loss of control, but just couldn't bother.

Jack tore his mouth away from hers, ignoring her groan of need, and tucked his head to the side to lick her sensitive earlobe. Whispers of naughty instructions swirled in her dazed brain, guided her to open her legs a little more, push her tight nipple into his greedy hand, touch her mouth to his salty, sweat-tinged neck. Jack tensed with pleasure under her tongue, and she caught his skin lightly between her teeth, suckling him. Jack swore again.

In the space of seconds, he was gone. It took her passion-fogged brain a few moments to realize he had dropped to her feet to pull on her jeans. As they hit the floor, he lifted one foot roughly and dragged the jeans over her boot. He didn't take the time for the other one.

Kicking her feet apart, Jack grabbed the crotch of her panties and ripped. She would never admit that the primal act burned her like fire, but it did. How, she didn't know—her body was open, vulnerable, unprotected, but it wasn't fear that filled her. Just a desperate need she knew would never be quenched without Jack inside her.

A quick rip, the crinkle of foil, and Jack was between her legs, the tip of his latex-covered cock tapping her entrance. When he'd found the time to open his pants, she didn't know. Didn't care. Didn't even bother to look down. She raised her thigh to his hip, opening herself more. Jack held her leg in position, centered himself, and drove straight in.

Maddie screamed before she could stop, buffering the sound with a harsh bite on the thick ridge of muscle along his shoulder. If she hurt, he would too. He seemed to get the message, because he paused, waiting, his breath rasping in her ear as her channel pulsed around him, trying desperately to accommodate his thick girth. Tiny rolls of his hips eased her tightness, the vise grip she had on his rigid length, and soon Maddie was moaning into his ear and pushing back against him. She needed him deeper, needed more. He gave it to her.

"Maddie. God."

Jack's tone was strained, the fight to hold back evident, but he set a steady, even rhythm, every thrust loosening her a bit more, drawing out her cream, easing his way until the tip of his cock grazed the mouth of her womb deep inside. Maddie's tight throat strangled her cry of pleasure. She angled her hips, needing him even deeper, needing him to fill her to the brim. The frenzy was returning, fire burning from her clit to her belly to her bare nipples as they rubbed the hair-roughened muscles of his chest. But the connection wasn't complete until she turned her mouth up and Jack met it, his tongue thrusting between her lips in a perfect imitation of his invasion of her body.

Jack tugged her knee higher, bent his slightly, and the base of his cock hit her clit with an electric charge. Breathless, arching, she sought the contact again and again, moaning his name into every kiss as she tightened on his pounding length. She was so close, so desperate she thought she just might die if she couldn't explode.

"Now, Maddie," Jack whispered, voice ragged with pleasure and his own rise to completion. "Come on. You're almost there; I can feel it. Come for me. Come for me, wildcat," he gasped against her neck, and she did. Her body imploded, squeezing down, muscles locked in painful pleasure as orgasm took her over. She was vaguely aware of Jack's muffled shout as he followed her, his thrusts continuing to milk every last spasm from both of them until they collapsed, replete, dazed, against the wall behind them.

Chapter Fifteen

Reality bitch-slapped her brain the minute it cleared. Caught between the wall and Jack's big, hard, sweaty body, she couldn't stop the panic that exploded in her mind, the need to strike out at the threat that stood too close and was way too strong. She didn't even realize she was throwing punches until Jack staggered back, a hand on his reddening chest, his "Goddamn it, Maddie!" like a cold cup of water to the face.

She sagged against the wall, shivers rattling her bones.

Jack figured it out before she had to tell him. His face softened, eyes concerned as he tucked himself back into his jeans. "Wildcat, it's—"

"Don't tell me it's all right. Don't! It's not all right and— God," she moaned, one hand coming up to cover her face, "what have I done?"

Jack stepped toward her. Maddie tried to move back, slide along the wall, but something was under her boot. Catching herself as she stumbled, she managed to grab on to the fact that her jeans were tangled around her ankles, keeping her from getting away. Embarrassment flooded her. She had to move, now, before he came at her again. Had to get dressed. Had to get away from him.

Maddie fumbled her jeans around until she could pull the leg back over her boot before yanking the material up her shaking limbs. Jack paced before her, not coming closer but cursing under his breath, his fists opening and closing as he moved. He sounded angry.

How had she gotten herself into this mess?

Keeping her eyes firmly on Jack, she moved back, one step, then another, until she came to the corner of the room. The wall at her back felt solid, safe. Maddie let herself slide down it to crouch, huddled, surrounded by walls. Not arms, never arms. A sudden, powerful longing for her mother to hold her, for her parents, who didn't even know where the hell she was, rose out of nowhere, a need so strong she shut her eyes, able to battle it and nothing else. Because she couldn't afford to give in to that longing. Her parents weren't here. No one was going to hold her. Nobody cared that she was scared out of her freaking mind and confused and trying desperately not to throw up. She had to get herself through, just like she had for four years.

God, she'd let him touch her. Let him take her. And she'd enjoyed it. How could she enjoy something so— Images rose to haunt her, not of Jack but of David, of the things he'd done, made her do. Of that last night, the pain. They flooded her mind, so sudden and violent that she gagged. The bile in her throat made her panic. David always punished her if she threw up, always.

Hold it in. Hold it in.

The words never broke from her clenched throat. She was screaming inside, going down into that place where she was bound, helpless, unclean. And her body was protesting in the only way it knew how. One more desperate heave and she sprinted for the tiny restroom on the other side of the room, barely stumbling to her knees in front of the toilet in time to empty her rebelling stomach.

It took long moments before she was aware of anything but the racking cramps. The next thing she felt was a cool washcloth, its nubby surface gliding along her sweaty neck, her arms, her forehead. She kept her head down, not wanting Jack to see her this way, not wanting anyone to see her fighting the convulsions, the memories. This battle was private—and humiliating. She'd been humiliated enough in the past; she didn't need more now.

Jack flushed the toilet. "Maddie, darlin', raise your head."

"Go away, Jack. Just…go away. Please."

"I can't, wildcat. Let me take care of you."

"No." She raised one shaking hand, waving it in his general direction. "I don't… I'm not sure I'm…"

"Finished. Okay." He moved behind her, letting her feel his warmth, but didn't touch her again. "I'll wait. Just…take your time."

They sat in the silence, Maddie's occasional shaky sigh breaking through, until she thought her limbs might hold her up. When she shifted to stand, Jack was right there.

"Jack, I… Please"—she pointed at the door, keeping her head averted, hating that she had to ask but doing it anyway—"give me a minute."

He hesitated but finally relented. He reached past her, set the cloth on the sink, and stepped to the door. "I'll give you a minute."

It wasn't funny—nothing about this was funny—but for some reason his parroting of her request brought a smile to her lips, almost as if all the emotion that had filled her up had been emptied out with her stomach, leaving room for this one small moment of humor. She held on to it with desperate hands as she cleaned herself up, but even that tiny bit of happiness couldn't help her face herself in the mirror. Instead she turned away.

When she returned to the break room, she couldn't look at Jack either. She could see his legs as he stood over by the door leading out into the hallway. The murmur of voices, Jack's and another man she thought was Con, drifted back to her, but the words didn't register. She made her way to the small table near the fridge and sat before her wobbly legs gave out. She'd get herself together, get her things, and then talk to Tommy Ray. Not only had she left the bar unattended, but she couldn't come back here after tonight. If Jack could find her, so could others, and she wouldn't risk these people. She'd learned that lesson a long time ago.

The *click* of the door closing brought her head up. She trained her eyes on Jack's chest, noting absently the missing buttons that left his shirt open most of the way down. "I need to go."

Jack didn't answer right away. Instead he crossed the room to take the chair next to hers. The sudden stiffening of her body was something she had no control over.

Jack noticed. Of course he noticed—he never missed a thing—but he didn't mention it. Maddie saw the flash of something she couldn't quite identify in his eyes, though.

"Maddie...about what happen—"

"I really, really don't want to talk about this." She rubbed her fingers over tired eyes.

A pause, then, "Okay, we can shelve that for now."

She threw him a sarcastic look. "Gee, thanks."

"But we do need to talk about Reed."

Yeah, she guessed they did. "How did you find out?"

Jack shrugged. "You caught my attention from the first moment I saw you, and...I needed to know more. My company specializes in security. It wasn't as difficult to get information as you might think, not once I had your name—"

"And how did you get my real name."

"I..." Jack rubbed the back of his neck. It was strange—all these years she'd spent closing herself in, keeping herself apart, she'd never thought to be close enough to someone else to be able to read them at will. Maybe Jack seemed enigmatic to others, but the dread on his face was as clear to her as the color of his eyes. "I looked through your backpack."

"What?"

"Marge asked me to run your background check. I do those for her, all of them. I dig a little deeper than most."

"When?" Had he violated her trust while she'd slept beside him? When she'd allowed him into her home, her bed?

"Here."

"But I keep my—" She caught her breath. "You broke into my locker."

"All of them, actually, until I found yours."

She stared at him, trying to let that sink in. Anger took second place to figuring out how he'd found out about her past. If Jack could do it, could someone else? "Still, my real name isn't on anything in my bag."

"I know Z."

That spiky-haired little punk. "He told you?"

"No. Not directly, anyway." He leaned his elbows on the table. "He and I have known each other for years. I recognized his handiwork and kept digging. I'm good at that, Maddie. It's what I do— whatever it takes to find the information I need."

"And you needed information on me."

"Yes."

"But…why?"

"At first…" He shrugged. "I was curious. And then Marge called. JCL does pro bono work for Hope Place. I had to clear you before Marge would even consider allowing you to volunteer. But even after…I couldn't let it go."

She didn't want to hear the rough note of pain in his voice. "Why?"

"Because it—*you* were different. Because you weren't just a job. Because I…care."

Maddie's eyebrows went up. "You care?"

"I care. Just give me a chance to prove it."

Let me show you, that's what he'd said the night she let him into her apartment, into her bed. The same sentiment echoed in his words now. She couldn't respond. She'd trusted him, and now… She didn't know what to say.

Jack reached up, stroking his fingertips along her jaw, across her heated cheek, down the length of her neck. Maddie trembled at his touch, but he didn't go farther. She didn't know if she was glad or disappointed.

"I have dealt with women on the run," Jack said, "and the asses that hunt them. I turn the tables, and believe me, I'm very good at it. It's time for you to stop running and start letting someone help you. Let me help you."

"Why should I give you a chance?" She tried to sound strong, in control, to draw on her anger from moments ago, but the truth was he wore her down with his very presence, not to mention his words. The knowledge sharpened her tone. "Why should I stay or even give a shit what you want, Jack? We're not in love; we're not even sleeping together. I can walk away without a backward glance and never think of you again"—*liar!*—"so why are we even arguing about this?"

Jack chuckled, actually chuckled. He knew she was lying as well as she did. That didn't make her questions any less valid.

She shot him a dirty look. "How do I know you're telling me the truth?"

"Really, Maddie? You've talked to Con, to Jess. To Tommy Ray and everyone else here. I'm more than willing to take you to my home, my job. Why do you think I wanted to get to know you? So that when you found out who I was, that trust would already be there."

"Are you seriously reminding me that you slept at my house while you were lying to me?"

Jack chucked her chin gently. "Keeping secrets, Maddie. That's not the same thing, and it wasn't intentional."

She turned her head away from his touch, his stare, hardening her heart. She couldn't concede this point or she'd concede all the others, and that was too big a risk to take.

Jack sighed. "Okay, so you tell me: what happened? You stayed what, six years? Why leave, why then?"

No. Hell no. She stared at the ticking clock on the wall, her lips tight against the chance that the answer he sought might slip out.

"See," he said without even a trace of smugness, "we both have secrets. Now you know mine. In time, you can tell me yours. In between?" He eased closer, slowly, carefully, and took her in his arms with a tenderness that shook what little composure she had left. "I'll protect you with everything I am."

She closed her eyes, dropped her forehead to his shoulder. Incredibly, a faint hint of arousal stirred low in her belly. "You don't know what you're asking, Jack."

"Maybe not, but you're going to help me figure it out. In the meantime, I'll be here to help you."

* * *

One night, two at the most. That's all the time Jack had to solidify the connection between them. And there was a connection. Not only had Maddie blown his every notion of how good sex could be out of the fucking water, but holding her, caring for her, easing her pain had done something to him that he couldn't explain. It was as if his every cell, every thought was drawn to her. Every instinct screamed at him to keep her close, to glue himself to her side—so that's exactly what he planned to do.

Once Gabe arrived and more intel came in, they'd be knee-deep in chaos, and before that happened, he had to make sure Maddie was with him, completely, no reservations. Not only because of the plan and because he could free her, but because his soul demanded it. If she walked away now, he knew he would never be the same again.

He had one mission when it came to Maddie: *make sure she stays*. Taking her back to his place was vital to that mission—and to her safety. Now he just had to figure out how to make it happen.

He was waiting when she entered the break room at the end of her shift.

"Haven't we talked about you stalking me?" she asked, a weary smile on her face. His chest squeezed at her attempt at humor.

"Not nearly enough," he said. He approached with caution, more because he knew she'd been through too much tonight than because he was afraid she'd attack. Of course, with this woman, he should always be afraid she'd attack—she was a fighter, and he was damn proud of that. Weak women had never drawn him, maybe because he'd lived with enough of that in his childhood. Maddie was nothing like his mama.

Tonight he needn't have worried. Maddie accepted his arms around her without protest, allowing him to tug her close, even leaning her head against his chest. It felt so damn good to hold her.

"I want you to go home with me."

She stiffened against him, just as he'd expected. He headed off her protests before they could start. "Maddie, I need this. I need to know you're safe. And I need you in my arms."

Her forehead pressed hard into his sternum. "What if...what if I can't, Jack?"

She had so little faith in herself, while he had all the faith in the world. "You can. But if you think you can't, then sex can wait."

"Is that right?" she asked, the faintest hint of amusement sneaking through.

"That's right," he said, tipping her chin up until her mouth met his. "Even if it kills me."

She laughed through their kiss, and he thought for a moment that the tentative happiness in the sound might just stop his heart.

"Okay," she said when the kiss ended, "but I need to go by my apartment first."

"That we can do." He took a second kiss, deepening this one, losing himself in the warmth of her mouth and the touch of her tongue. His cock went rock hard against her.

"You also have to feed me."

"You're just demanding all kinds of things tonight, aren't you?"

She gave him a little punch to the ribs. "You bet I am. I want a Coke and a big, greasy burger. And fries."

He ran his hands under the hem of her T-shirt. Her skin was smooth as cream beneath his fingers. "Fries, huh?"

Maddie shivered, gooseflesh peppering her skin. The reaction made him feel about fifteen feet tall.

"Yes, french fries. Salty ones. I don't think I could agree without the french fries."

"French fries it is. Come on." Jack pressed his lips to hers for one more hot, hard kiss before he stepped back.

"Okay then."

By the time they'd swung by her apartment for Maddie to pack an overnight bag, and gone through the drive-through for the required fries and burgers, Jack was as hungry as Maddie. They ate on the drive out to his place. About twenty minutes later they hit the long driveway that led to his house, but Maddie was already drifting off to sleep on his shoulder.

"No wonder you're at the Halftime so much. It doesn't take you long to get there," she said, rubbing her eyes.

"It's also on the drive home from JCL."

In the glow of the motion-sensor lights surrounding the house, he could see Maddie's lips tighten. Reminding her of the secret he'd kept didn't make him happy either, but they both had to move on, and talking about it was the only way to do that.

"Our offices are in downtown Atlanta, so it's a long drive to an empty house. Might as well stop along the way."

Maddie nodded, then reached for the door handle. Jack did the same, taking her bag with him. After he locked the truck, he led Maddie around to the back deck.

"Why is it Southerners always use their back doors?" Maddie asked.

"Don't you know? You grew up in Nashville, right?"

"I grew up as an upper-class Southerner. My parents are sweet, but they're not country in any sense of the word."

He held the door open for her to step through. "So they're still alive." He hadn't found obituaries, but with Maddie it was probably best to ask.

"Yeah."

The word was soft, filled with longing. So she hadn't left her parents voluntarily. He opened his mouth to ask more, but Maddie shook her head as she walked inside. "Not tonight, okay? It's…just too hard tonight."

He nodded, though she couldn't see him. He reset the alarm, flipped on the kitchen light, and gestured Maddie toward the living room. "We use the back door because it's more casual. At least I think that's why. Or it might be because we're too lazy to walk around to the front after parking in the back."

There was the light he longed for in her eyes. "Says you," she teased.

"Says me."

He watched her take in their surroundings. His house was decorated to blend with the outdoors, the reason he'd moved out here. Con was lucky in that his family had owned property on Lake Lanier for generations. Jack had been searching for the same feel as Con's family home but also a chance to start his own tradition, his own family. He'd built a brand-new home, one exactly like he'd dreamed of since he was a kid sleeping in the closet of his mom's cramped one-room apartment. It was the perfect house, with a view of the woods and the river out back. All it had needed was one little detail: someone to share it with.

He couldn't wait to get her in his bed.

Maddie was talking as she glanced into his darkened den. "It just seems like the South calls to you no matter where you are."

Jack grunted. "Yeah, I felt the same way when I was in the marines. No matter where I was, what it was like, it wasn't the South."

Maddie moved back to his side, and he turned, leading the way down the hall toward the bedrooms. "Where were you stationed?" she asked.

"Around. Mostly Iraq." He flicked on the overhead lights to guide their way.

"Iraq? Dangerous place."

"Yeah."

"What was it like?"

He paused outside his bedroom to glance down at her. Maddie's hair, swept back in its customary clip, left the soft lines of her face revealed. "Scary," he said, drinking in the sight of her. "There's nothing like facing the muzzle of an AK knowing the guy on the other end thinks you belong in hell anyway, so killing you ain't a sin."

Maddie reached up, her fingers tentative as she traced the tight lines of his lips. A shiver of need tingled down his spine to his balls.

"Was there anything you liked about it? Your time in the marines?"

He grinned under her finger. "My men." He stepped into the darkened room. "Some nights, when we weren't out in the desert on missions, we'd spend time jawin' over a round of beers, eating cookies J. J. got from his wife in his care packages, blowing off steam. That I do miss. Working together, putting your life on the line for each other, living through thick and thin together. That's what made me work so hard on our team at JCL." He tossed Maddie's bag onto the king-size bed and moved to turn on the bedside lamp. "It's like I'm the daddy and they're all my little children; I get to build for them what I found with my team over there."

When he turned back to her, Maddie's eyes were round, her stare fixed on the bed. Hoping to ease the obvious fear he saw in her face, he asked, "So what about you?"

Maddie jerked her head around. "What about me?"

"You know what I do for a living." He took a step toward her, then another. "I know you haven't bartended all your life." Another step. Maddie's stare was fixed on him now, not the bed. "What did you want to do before all this happened? You went to college, right?" He thought he remembered something along those lines, but right now he couldn't for the life of him draw the details to mind. All he could think about was getting closer and closer to Maddie.

"Yeah. Early childhood education." Her gaze dropped to the floor. "Don't know what I was thinking. Can you imagine, me, with kids?"

Oh, Maddie. "I can very much imagine it," he said, taking the last step to bring them face-to-face. Maddie lifted her eyes to him. "And even if I couldn't, Marge has been glowing in her praise."

The muscles around her dark eyes tightened. "Yeah, well, Charlie is a special kid."

"He's been through a lot," Jack said.

"I know."

"So have you." He took her hand, fiddling gently with her fingers, letting the silence play out between them. He stroked each digit, making tiny circles around her knuckles, tracing the calluses on her palms from work, the rough spots from so much dishwashing.

Maddie shivered. "Jack…"

He glanced from her hand to her wide eyes. "I want you again, Maddie. Just like before. Well, not just like before." He let a smile tug at his lips. "I want to go slow this time, savor you."

She started to speak, to deny him. He pressed a finger against her mouth. "We've already established the ground rules: If you're okay, we move forward. If you're not, we stop. Why wait to try?"

Chapter Sixteen

"Because…" Maddie tugged her lip between her teeth. Jack waited, letting her gather the words, tracing her chin with his forefinger.

She took a deep breath. "Because the only thing that scares me more than sex is the thought of disappointing you."

His heart hurt. "We didn't have sex Friday morning. Did I act disappointed then?"

"No."

He lifted her hand to his lips, kissed the trembling fingers, licked between each one as she watched, her eyes glazed with desire and indecision. He knew which side he wanted her to come down on. Without waiting, he used her hand to tug her closer, right up against him, and then he took her mouth, delving deep, shaking with the fierce need to throw control to the wind. He wouldn't. Maddie deserved time and tenderness, and he deserved to give it to her.

Her lips were salty from the fries he'd fed her. He savored her taste, the soft texture of her skin, the pressure of her tongue against his. When she kissed him, everything else fell away. There was only Maddie—her gasps as he nipped at her kiss-swollen lips, her moans as he stroked the inside of her mouth, the pulse of her pelvis against his, picking up the ageless rhythm they'd known together just a few hours before. Finally, *finally* Maddie's hands came up, her fingers digging into his hair, pulling him close, taking the lead to explore his mouth as well.

He needed more and sought it out, leaving her lips to trail lower until he could lick and suck the tender skin of her neck. Maddie shifted restlessly against him.

"I want to take you right here. In this bed," he told her on a groan as need tightened his shaft. He nipped the sensitive lobe of her ear, sharing the bite of pain. "I'm gonna lay you out. Spend hours tasting your body, sucking your nipples, feeling all that hot cream drip over my cock as I drive into you."

Maddie moaned. "Jack, I…"

Her words strangled off to nothing as he traced the edge of her collarbone with his tongue. He started a downward trail toward the sweet hollow of her breasts. Maddie's chest heaved against him, her breath quick and hard and loud in his ears. "Jack, I don't know if I can do this."

The tears rumpling her voice just about killed him. Lifting his head, he cupped her flushed cheeks and stared into her eyes. "Talk to me, Maddie. That's how we get through this."

She took a deep breath, closed her eyes. When she opened them, he could read, so clearly, that steel core of strength, of resolve that was her foundation. "I haven't…done this, not since David. And not before."

Her ex-husband's name made Jack want to rage, but he kept his touch soft, his voice quiet. The stroke of his thumbs back and forth across her cheekbones was hypnotic, easing his tension, focusing him when the emotion wanted to take over. He couldn't risk it. He had to be what she needed, right now more than ever. "So David is the only man you've slept with."

A teardrop slithered from the corner of each eye. "He told me that's why he chose me," she whispered, voice hoarse. "His virgin bride."

The last word ended in a choked laugh that tore him up inside.

"Was it ever good, between the two of you? Or was it always—" The rest of that sentence refused to leave his lips.

Maddie looked down, hiding her face, herself. "Always."

He wanted to get down on his knees and thank the Lord that she'd ever let him touch her, but right now she needed something more. She needed his belief in her.

Jack tilted her chin back up until her shadowed eyes met his. "Never do that," he said, his voice like gravel. "Never feel ashamed for what that bastard put you through. That shame is his burden to carry, not yours. And so is the fear." Deliberately he forced his voice lower, rumbling with sex and need and hunger instead of anger. "Come to bed with me, wildcat. You know already that there's no pain with me, even when it's rough. I won't hurt you, and I can give you so much pleasure. It won't be like it was with him. Ever. Lay with me, right here, in this bed, and let me show you how it should be."

He returned his lips to her neck, warming her nerves with hot breath and sex-laced words. His hands he moved to cup that full, firm ass, to push Maddie against his erection. "I promise, Maddie. Let me show you."

For long minutes he coaxed her, utilizing a patience he hadn't known was hidden somewhere inside him, but that patience was finally rewarded when Maddie dropped her head back, giving him access, and raised herself up on tiptoes to crowd against him. "Okay, Jack. Show me."

He pulled her roughly to him, nestling his face between her breasts to hide the sheen of moisture he knew coated his eyes. "You can trust me, Maddie. You can—and I'll earn that trust or die trying."

Maddie gripped him tight, used the leverage to wrap her legs around his waist. "Take me to bed, Jack."

All it required was a turn and a few steps to comply. Settling Maddie on the mattress, he knelt in front of her, between her thighs. Once more he took her face between his hands. Her eyes locked with his.

He took his time, studying her, wanting to be sure of what he was seeing. The soft flush of passion was still there, the determination to follow through with her decision, but both warred with rising panic as her hands went to the bed and clenched down. He kissed her gently, a sweet salute, tempting her to open to him, overrunning the fear with warm caresses. When her lips parted, he accepted the invitation, delving inside to caress, explore, enjoy. He kept a tight rein on his own passion; Maddie needed to match his hunger, needed to completely let go before he could follow.

Within moments a soft moan escaped her. The sound vibrated across his tongue as he slid it across hers. Her hands came up to clutch his shoulders instead of the covers. She held him so tight he thought she might break the skin, but it didn't matter. Her touch was the signal he needed. One piece at a time, lingering over every inch of skin he uncovered, Jack undressed her until she lay bare on the mattress before him. That night in her bed, and earlier at the bar, her body hadn't been totally revealed to him, only enough bits and pieces to drive him quietly insane. Now... He caught his breath in awe. Lamplight kissed the long, pale lines of her body, from her firm, athletic thighs, across the shadows between her legs, to the softness of her stomach. Her rib cage narrowed just below full breasts with dark, tight tips that made his mouth water. She was everything he could have asked for in a lover, and so much more.

Maddie lifted silken arms to cross over her breasts, hiding them from his sight. He couldn't stop the growl that rose in his throat.

"No." He clasped her wrists gently and pulled them back to her sides. "Don't hide from me."

"Then why don't you get undressed so we can be a bit more equal?"

He smiled at the return of her sassy mouth. Of course, there was so much more that mouth could be doing. The thought had him tearing at his clothes. He was naked in seconds.

The feel of one tentative hand sweeping up his naked thigh brought a groan to his lips. He quickly

214

dug a condom from the bedside table drawer and tossed it on top where he could find it later. He turned back to see that Maddie had shifted away from him, lying now dead center in the middle of the big bed. Her breasts shook with each heaving breath she drew, the sound choppy in the quiet of the bedroom.

"Shh, darlin'," he whispered as he climbed onto the bed. "It's all right."

Maddie gave him a faint, strained grin. "Why do you always tell me that?"

He crawled to her side and slowly positioned himself, limb by limb, on all fours above her. "Because it's true." A good sixteen inches separated their bodies, giving Maddie free access to him. Room to breathe. He kept his hands and knees a few inches from her body, but still her eyes went wide, her heartbeat fluttering at the base of her throat. "All of what we do is right, and it will all be good." He held himself still, murmuring quietly to her until finally, slowly, her breathing calmed and her muscles relaxed.

"Touch me. Take it at your own pace."

Maddie visibly braced herself and lifted a finger, tentatively tracing the lines of his face before plunging both hands into his hair. The drag of her fingertips through the strands sent tingles across his scalp. She stroked down, ruffling the shorter almost stubble along his nape, massaging the tight cords of his neck and shoulders as he balanced above her. The light dusting of hair along his arms, the muscles of his chest, even the hardness of his abs didn't escape her touch. The farther down her hands wandered, the tighter his sex got, the quicker his breath, until he thought he might explode with the first stroke along his cock.

Maddie grew bolder as he remained still, though nothing could still the hard jut of him bobbing with every surge of lust her touch generated. Sweat broke out along his spine as he struggled not to move, to allow her the time to explore, to relax. He focused in on her breasts, watching the pinkish-brown tips darken with arousal and lengthen as if reaching for him. He wanted them in his mouth, wanted to weigh the rounded globes in his hands and see if they were as heavy as he remembered. He contented himself with blowing gently on her sensitive nipples, the sensation causing her to bow her back in response.

When she clasped the thick length of him, Jack couldn't hold back a grunt, couldn't stop himself from bucking into her touch. Her hands were hot with friction and passion. They seared him. The massaging rhythm she started up hardened him to the point that he questioned the control that had always been ironclad. He had no choice but to thrust into her clasp, seeking relief, needing her grip tighter, drawing the tension in his balls to the boiling point.

"Jack." Maddie's voice was breathy with her passion, the beautiful sheen of it coating her face as she stared down at her grip on his cock. She rubbed the length, balls to tip. Every stroke sparked rising excitement in her gaze. He could see her readiness in the lines of her face; God knew he shared it.

He didn't ask; he simply leaned down and took one tight nipple in his mouth, his lips snug around it as he sucked her in hard. He cupped the opposite breast, loving the heavy weight, tweaking the jutting tip between thumb and finger until Maddie was pushing up against him, tiny cries escaping lips still swollen from his kisses. He gave her the harder touch she needed, the fuel for her rising desire.

Jack switched sides, suckling at her breast in rhythmic waves. Her taste drove him wild, the slightly salty tang of sweaty desire spiking her natural sweetness. Maddie bucked against him when he forced her nipple to the roof of his mouth and rolled it with his tongue. Her pelvis met his again and again, and he sucked harder, needing that full-body contact as much as she did.

A tingle shot down his spine. If he didn't get inside her soon, he wasn't going to last.

Sitting back on his knees between her legs, Jack smoothed his hands down her belly to the dark, neatly trimmed hair at the juncture of her thighs. She was writhing, desperate little mewls escaping her lips as she undulated beneath his touch. The scent of her was like a punch to the nose as he bent to nuzzle the crisp brown curls. Immediately her thighs clamped down on him, and her entire body stiffened.

"No," Maddie cried. She scrambled to back up despite the headboard behind her and Jack's firm grip on her hips. "No, Jack. Not that. Please."

The lamp beside them clearly revealed the terror that had replaced the need in her eyes. Jack sat back immediately. Kneading her hips and thighs, he soothed her with words and touch—and soothed himself, trying not to think about what could've

217

caused her reaction. "Shh, wildcat. Calm down; catch your breath. I won't do anything you don't like."

He allowed his fingers to take the path he had planned for his lips, to circle her inner thighs, dip to the shyly closed labia shielding her from his gaze. Down and up, over and over, one side, then the other. Slowly Maddie relaxed and her thighs opened the slightest bit more.

"It's all right, darlin'. No mouth for now. Just relax for me." He trailed one finger between her lower lips, opening her to his gaze. Cream bathed her slit. Her pinkened clit peeked shyly from its protective hood, and Jack longed to stroke it with his tongue. But not right now. Trust first.

And he had it. As he watched, Maddie relaxed, her passion returned, her body wept. She believed him. Triumph rocked his heart, but his fingers were steady, tracing and teasing her. Their breathing and the moist sounds of his touch trailing through her cream were all he heard, all he needed. When her hips tilted, seeking out his touch, he tugged down on the hood of her clit, then pushed it back. Maddie hissed, bucked. He did it again.

"God, Jack," she groaned. "Please."

"Please what, wildcat?"

"Please." She whimpered, pushed into his touch. "More."

Jack eased a single finger inside. She met him, driving herself onto his penetration. He pulled back and added another finger.

"So tight," he whispered. He knew already that she would strangle his cock when he finally got inside her. Just the memory of how tight she'd been drew his balls up, ready to spill at any moment. Her inner walls rippled around his fingers, and he groaned. It was impossible to wait any longer.

Removing his hand from her body was the hardest thing he'd ever done; only the promise of greater pleasure to come allowed him to do it. Thirty seconds was all it took to snatch open the foil wrapper and get himself sheathed and ready. He surged over her, enjoying her needy moans, and laid his body down full length atop hers.

Instantly Maddie's eyes snapped open, and her fear returned. He took her kiss quickly, drawing her lower lip into his mouth, nipping, pushing his tongue inside. But no matter how he teased and taunted, her body didn't relax.

He lifted himself off her, giving her space to breathe, but didn't sit up. "Maddie?"

She gripped his shoulders and wouldn't let go. "No, Jack. I can do this. I can." Tears thickened her voice. "I can, please. Just get it over with. It will be better after."

Her begging tore at his heart. "We have time, Maddie, all the time you need. I can wait."

"No, please. I can do this, I promise."

Looking into her eyes, he could see the same determination that had gotten them to this point. Hell, with as much as she'd been through, he was surprised she had even allowed him to see her naked. Her trust in him strengthened his resolve. He would not let her down.

Here we go then, wildcat.

The white lines surrounding Maddie's mouth showed the gathering fear she was just managing to hold on to. The sight tore at his desire enough to make him afraid he couldn't finish. He'd have to make this quick before either one of them lost their nerve. He had no doubt he could climax, but actually forcing his way into her if she was fighting him might be more than he could accomplish, even if she begged him to.

Gathering his courage—and praying to God he was doing the right thing—Jack pulled his knees up under her thighs, positioned himself at her entrance, and pushed inside quickly. He knew he was being rough, hated it, but didn't know how else to get them both through this. A keening cry burst from Maddie's lips, and then she was hitting, kicking, hurling her body from side to side to get away. He couldn't bear it, couldn't stand her pain. But he also couldn't abandon her, not when she'd asked him to take her. Not knowing what else to do, he laid his weight heavy on her breasts, immobilizing her long enough to get one arm under her shoulders and one under her hips, clutch her tight against him, and then roll quickly to his back.

Immediately the fighting stopped. No longer confined, not bearing his weight, Maddie stopped striking out, but her fear continued. He could feel it in the tremors shaking her, the racing breath, the slam of her heartbeat against his chest. He held her tight as the adrenaline faded and her incoherent cries transformed into his name, repeated over and over in a shaky mantra that eased as the minutes passed.

Maddie finally dropped her head to his shoulder, her lips against the crook of his neck. Her teeth sank lightly into the thick layer of muscle above his collarbone as if she needed every anchor she could get, including the taste of his skin. The feel of her needing him, clinging to him, surrounding him shook him almost more than her fighting had.

His first stroke along her spine had Maddie sighing, the sound almost like relief. He stroked again, massaged her sleek back, soothing away the chill of her skin and the lingering tension. He dipped down to her butt, held back his groan of pleasure as he kneaded the taut muscles, then up to her shoulders and back down again. She was all right. They were both all right.

Gradually he began to use the downward glide to push her hips onto his semihard penis, the tiny thrusts intended to renew passion for both of them. Slow, careful. When Maddie's breath hitched in his ear and her hips responded with a tiny swivel, barely grinding against his pelvis, he knew she was coming out of the last dregs of her panic.

He increased the power of his strokes, keeping to the same easy rhythm. Time went molasses slow, but the feel of her barely opening for his swelling shaft, the renewal of her liquid arousal pulled him along with her. Finally Maddie was moaning against him, her pelvis hitting his with every upstroke, her nipples tightening once more against the sparse hair on his chest. And Jack knew the time had come.

A slight push tilted her upper body away from him. "Up you go, wildcat." Guiding her hands to his chest, he watched as she sat up, searched her body for signs that she was truly ready. The rosy blush of passion had returned to her cheeks and spread down her chest. Her eyes were glazed, unfocused. Needy. He could give her what she needed, what they both needed so much.

When he gripped her hips and pushed her down hard on his next thrust, Maddie threw her head back and gave a wild cry. Her nails dug into his chest, and he thrilled to know tomorrow he would carry the evidence of her passion, not her pain. The thought added to the oncoming rush of his climax. He quickened the thrusts, lifting his hips off the bed to meet her downward plunge, and felt her tight sheath begin to pulse and flutter and then clamp down around him.

Maddie in climax was so damn beautiful she took his breath—and his control. The tingle along his spine returned, exploded, blasting him forward until he was buried to the hilt, held there by a freight train of an orgasm that shot through him for what seemed like forever. He savored the force of it, the force of Maddie's muscles squeezing the life out of him, until his vision grayed and he fell back to the pillow, dragging Maddie's lax body back with him.

Their breathing huffed in the stillness that followed. Jack shut his mind off and just held Maddie in his arms, the quiver of aftershocks pulsing around his softening penis still tucked inside her. Sweat glued their bodies together, and he knew he should get up, take care of her, get them cleaned up, but it wasn't happening anytime soon.

As Maddie's breathing deepened and sleep came for Jack as well, only one thought floated through his mind: She was his. She was finally his, and nothing, no one, ever, would take her away.

Chapter Seventeen

"Wake up, sleepyhead."

Maddie groaned, unwilling to surface from the best sleep she'd had in… Her brain couldn't work out the number, but years. Years, and someone was trying to steal it away from her. "Go away."

Something hot touched her breast, surrounded her nipple. The sensation nudged her closer to waking, then left. Cold air tightened the wet, naked skin next.

Naked skin. "What the heck?"

She forced one eye open and glanced down at her body. *Her unclothed body.* The realization jarred her awake so fast she nearly banged heads with Jack on her way up.

Jack laughed. "Good morning." He glanced at the alarm clock on his bedside table. "Or, afternoon. Almost."

She opened her mouth to give him her opinion of his opinion of her wake-up time. The scent of sweet, hot coffee forestalled the tongue-lashing. "Coffee?"

Jack brought the largest coffee mug she'd ever seen from behind his back. "Thought you might like some."

She took the cup in greedy hands. If this was how he treated her after two rounds of sex, she'd have to make sure she gave it to him every night. *Or…er…hmm.*

She took a sip.

Jack watched her drink, looking awake and disgustingly refreshed. Maddie felt like fish bait. And uncomfortably bare. She tugged the soft sheet higher on her body, eyeing Jack the whole time to see if he would pounce. He didn't.

Part of her was disappointed.

"I take it you're not a morning person," Jack said.

She took another sip of coffee.

"Okay." He drew the word out, the amusement in his voice almost, but not quite, pulling a smile out of her. "I guess that means asking for morning nooky is not an option."

"Uh…"

He stole whatever else she was going to say with a hard, quick kiss. "All right. Breakfast—or lunch?—will be ready when you get to the kitchen."

She was still staring at him as he walked into the hall, his laugh trailing behind him. Automatically Maddie raised her cup to her mouth, but before she took a drink, she slid her tongue along her Jack-kissed lips. Coffee and man.

That smile finally made an appearance.

Wandering through the house on the way to the kitchen, Maddie took a closer look around. With earthy tones and casual furniture, Jack's home felt more comfortable than anyplace she'd ever lived. A place where she could take her shoes off and relax, sit back with a margarita or cook up a fancy dinner, whichever the occasion called for.

Jack apparently thought BLTs were the perfect mix of breakfast and lunch, because that's what awaited her when she wandered into the kitchen. He set the final piece of toasted bread on the sandwich in front of him, cut it neatly in half, and slid the plate into place in front of one of the bar stools at the island. "Come eat."

She shouldn't feel this awkward. She'd had plenty of mornings after, but all of them had been after David, and she'd been the one taking care of him. It hadn't mattered that she could barely walk or that she dropped things because her wrists or feet or back were bruised. It only gave him an excuse to punish her. Jack wasn't punishing; he was providing, both last night and this morning. A feeling unlike any she'd ever known unfurled in her chest, but it took long moments and a couple of bites of the food before she was able to identify it.

Trust.

"So"—she cleared the lump out of her throat—"I have a shift tonight."

Jack nodded. A quick slice and his sandwich was ready too. He sat next to her at the island. "I'll take you in."

She picked up a half, brought it to her lips, but set it back down. "I need to work, Jack." Not just for the money, though she did need cash, but for the independence. The control. "But I need to know if it's safe. I won't risk anyone there if David…if he knows where I am. Might know where I am."

Jack chewed and swallowed in silence. After a sip of his water, he said, "I have to tell you, right now,

I don't know if that's a concern or not. Without knowing what I'm looking at, without more information, I'm stumbling around blind. I did a pretty thorough background check, both on you and Reed, but I didn't access anyplace officially that should set off red flags. I made sure to hack the financial records so there was no—"

"You hacked David's financial records?" She felt a gray haze fall over her.

"Maddie, hey…" Jack cupped her cheek, the warmth of his touch more powerful than the faint that she really wanted to let take her. "It's all right."

She was no longer sure if she hated that phrase or reveled in it. "Jack, you have no idea what you're getting into."

"I would if you would tell me why you left."

"I left so I could keep my silence." She stood, unable to sit still any longer. The back windows, open to the sun, drew her. "The fewer people I had connections to, the fewer people David might think I'd tell…what I knew. If I wouldn't tell strangers, acquaintances, why would I tell you?"

Jack crossed the kitchen, his boots clicking on the hardwood floor. "Now, wildcat," he teased, "are you saying you want to protect your lover."

Teasing or not, she whipped around to face him. "You're damn right I do."

His grin tugged at her heart. "So you admit that I'm your lover."

"Jack, this is not a joke."

"No, it's not. But it still feels good that you want to keep me safe."

She backed away, her spine meeting the sun-warmed glass, her hands coming up to meet his broad chest. Without waiting for permission, he cupped her bottom and pulled her to him, crotch to crotch. He was already hard, thick. She couldn't stop herself from tilting her pelvis to nestle more firmly against him.

The man had made her into a freaking nymphomaniac in only one night. How was that even possible?

It wasn't. She knew it in the back of her mind, knew that sex, no matter how good, no matter how much she wanted it, could never "fix" her. But the miracle of standing here, in this man's arms, in this moment, and wanting him without fear…it filled her heart so full it hurt. She closed her eyes, stopped thinking about it, and surrendered to Jack's kiss.

When his lips finally left hers, he stayed close. The amber streaks in each iris shone in the sunlight as he looked down at her. "I've told you before, I'm very good at what I do. The likelihood that anyone detected the breech is almost nil. And just so you know, whether you like it or not, I or one of my men will be at the bar with you at all times.

"And…I will be keeping you up-to-date on anything I know. No more secrets. If the risk assessment changes, if I see anything that makes me think you are in danger, you'll know immediately."

She couldn't rely on that, couldn't count on help. She'd taught herself not to. Except Jack had proven himself reliable. She wanted to believe in him so badly.

She could tell him everything; she knew that now. But as she tried to get her tongue to work, tried to form the words, Jack spoke instead.

"I want to ask you a favor."

"Okay." What she could offer him, she had no idea, but she'd sure as hell try.

"I want you to go with me to see Charlie."

"Sure. Why do you need me to go with you?"

"Because Charlie won't see me. He's upset that I haven't found his sister…"

Jack kept talking, and Maddie kept nodding, but the last words to register were *haven't found his sister*. Jack was investigating Vaneqe's disappearance. Jack, the man she could trust. The man who could help her.

"Maddie?"

"Jack." She hesitated, took a breath. "You need to know—"

Ding dong.

Jack groaned. He glanced from the living room back to her, regret shimmering in his eyes. "I'd really wanted a longer time with you."

"Why—"

Ding dong.

"Impatient bastard," Jack muttered. He took her hand and led her toward the front door. "Come on. You might as well meet him."

"Meet who?" She didn't want to meet company. She needed to talk to him, tell him about her investigation, what she knew. Maybe, if they shuffled their evidence together, they might find a clue they didn't know they had, or a route toward a clue that could take them to Vaneqe. But though she tugged on Jack's hand, he moved inexorably toward the living room.

"Hold on, hold on," he yelled through the door, keying in the security code. She was surprised he didn't check first to see who was outside, but on taking a closer look at the panel, she noticed a tiny monitor on the far side, maybe two inches by two inches. Shifting on the monitor told her whoever was outside was moving, probably to knock again. Jack got the door open first.

"What's the matter with you, dickhead?"

"Finally," a deep voice said, and then Jack and the man were doing that bro-hug thing that, for some reason, always made Maddie's throat clog up. Maybe because she could relate to trying to hide the true depths of her emotions, even when she touched someone. Thank God Jack accepted nothing less than all that she felt.

When Jack ushered the man inside, Maddie stepped back. He was big, almost as big as Jack and just as muscular. Definitely had to be Miracle-Gro in the water, although this one carried an overnight bag, so maybe he got his magic growth from a different water supply. His reddish-blond hair was cut ruthlessly short, but she could see the tendency to curl in the whirls that circled his face, a face full of harsh angles softened by full, sensual lips and light blue eyes she couldn't read. What she could read was the same thing she'd seen in Jack when they first met, the same still awareness that said he missed nothing. That said he was dangerous.

Maddie closed her eyes, aware of every millisecond, as she struggled to allow the mask that had protected her for so long to slide back into place. A blink, that was all, but she felt the weight settle on her shoulders. She hadn't even realized how freeing it had been not to hold everything back, not to be just the charming bartender. Jack had given her that freedom, but she wouldn't risk it with anyone else.

"Hello," she said, taking the advantage.

Jack turned from resetting the alarm. His arm came around her waist. "Maddie, this Gabriel Williams. We served in the marines together."

The man turned slightly, reaching to shake her hand, and light from the window hit his face. There, from cheekbone to chin, a thin scar marred his masculine beauty. Or maybe enhanced it. Like a cobra, he was fascinating to watch, but the threat could not be missed—or ignored.

And then he smiled, and Maddie watched the danger submerge beneath his charm. He extended a hand to her. "Gabe."

Maddie returned the smile, thankful for the mask under the intensity of this man's stare. "Maddie. Nice to meet you."

The man snorted. Jack laughed. Maddie glanced at him, confused.

"It's all right, wildcat. Gabe's one of the good guys." He turned her fully to face him, keeping her close, his body heat warming her down where the effort to hide made her cold. "But since he's here, our visit to Charlie is gonna have to wait. Let me get Gabe settled, and then we have to talk."

Maddie frowned. She wanted to talk, but not to Gabe.

Jack pulled her close, his head tucked against her ear, hiding her from Gabe's sight. "Talk. I'll show you my cards, and then I hope you'll show me yours." He nipped her ear, then started off down the hall. Gabe threw her a cocky little salute and followed Jack.

I'll show you my cards, and then I hope you'll show me yours.

I'll protect you with everything I am.

You can trust me, Maddie. You can—and I'll earn that trust or die trying.

Like a guillotine coming down out of nowhere, Maddie's breath cut off. Choking, gasping, she ran for the back door. She needed air, needed space, needed...

No alarm blared when she yanked open the door and rushed out onto the back deck. Maddie heard the screen door slam, heard her pounding footsteps on the wood, felt the railing beneath her trembling hands, but it was all hazed by the screaming need to get air into her tight lungs.

When heavy hands settled on her shoulders, instinct had her lifting her knee and kicking back. Jack's laugh rumbled in her ear as she hit empty air.

"Whoa, wildcat. Settle down."

She couldn't settle down; she couldn't breathe. She bent over the railing, adrenaline and panic and embarrassment a noxious flood in her veins. "Jack."

He moved in close, his groin cradling her butt, his hands warm and heavy on her back as he stroked her. "It's all right, Maddie. I'm right here, no one else. Just relax."

The man was so good at calming her. How did he do that? When she asked, she heard his shrug, felt it in the minute lift of his hands. "Your body trusts me." He gripped her hips, squeezing her in quick reassurance. "*You* trust me." He tugged her up to lean against his chest, nuzzling the sensitive skin just below her ear. "Keep trusting me, Maddie. I won't let you down."

"I'm sorry," she whispered. Jack was a good man. He'd done everything he'd told her he would and more, despite her attempts to see it otherwise. He shouldn't have to keep proving himself.

"I'm not," he told her. The next instant his arms were crushing her against him. He surrounded her, his grip at once so tight but so... She didn't know how to describe it. There was an emotion there she couldn't put a name to, but it overwhelmed them both. Maddie let herself relax, let Jack submerge her in the moment until everything else fell away.

Reality couldn't be avoided, though, and they both knew it. Finally, his arms loosening but not letting go, Jack whispered in her ear, "Come on. We've got talking to do."

Chapter Eighteen

Reluctantly she let Jack lead her back to the living room, where Gabe waited on the couch. If the newcomer had seen any of her emotional display, he didn't mention it, didn't look at her any differently than he had before. Maddie scrambled like hell to pull the pieces of her mask back together. It wasn't happening. Jack was systematically destroying her ability to close herself off, and for once she wasn't certain she was unhappy about that.

She chose the matching leather chair instead of the couch where Gabe occupied one end. She needed the space. Jack didn't comment, just stood beside her as calmly as if they were about to decide what to have for dinner. Maybe for him it was that easy. Maddie felt like her world had just been shattered, and now, instead of picking up the pieces, she got to break them into tinier bits.

Except he saw exactly how she was feeling. She knew that by the gentle touch that tucked her hair behind her ear. A tiny bit of the tension in her relaxed. She wasn't alone. No mask, no need to do it all herself… Jack was taking her all kinds of places she hadn't been before.

She glanced up at him, knowing he'd seen her gratitude the minute he smiled.

"Maddie, Gabe is here because—"

Ding dong.

Jesus. What was this, a three-ring circus? But Jack didn't seem surprised. "Because he has had some dealings with Carson Alexander."

He walked toward the front door. He wasn't even looking at her, but she could feel his attention sharpen, feel Gabe's stare searching for any reaction they could find. And she couldn't help but give it to them. No one terrified her more than David—except Carson. His name was like a four-ton truck hitting her head-on. She reeled, unable to hide it, using all her strength just to stay upright. The next thing she knew, Jack was at her side.

"That answers one question."

Maddie glanced up, only now aware that Con had arrived. His gray eyes were dark with sympathy. It pissed her off. It all pissed her the hell off. She wasn't some sideshow for these men, some experiment in a petri dish for them to dissect and examine. She surged to her feet, ready to attack—and caught sight of Jess, so delicate, petite, standing just behind her husband.

"Maddie," the woman said. If Con's eyes were sympathetic, Jess's were something else altogether. Understanding. Fierce with determination and anger, but not anger at Maddie, it didn't seem. At someone else.

"You told them," she whispered to Jack, wishing she could crawl into a hole and die there.

"I did." Remorse wasn't even a tinge in the words. "They're here to help, all of them."

Maddie was already shaking her head, backing away. The chair caught her at the knees. She stumbled, her hand landing automatically in Jack's as

235

he reached to catch her. The touch, the stares, the lack of air seared her senses until she thought she would scream. "Jack, I can't. I can't talk about this, not with all these people." She'd barely been working up to telling him.

Jess circled her husband, moving forward until only the coffee table separated her from Maddie. "I get that it's hard to talk about, but we can—"

"Jess." Maddie couldn't stop the sharp edge as the word left her lips. "You cannot possibly 'get it.'"

"Yes, I can." Her hands went to the buttons holding her shirt closed. Con made a sound deep in his throat, his hands coming up as if to stop her, but she threw him a look and he retreated, if reluctantly. Jess turned back to Maddie, peeling off her shirt. Beneath, a cotton cami covered her chest and stomach, but her arms...

God. Maddie sucked in a shattered breath. Jess's arms were covered in pinkish-gray scars, methodical slices all the way from wrist to armpit. As Maddie watched, Jess raised her cami to reveal scar-covered skin on her belly as well. What someone had done to this woman... Maddie just couldn't comprehend it. She'd seen horror, lived with its aftermath for years, and yet...this she couldn't even fathom.

She looked to Con, caught a glimpse of the agony he must have lived through in the near-black shade of his eyes. They echoed the emotional scars Maddie carried, only amplified. Jess's eyes were the same. Maddie shuddered in sympathy. "I'm sorry."

Jess lowered her cami and reached for her shirt. After she slid it on, Con folded her into his arms, speaking over his wife's head. "We know abuse, Maddie, intimately. We know how terrifying it is to speak out. But we can help you stop him. We've done it before, and we'll do it again, now, for you."

Maddie looked into his eyes, read the truth there. She glanced up at Jack, saw his tight lips and the sorrow as he looked at Jess. He met Maddie's eyes and nodded.

What if I can't?

Jack's words from last night flashed into her mind. *You can.* And she had. With him beside her, she'd done what she thought she could never do again.

She wasn't a coward.

She sucked in a long, slow breath, tucking the courage he gave her deep inside where her fear couldn't eat away at it. "All right. I'll try."

Jack nodded again, then took her hand and led their little group into the den.

The room was a typical man cave, with dark furniture, a massive wall-mounted TV, and in one corner, a bank of computers Maddie had a hard time imagining could be used all at once. Jack grabbed a stack of files from the nearby desk and joined them in the seating area that occupied the middle of the room. The coffee table in the center, wider and longer than the norm, became their conference table.

Jack's evidence shook her. He'd dug deep into David's past, pulling at threads and unraveling secrets even Maddie hadn't known, and she'd lived with the man for five and a half years. That Jack had done all this based only on his instincts, the instincts that told him something wasn't right with her, was nothing short of scary. Those instincts were very good—and so were Jack's hacker skills. She shuddered. Looking over the lists of companies, the tracing of money from one to the next to the next, she had to wonder if anyone else, law enforcement or not, would've bothered to go this far.

Not without probable cause, and David had made certain they didn't have it.

"What we need," Jack said, his gaze holding her steady, his hand keeping hers warm, "is the key to what all this means. What are they doing? I think you know, Maddie. Even if you can't make the connection now, something in your story will make that connection for us."

"Okay." Jack was right; she had clues they needed. Together they could figure out where Vaneqe was, how to stop David and Carson's little enterprise. It was the same conclusion she'd come to this morning; she just hadn't realized she'd be spilling it all in front of an audience. Still, she sucked it up and started her story.

"After David and I married, it became obvious he had certain...tastes."

Jack squeezed her hand. "Sex?"

She swallowed, her throat like sandpaper. "That, but it was more. I'd known he was powerful in the world of law; I had no idea how far he took that power at home."

"What do you mean?" Jess asked softly.

How do get them to understand what it had taken hell to wrap her mind around. "He was... The family, that land...it's a closed community, a cult. It was like going back to before the Civil War. David claims he lets no one onto his property because of spies, paparazzi, but the truth is, no one goes there. No one. I realized pretty quick that the servants weren't really servants; they were slaves. David is their master, and he made certain they didn't forget it. He doled out their punishment and their food and their education. He controlled their well-being. He had a private physician on staff so there was no risk of hospital visits." She stared down at her hand in Jack's. "No records to track."

"How could he get away with that?" Jess asked.

"The rich live in their own little bubble." She knew; she'd grown up inside that bubble. "David's eccentricities didn't appear all that odd unless you were on the inside. Even the abuse... It was always subtle things, you know—cuts from a strike or fall, a sprain, bruising, things like that—but altogether they would've added up to a pattern. David never risked anything he didn't have to."

"How many people live there?" Gabe asked.

"About twenty, twenty-five, maybe?"

He cursed.

"I can see how hard it would be for you to gain the courage to leave," Jess said, "but why stay employed there?" Jess asked. "Why did the staff tolerate it?"

Maddie dug her nails into her palms. She had to get this right. "Because of the children."

Jess shook her head, confused. "They tried to protect their children by staying?"

"Not their children, *his* children." She glanced up at Jack, saw the dawning revulsion there. She dropped her gaze back to her lap. "The children are his. All of them. If they aren't family, they don't stay. Women don't go outside the compound, but even if they snuck out, getting pregnant by an outsider meant automatic termination of the pregnancy. When the girls were old enough"—her stomach twisted, forcing her to take a steadying breath—"well, it became clear to me pretty quick that David 'serviced' his women on a regular basis." To her shame, she'd often been relieved when it happened; it meant he wasn't using her.

Jack uncurled her fingers to rub at the crescent moons her nails had left in the skin.

"Many of the servants are third- and fourth-generation. They were born and raised on that land. They didn't know anything else. And…once you live there…you understand that there is nowhere to run that David wouldn't follow, not if you took his child."

"But you did run," Jack pointed out.

She nodded. It took a few minutes to clear her throat enough to speak. "David and I argued during our engagement. I wanted time together before we had a family; he didn't. Without his knowledge I had an IUD implanted before the wedding." Even then she'd known something wasn't right. "After so many years with no pregnancy…" Her nose stung, and

240

Maddie stopped, focused, pushed back the pain. She closed her eyes, unable to bear so many stares. "I had to leave before he— I had to leave."

Jack stroked her fingers, her palm, waiting for her to open her eyes again. "What happened?"

"I couldn't go to my parents. David had threatened them, told me if they ever found out, he'd make them disappear. I knew he could do it. But I needed help, so one day I managed to sneak out of the house, said I was meeting my mother for lunch, but I went to a divorce lawyer. They told me I needed papers, information. I didn't have it, didn't have the money they wanted up front. So I went searching. David's home is an old antebellum mansion, massive. After a week of looking, I couldn't find what they wanted." She remembered the desperation she'd felt, the fear that grew every day. "I looked and looked for clues, but nothing. So I searched the butler's room and found a list of passwords. One was labeled 'Door.'

"David had an office in the basement. He even slept down there sometimes." She'd been grateful on those nights. "Since I'd searched everywhere else, I thought it must be the door to the basement. I was desperate. So that night when everyone was asleep, I went down there." She hated the faint wobble in the words. Hated that David still had that kind of power over her. "Except, when I got downstairs, it wasn't an office."

"What was it?" Jack asked.

"It was a dungeon. David wasn't there, but Carson was. He had a woman down there, training her. It...wasn't voluntary."

Jack grunted as if he'd been punched. She couldn't look at him; she didn't dare. Didn't want to see disgust on his face and wonder if it was for her too.

Suddenly his thigh was against hers, his hip, his arm coming around her to pull her close on the leather love seat. She turned her face into his neck, speaking the rest against his skin, surrounded by his calming scent. "I didn't know until... Carson is...very talkative...when he trains. That's what he calls it, training. Some of the things he said..." She swallowed hard, trying to keep control of her stomach, of her tears. "There was no way to get her out," she whispered.

Jack didn't pursue it. "What happened next?"

A lot. But she couldn't say that, couldn't speak the memories that terrorized her in her dreams—hell, even when she was awake.

"I left that night, ended up at the Sisters of Charity Women's Shelter in Nashville. There was a cop that worked directly with the shelter...Darren Hendley. I started talking to him, telling him the bits and pieces I'd put together from living with David, the details that hadn't made sense until we matched them with the things I'd heard Carson say...that night."

"Like what?"

"He kept telling her how much she would bring on the open market when she learned to be obedient, how bidders would go crazy over her white skin at their auctions." She sat up straight to look Jack in the eye. Needing him to believe her. Needing him to see the truth. "It's a trafficking ring."

Jess's gasp filled the air, but the men were silent. Maddie could see the understanding, the knowledge of how the pieces fit together in Jack's expression. He slid a palm up her thigh, the touch comforting, warm. It steadied her enough to keep going. "All I had was hearsay, so Darren was working on finding more evidence. But...we ran out of time."

"Why?" Jack asked.

"Because—" Maddie's voice broke. "I took Amber with me."

"Who is Amber?"

She could feel herself shaking inside, feel herself coming apart at the seams, but she pushed forward anyway. "Not long after we married, one of the women gave birth. A little girl, Amber. I helped raise her like my own." She clutched Jack's shirt in her fist, drawing on his strength. "I couldn't leave her with him, Jack. I loved her."

"Her mother?"

"Refused to leave. She could choose; Amber couldn't. So I took her with me. I swear I never left the shelter, never. I didn't want to be seen, didn't want anyone tracing me back there." She shook her head. "He found me anyway. One day, Amber disappeared from the courtyard where the children played. David—"

"What did he do?"

"He contacted me, told me I had a choice: Amber or me. Without me, there was no way to convince the police of what was going on at David's estate. He— She was his daughter. I thought she'd be safe, at least until I could get her back."

"But she wasn't, was she?" Con asked, his voice hoarse.

"No." Maddie started to cry then; she couldn't hold it back any longer. "He killed her. And Darren. Both shot, execution-style, both left in a dumpster one block from the shelter."

Jack's muttered curse was echoed by three more around the room. Jack cupped her nape, pulling her close to bury her face against his chest as she cried. She could hear more discussion going on around her, but she didn't have the capacity to care. All these years she'd kept the pain of Amber's death, her parents' loss, her own terror at bay with the sheer will it took to survive. Now that barrier had been torn away. Only Jack's arms around her kept her from breaking apart. It was long minutes later before she came back to the reality of tissues clutched in her fist and Jack pushing her hair out of her face.

"Come back to me, wildcat."

His whisper tugged the broken pieces back together. She wasn't sure she could take much more, but she sat up anyway. Everyone staring sent a shudder down her spine.

Gabe drew her attention first. "Why come back here?"

She'd had good reason to stay away. David wanted his legacy, and without remarrying, he couldn't establish it legally. He needed a divorce or her dead, preferably the latter. Still... "Because I want the evidence. I want to prove what he's doing—and have it stick."

"How?" Jack asked.

She stood up, needing to move, needing to feel something besides tears. "I knew they were running a trafficking ring, not just prostitution but selling women and children—that's what the auctions were for. Carson said their clients had diverse tastes. I figured a steady stream of illegal immigrants wasn't enough to meet their demand, so I started tracking kidnappings through the papers."

Jack followed her progress across the room. "And what did you find?"

"I found that, though the major cities like Nashville and Atlanta had more disappearances, the smaller towns had seen a rise in the amount of homeless women and kids, especially what you would consider the 'pretty' ones—the sellable ones—that were disappearing. Permanently. And since David obviously had inside knowledge about the shelter in Nashville..."

Jack rubbed his chin. "So they could choose candidates by watching the shelters, which only select people should've had addresses for, and know that the risk of a small town paying more attention to a disappearance would be offset by the victims they chose."

"People the authorities wouldn't be surprised just up and left," Con added.

"We tend to think homeless populations naturally drift," Maddie said, "so a woman who decided to up and leave her kids behind in a shelter isn't going to necessitate the kind of search an upper- or even middle-class woman would."

"And they'd need local eyes on the shelters, someone above suspicion…" Jack was staring at her again, calculating. She saw the moment he made the same connection she had. "Vaneqe. You're looking for Vaneqe."

She nodded. "Pretty. Homeless. Her disappearance received a cursory search but not much more."

Jack grabbed her hand as she walked by, squeezing down so hard that she winced. He let up immediately.

A beep sounded, and Con pulled out his cell phone.

"What leads have you got?" Jack asked her.

"Not many. I've researched everything I could find in the papers, canvassed as much of the area as I could, talked to Charlie a little bit. I've been looking into people connected to the shelter, the board of directors, gathering any clues I could. I'm afraid I haven't found much." She shrugged. "I'm not experienced in this like you are. I needed more clues."

"Well," Con said, still looking at his phone, "we may have just gotten the clue we all need."

Chapter Nineteen

He could tell Maddie wasn't happy by the tightness of her lips as she strapped him into his Kevlar vest, working around the full weapons belt he was already wearing. After everything she'd been through yesterday, the things she'd had to relive as she spoke them, the embarrassment of strangers hearing it all, the nightmares she'd suffered during the night, he hated upsetting her. There was no way around it, though; she wasn't going with them, and that was final. Maddie and Jess would stay here at their office with Mark, a JCL bodyguard Jack knew would give up his life to protect them—he almost had for Jess last year. No way in hell would anything get past the man.

Of course, Maddie acted more as if Mark was there to keep her in than to keep anyone else out. She might not have been too far off the mark on that one.

"I am trained for this, you know," he told her.

Maddie ran her hands along his body armor as if ensuring it would protect him better than she could. "And I'm not. I know."

"There's no guarantee she's there."

"And there's no guarantee she's not." Maddie glanced up, meeting his eyes. "No matter how unlikely, I need...I want to be there when we find her."

When, not if. *That's my woman.*

The surge of emotion threatened to bust him out of the Velcro straps holding on his vest. Taking Maddie's face in his hands, he stared at the dynamo that had upended his life in such a short time. He'd refused to admit to Con that he loved her—it was too soon, too out of control—but standing here now, seeing her courage, her resolve, her need to do whatever it took to rescue one young girl, he realized he didn't give a damn what anyone, even his own psyche, said. He loved Maddie Brewer.

"What?" she asked, quirking her brow up at his stare.

Jack just smiled and leaned down, inch by inch, savoring the way her dark eyes grew darker in anticipation of his kiss. When his lips met hers, he didn't wait, just pushed on through, taking her deep, sharing the power and the need that shook him to the bone. Maddie moaned around his tongue. Wet heat welcomed him, surrounded him, pulled him in. This woman was everything to him, and he let her know it with just a kiss.

"Ahem."

"Can I shoot him?" he asked, lips still brushing Maddie's. "Please?"

"Not if you want this to be a successful raid," Con said, laughter jostling his words. He was enjoying Jack under a woman's spell far too much.

Maddie patted Jack's vest. "Go."

He stole one last peck, then walked toward Con.

"Yeah, Jack." Con patted his vest too, a little harder than Maddie—*thump, thump*. "Let's go."

Gabe stood near the door, watching them all with enigmatic eyes. The plan was for the three of them to join up with T. C. outside the warehouse he'd been watching for the past two days. It stood on the property owned by a manufacturing plant on the list of companies suspected to belong to Alexander, one of the places they'd decided to stake out for possible intel. T. C. had observed a series of deliveries at regular intervals. Mealtimes. Whoever ran the warehouse was receiving meals, but no workers were coming and going, not over the weekend, not on a Monday. When he realized what he was seeing, he'd called it in. Jack hoped it meant Vaneqe or some other victims of Alexander's schemes were inside. Hell, he hoped Alexander was inside—he had business to take up with the fucker in very short order.

T. C. met them about a mile outside the security fence for the facility. They hadn't called in the cops, not knowing who might be on Alexander's payroll. Jack didn't want to think it of any of the men he knew on the force, but neither was he willing to risk Vaneqe's life by trusting the wrong person. Get in, get out, minimal fuss, report to the cops if necessary. "Better to ask forgiveness than permission" was the motto of the day. Or night, rather.

"The evening delivery should be any minute now if they stick to schedule," T. C. told them. He pulled out a hand-drawn map of the building, notations showing exits and known guard locations, windows, anything they could use to plan. Though young in years, the Georgia farm boy had already done a stint in the military, and his actions were testimony to his experience. "I recommend going in about an hour later. Full bellies mean lax guards."

Jack nodded. "You did good."

A wide grin split T. C.'s earnest face, but he didn't let the praise faze him; he got right back to work. "I can't tell you much about the main part of the building, but I do know it's not all one big space." He pulled out a digital camera with a zoom lens attached and scrolled through some photos. "I managed to get a few shots through the windows."

There wasn't much to see. The warehouse was old, having been built in the seventies from what they could find in county records, and it hadn't received much updating, at least on the outside. They couldn't ignore the possibility that the neglected facade could be a decoy. T. C.'s photos showed standard offices, mostly dim, but one or two lit from an open door at night showed a lack of personal details or office supplies. That told Jack there weren't a lot of standard office workers to go with the rooms. One photo taken from a good distance away allowed them to see into what looked like a second-floor conference room and another office like the downstairs, but again, not a lot of detail.

"So, could be good, could be bad," Con said. "We can get through a window into one of the empty offices, but we have no idea what we're facing once we go past the office door. Might be more offices, or it might be a big open space with just the offices around the perimeter."

"I do know one thing we're facing," T. C. said. A couple of clicks and he brought up another picture. This one showed a man in camo opening the door for their delivery. The glint of sun off the scope and barrel of an assault rifle was barely visible through the gap. Jack whistled softly.

"Okay, we know they're weapons ready."

Gabe grunted in agreement. Jack did a visual on his friend. "Got what you need?"

A short, sharp nod was his answer. Gabe's job was to set off their diversion: a pulled fire alarm and smoke grenades. The alarm should clear the building of any nonessential—and possibly uninvolved— personnel. If anyone came to investigate, the smoke should convince them the threat was legit. And hopefully convince the guards they now knew were present to move whatever they were guarding.

There was nothing Jack could do to block cell phone contact, but T. C.'s job was to cut the landline for the phones just before they went inside. At least that way they knew the fire detection system wouldn't be making any unwarranted 911 calls, though Jack was willing to bet Alexander didn't want the police nosing around this particular warehouse, fire or not.

It was Con and Jack's job, joined by Gabe and T. C. when they finished, to find whatever they could find. Possibly it would only be guards needing to be fed while watching over a stash of illegal drugs or stolen weapons. Who knew? But if they got lucky, they'd be pulling people out tonight. In that case, Jack kind of hoped the guards resisted. They planned to go in as silent as possible, but if he had to, he could kill just as silently as he could search. He had no problem with it either way.

The delivery came and the delivery boy went. The same guard from T. C.'s photo let him in and out. The team hunkered down, waiting them out, letting the food do its work. Jack spent the time hacking the security system, which he'd learned was separate from the hardwired fire detectors, and looping CCTV cameras, shutting down automatic alarms for points of entry, discovering no motion detectors were present. Must not want to limit the guards' movements in the building. At 0830, they pulled on their pro masks to protect them from the fumes given off by the smoke grenades, and moved in. T. C. led the way to the entry point he'd "found"—i.e. created—in the company's fencing, where Jack took point on the decided path to get to their target destination.

T. C. peeled off first, Gabe second. He was entering his selected window on the first floor, the corner office, as Jack and Con reached their entry point at the opposite end. Con removed a square of glass, unlocked the old-fashioned sash-style window, and gave Jack the go-ahead.

The office was dark. Jack made his way to the door, Con right behind him. He pulled his Glock, threaded on a suppressor, then put his hand on the doorknob. When Con signaled ready, he cracked open the door, getting a good look at an empty hallway with what appeared to be identical doors across from the ones on their side.

They'd tagged this office because it was on the opposite end from their entry point, wanting to be away from the origin of the smoke before someone came to investigate. Jack and Con waited for the signal, watching for potential targets in the meantime. The only sound Jack heard was the rush of their breathing within the confines of their masks.

Ten minutes later, the fire alarm blared from down the hall. Jack peered through the minute crack in their door, watching for Gabe. A sudden billow of smoke into the far end of the hall was split by his friend's massive body. Gabe reached their location with a three-second sprint. Jack reset the door to its slightly open stance and continued his watch, heart thumping a steady rhythm of determination. Behind him, a barely audible squeak signaled Con raising the window for T. C.'s entry.

The sound of running footsteps, more than one pair, approached their door. Confirming the fire, just as Jack had anticipated. Two men in dark fatigues and T-shirts rushed past, rifles at the ready. Gestures and shouting added to the chaos of the billowing smoke, and then both men ran back up the hall and out of sight. Jack signaled his team to wait a couple more minutes, then pointed to Gabe and the door.

Gabe took point this time. T. C. covered their back trail. Their door was mere feet from a blind corner, in the same direction the targets had taken. Jack watched Gabe clear the corner with a glance, keeping low out of any enemy's line of sight. "Empty," he said. The word came through the communication system in their masks. Gabe checked once more, then pushed to the far wall, where he held the line for the others.

Jack led the way down the second hall. They figured a secure room wouldn't be on a main floor, so they were looking for access to a basement of some kind. He hoped the lack of personnel meant whoever was occupying the building was clearing out, but it also increased the possibility that they'd catch the enemy in a group. If they'd gone to retrieve their merchandise, Jack knew that possibility was higher. It also meant possible civilian victims in the line of fire.

Smoke made the air hazy. Jack focused on his breathing, a calm in and out, and putting one foot quietly but quickly in front of the other. Nice and easy, moving down the corridor. About twenty feet along, a stairwell opened on his right. One set of stairs went up, the other reversing direction to go down beneath the concrete floor. Jack stationed himself this time, and Gabe took lead.

Down they went.

Their first target met Gabe near the bottom of the stairs, coming up. Not one of the men from before. This man's eyes were down, watching his feet, his M16 pointed toward the floor. *Lazy.*

Gabe caught him with an uppercut to the chin. A perfect swan dive took the target back to the ground, the crack of his skull on impact louder than Jack's breathing. The target didn't move after that.

Gabe followed the man down, weapon at the ready. He stooped to assess pulse and respiration. A nod—*still alive*—and he moved on. Jack followed, Con bringing up his rear. From the corner of his eye he saw T. C. stopping to secure the downed man. He would stay at the stairs, safeguarding their exit.

Jack could hear shouting now. Like the floor above, a long corridor lay before them, another to the left. Gabe took the left, following the noise.

A set of steel double doors opened ahead. Gabe approached cautiously. Jack stayed on his heels, close enough to assist but not close enough to crowd. The area beyond opened up; they could hear it in the echo of the voices as they argued.

"Leave her!" one said.

"If you want to face the boss without this girl, you can do it. I'm not that stupid."

"Brian and Jay are securing the data," a third voice said. "We just have to get the girl and get outta here. What's taking so long?"

"It's not like they oil anything down here, dickhead. The lock's stuck."

From the shaking in the guy's voice, Jack would bet the problem was in his aim, not the lock. Didn't matter. Dickhead had given them the location of the rest of their team and a number: five; three in the room, two above. One girl.

Jack signaled Gabe forward.

Gabe eased around the doorjamb, staying low. One of the targets stood with his back to the door, just inside. Gabe was close behind him. Jack left Gabe to take care of his target while he moved to the next closest. Two men argued and played an aggressive game of tug-of-war with the keys to an old-fashioned padlock. Before them, the length of the room was lined in bars, small jail cells waiting for their occupants. As Jack approached, he caught a quick glimpse of a cot, a body, and then all his focus was on the enemy.

Gabe took the man near the door by the throat.

The sound of their buddy choking out finally caught the two guards' attention. They raised their heads and came face-to-face with the business end of Jack's gun.

"Hands up, gentlemen."

The lock clanged as the target who'd been whining earlier dropped it. His shaking hands went up. Dickhead wasn't so nervous, but he was stupid. He charged.

Jack slipped the attack, shifting to one side and putting out his foot. The target tripped himself over it. Jack brought a knee down on the man's spine, not bothering to be nice about it.

Con was ushering his new friend toward the door. "Over there."

The man followed the nod of Con's head and the urging of Con's ready weapon. Gabe had secured the passed-out guard with gag and cuffs. When he got close enough, Con instructed guard number two to turn around, then did the same. Gabe collected Jack's prisoner while he put away his weapon and retrieved the keys to the occupied cell.

He didn't dare look inside, didn't think his heart could take it if the small, limp form he'd seen moments ago was dead instead of unconscious. It had to be one or the other, because the noise of the alarm still hadn't stopped, and the figure hadn't moved.

With fingers much steadier than the guard's nervous hands had been, he managed the lock in seconds. Only then did he raise his eyes.

A single hitch of breath was all he allowed himself. He moved through the door toward Vaneqe's motionless figure, assessing injuries, adjusting plans for an unconscious victim. She had to be unconscious. Had to be.

Those ten steps seemed the longest of his life.

Finally, one foot from the edge of the cot, he got a good enough look to see her chest rise and fall. She was covered in a flimsy cotton nightgown, her eyes closed, face unmarred except for a split lip. Jack reached down to smooth her hair back from her face. She didn't stir.

"Gabe?"

"All clear."

Relief sagged his shoulders. He bent, slid his arms under Vaneqe's shoulders and knees, and lifted her into his arms. "Let's go home, darlin'," he whispered, not caring whether she could hear him or not. "Charlie's waiting."

Con and Gabe led the way around the corner. T. C. stood ready, eyes and weapon up, at the bottom of the stairs.

"Up you go, boy," Gabe told him. T. C. nodded, grinned. Took the first step up the stairs.

The sound of a voice reached them. Two guards, guns drawn, rounded the end of the staircase, took one look, and charged. T. C. dropped to the stairs as the first shot came down. Returned fire. Gabe took the second guard by surprise. From the bloom of blood on each man's chest, Jack knew they hadn't been wearing Kevlar.

Gabe advanced. Con helped T. C. up, confirmed a lack of injuries, and they proceeded to the top. Jack followed. Stepping over the two bodies at the top of the stairs, he tried to feel regret, feel anything, but the weight in his arms made it impossible. Whoever these men had been, they didn't deserve his remorse.

T. C. hung back, taking the rear as they retreated to the exit point. Jack had to hand Vaneqe down into Gabe's waiting arms, but within minutes they had her through the fence and secure in their vehicle. Jack tore off his mask and passed it and his weapons belt back to T. C., then took the wheel. He'd made a promise to a little boy, and by God, he was finally gonna keep it.

Chapter Twenty

"They're almost here," Jess said over Maddie's shoulder. Her voice was quiet with the strain of hours of waiting. Maddie had no doubt hers would be the same, but she couldn't speak. All she could do was gaze at Jess's reflection in the window and remember.

The stares. The speculation. David had found her that night after she'd seen Carson in the basement. She hadn't told Jack that. She couldn't. Some things it was better if no one knew but her. When she escaped, she'd gone straight to the ER. It had been a beehive of patients and nurses and equipment and buzzing white lights, but she'd made herself stay. She'd endured the tests, the pain and humiliation, even the critical why-didn't-you-leave-earlier tone of their voices. She hadn't cared as long as she survived. Vaneqe would survive too. That didn't mean Maddie's heart wouldn't break before tonight was over.

A hand on her shoulder made her jump. "It's okay, Maddie."

The instinct to attack was curbed by Jess's voice. She kept her touch soft, light, until Maddie's heart left her throat and she was able to nod her understanding. Only then did Jess give her a light squeeze and move away.

The *ding* of the elevator's arrival had them all surging forward—Maddie and Jess; Lori, JCL's fierce receptionist; and Mark, the guard who rivaled John in size and width. When the doors opened, a slight Indian man in a white lab coat stepped out. The collective release of held breath in the room should've knocked the man over. He paid no attention.

"ETA, Lori?" the doctor asked.

"Ten minutes behind you, Roger."

"Good." He swung the duffel bag in his hand toward a hall leading back into the offices. "Let's get set up, then."

The two left, and Maddie, Jess, and Mark continued the wait. It seemed like the longest ten minutes of her life before Maddie heard the elevator moving again. Mark ran down the hall to retrieve Lori and the doctor.

The elevator doors finally opened half a minute later, their loud *whoosh* echoing in the silent lobby. Maddie wanted to rush forward, find out what happened, get her first real glimpse of the girl whose picture she'd lived with for weeks. She wanted to take Jack in her arms, pat him down and make sure there weren't any holes where there shouldn't be. Kiss him like mad and then hit him for leaving her here to worry. She didn't do any of those things. She held herself back, let Jess do the rushing forward. Let Mark begin sorting through the chaos of men and voices and equipment. Let herself fall apart a little when she saw Jack walk off the elevator with a teenage-size bundle in his arms.

Lori took charge, guiding Jack toward the hall to the right. Maddie followed. The corridor led to a back office whose details were lost on her; all she paid attention to was the black leather couch on which Jack laid his blanket-wrapped load.

Maddie held her breath. Waited.

Jack turned to her, his eyes dark and his mouth hard. She could read the mission as if it was written on his face. Nothing good had come out of tonight except the bundle now being fussed over by Lori and Roger.

And then Jack had her in his arms. Maddie did the only thing she could: let him in, let him wrap her up so tight she could barely breathe, and hugged him back with all the fierceness she could muster.

But even through the roar of emotions, she couldn't take her eyes off Vaneqe. Jack hadn't forgotten the girl either. His whispered words finally registered, shaky and wet with tears against her neck.

"We found her. We found her. We found her."

His tears hurt so damn bad. She held him, rocked him. He'd been her comfort the past couple of nights; now she did for him what he'd done for her.

A throat clearing finally caught her attention. She glanced up, meeting the doctor's expectant eyes, and realized they had an audience.

A big one. Lori, the doc, Jess, Con, Mark, Gabe, and a man she didn't know filled the room to capacity. All of those eyes were on her and Jack. She stared right back, daring any of them to say a word as Jack gathered himself and turned to face the room.

"What can you do, Roger?"

The man looked back with serious brown eyes. "I want a more thorough exam. What I can see is…" He shook his head. "I need to check for more extensive injuries."

Injuries caused by sexual abuse. Maddie had known it was coming, but that didn't stop her welling nausea.

"Okay." Jack ushered everyone toward the door, and the crowd slowly filtered out. "Can you…take care of her here, depending on how bad…? I don't want to put her through the hospital and a million strangers touching her if we don't have to."

"Depending on the extent, it's possible. But I want to find out quick, while she's unconscious. No need to put her through the trauma."

"Of course. We'll be right outside."

Maddie followed Jack out the door, which he closed firmly, leaving Lori and the doctor inside with Vaneqe.

"Why is she unconscious?" Maddie asked. She wanted to know, but she also wanted to keep her mind off what was occurring in the room behind them.

"We think she was drugged, possibly in preparation for transport," Jack said, voice grim. "She was out when we got there, and the guards were minimal. She was the only one there, so they didn't need a heavy team." He leaned back against the wall beside the door, his eyelids sliding closed, the heavy ropes of muscle along the sides of his throat working as he struggled with the words. "We took out two."

"Took out?"

"Dead," Con said behind her.

"What? What about the police? Won't it be reported?"

Con shook his head. "The place was set up for this. Even if they used the upstairs for an actual business, which is unlikely—that would bring too high a risk of exposure—they had a virtual jail in the basement. Bars, locks, armed guards…the works. They won't be reporting a shooting or a dead guard or a theft or anything else. They couldn't allow the cops in to investigate; it would be hanging themselves."

Gabe shifted where he leaned on the wall across from her. "You know you've started a war, right?"

"Reed won't care about a couple of low-level soldiers," Con told him.

"No, but you heard what they said. For some reason that little girl in there is special to their boss— whether that's Reed or Alexander, I'm not sure. But they'll want her back."

Maddie took a step forward. "They're not getting her."

Jack's hand on her arm held her back. "Gabe's not the enemy, Maddie. And he's right."

She turned to argue, but Jack shook his head. "They're not getting her, but they will come after her. Their contact in town will know who took her, know it's us; I have no doubt." He pulled her toward him. Maddie bumped into his side, unused to the intimacy of someone taking her into their arms in a crowd. Jack ignored her awkwardness and wrapped his arm around her shoulder. "We just have to be ready."

"Any ideas on who the motherfucker is?" Gabe asked.

Jack shook his head. The scent of sweat and a hint of something metallic reached her as he moved. "No, but I bet I know who might."

A voice at her elbow startled her. The man she hadn't recognized. "The bastard we brought back?"

"We'll see what we can wring out of him," Con said. He didn't sound happy about the prospect.

"I'll do it."

Gabe's voice was devoid of emotion. She stared at him, seeing not someone for whom the mission was over, but a soldier still in mission mode.

Her heart thumped so hard in her throat it hurt. "Who are you talking about?"

"One of the guards," Jack answered. She couldn't read his voice, his eyes. She'd seen David and Carson contemplating violence, had seen the gleam that announced their sick fascination with hurting those weaker than themselves. That she knew, but it wasn't what she saw in these men. Jack looked almost...resigned.

Reassurance left her limp. If she hadn't already known that Jack was nothing like David, his reaction right now would've been all the proof she needed.

She leaned her forehead on Jack's chest and closed her eyes. "And then?"

Jack went rigid against her. "Then we regroup and find a way to stop these bastards."

At that moment a piercing scream split the air, muffled only slightly by the door it passed through.

"Fuck!"

Jack was through the door in two steps. Maddie followed, anticipating another scream, but what she heard instead was Jack's name shaken by a sob.

Vaneqe, awake and clutching the blanket to her like a lifeline, had one hand out, simultaneously trying to keep the doctor and Lori away and reach Jack, who raced toward her. Maddie could see the confusion in the teenager's drug-hazed eyes. Jack was familiar, safe, and as he gathered her quickly into his arms, that knowledge flowed through Vaneqe in a wave Maddie could clearly see. The girl went limp once surrounded by his protection.

She was small, smaller than Maddie had expected. She sat curled up tight in Jack's lap, brown eyes flickering with distrust, looking more like a little girl than a teenager on the verge of adulthood. Her first words, whispered just loud enough for Maddie to hear, brought a sting to the backs of Maddie's eyes.

"Where's Charlie?"

She watched Jack's eyelids slide shut above Vaneqe's head. The sting got stronger.

Jack cupped Vaneqe's cheek carefully. "He's with Marge, darlin'. He's safe. I'll take you to him as soon as possible."

"I want Charlie," the girl said with a whimper.

"I know you do, but we don't want to wake him, okay? It's the middle of the night."

Vaneqe jerked her head around. "What? When?" Jack tensed, preparing to stand, maybe take her to the blinds-covered windows, but Vaneqee subsided against his chest. "I want Charlie," she whispered, blinking hard as she struggled to keep her eyes open.

"Soon," Jack crooned. He glanced at Roger as Vaneqe drifted off. "Any idea what she was dosed with?"

"Could be a couple of things or even a mix. Propofol, maybe Ativan? She's breathing fine, which is a good sign, but she'll likely be in and out."

"Okay." Jack glanced toward the door. "Mark, call Marge, please. Tell her to bring Charlie down. I'd like to keep her as calm as possible, and seeing him will help."

"You got it, Boss."

The others shuffled out, leaving the door open. Maddie settled onto a spot on the carpeted floor, close enough that she could help if Jack needed her, far enough away that Vaneqe wouldn't feel threatened. Jack slumped back into the couch cushions, his arms still around Vaneqe, looking like he never wanted to let her go. He probably didn't. He'd searched as long as she had, only he'd known who he was looking for. Maddie'd only had a picture to guide her. And now, looking at the two of them together, the guilt she felt at not working faster roared back to life.

Vaneqe shifted, one small foot peeking out of her blanket cocoon. Maddie glanced down, a small sound escaping as she caught a glimpse of the welts on the bottom of the girl's foot. She remembered those welts well; it was David's favorite form of punishment. The man had been particularly fond of his thin, flexible canes. She closed her eyes, trying to blank out the memories, feeling her toes curling up in her boots in remembered pain. God, she hated that man. There were no words to describe the depths of evil inside him. So many people said life wasn't fair, but sometimes she wondered just when the fuck it was at least going to be endurable, when girls like Vaneqe and Amber and women like Jess were going to get to play God the way these men had played God. When did Maddie get to make them pay the way she had paid? The way Vaneqe had paid?

It was never going to end until David was dead. She needed to be the one to stop him. And as she opened her eyes and watched Jack murmur quietly to Vaneqe, stirring in his lap once more, she realized all over again that the moment couldn't come soon enough.

Vaneqe lifted her head from Jack's shoulder. "Where is Sarah? Gracie?" She mumbled a few words Maddie couldn't hear, her head swaying as if she wasn't quite awake enough to hold it steady.

"Who are they, Vaneqe?" Jack asked.

"The other girls."

Maddie tensed. Jack's narrowed gaze said he'd gone on alert too.

"The other girls in the basement?"

A shudder shook Vaneqe so hard her blanket slid from her shoulder. Jack quickly tucked it back up, covering a wide yellowing bruise.

Vaneqe nodded. "Did you get them too? We were afraid they'd be moved. One of the guards said there was gonna be an auction. We tried to stay together, keep each other safe if we could, but...I couldn't stay awake." Vaneqe clutched Jack's T-shirt in her fist. "They weren't there, were they?"

"No, they weren't, darlin'. But we'll find them."

Would they? Maddie's stomach churned at the thought.

Con moved into the room, and only then did Maddie realize the others were clustered around the doorway. The big man stopped a few feet from the couch and crouched down to Vaneqe's level. She couldn't see his face, but Vaneqe didn't flinch, so she figured he must be managing not to look scary. "Vaneqe, I'm Con. Do you remember any details about the auction? When it would be, where it was?"

She shook her head. It fell back to Jack's shoulder midshake.

Gabe stirred near the door. "Don't worry; I'll find out."

Because he was going to question the guard. One look into Gabe's eyes, focused on Vaneqe's dangling foot, showed the emotionless windows now filled with fire. That look made Maddie supremely grateful she wasn't said guard.

Roger interrupted quietly. "Jack, we really need to finish up."

Maddie stood. Jack called her name.

"Hmm?"

He finally let go of Vaneqe, just one hand, to reach out to her. Maddie walked over and took it, crouching like Con had.

"Vaneqe, this is Maddie."

The girl stared at her with wary eyes. Maddie didn't smile; Vaneqe wouldn't buy it. She knew what it was like to have trust stripped away, faith, belief.

"Maddie helped me find you," Jack whispered.

Vaneqe glanced up at him, then back at Maddie. "Thank you."

Maddie looked down at Vaneqe's foot. "I'll see if we can find some arnica, okay? That might help." It was what they'd always used at the estate, the only thing that had helped reduce the swelling after a session with him.

"'Kay." Vaneqe closed her eyes again.

Maddie stood. Her legs were shaky, but she made it to the door. Jack called her name. She turned back to him, not bothering to hide the blaze of emotions she knew must be clear in her eyes. "What?"

Jack smiled. "Thank you."

She turned to leave.

"Maddie."

This time when she turned, she could see Jack's fatigue and something else: need. Not sexual need, just...need.

"Wait for me?" he asked.

She smiled back as best she could. "No problem." She stepped into the hallway and closed the door, holding on to those three little words and the way he'd looked as he said them. As she went in search of the cream she'd promised Vaneqe, those words gave her strength.

They'd done it; they'd found her, but there was still a long way to go.

Chapter Twenty-One

"Sissie!"

Vaneqe startled awake at Charlie's shout. For a moment Jack could read the fear and confusion in her eyes, and then she was smiling, crying, reaching out. Charlie rushed into her arms. The two huddled together like shipwrecked passengers who'd finally found land. Jack thought his heart might just tear apart at the sight.

"You did good, Jack," Marge said beside him, voice quiet so as not to disturb the kids.

Jack just shook his head. After talking with Roger, he didn't think anything was good. Jack should've had her away from those men weeks ago. As it was the only thing that seemed to have saved Vaneqe from an even worse nightmare was the fact that she was a virgin.

Marge patted his shoulder despite his denial. "Look at them," she told him. As if he could do anything else. Vaneqe was sore and tired and still afraid, but she had Charlie in her lap just as Jack had held her in his. The two of them together... Jack closed his eyes.

"They wouldn't be here if not for you," Marge told him. "Don't let what you can't control take that away from you."

Jack turned to face her. "Maddie is the one who made this possible."

"Maddie Baker?"

"Maddie...Baker." The name thing was a little too complicated to go into tonight. He pushed it aside and instead launched into the story of the last couple of days. When he got to the end, Marge eyes were round.

"Good...God. I figured she'd been in trouble at some point, but never this."

"I know." Vaneqe shifted under Charlie's weight, stretching one leg out on the couch. Her feet were uncovered. All Jack could see was the way Maddie had looked at Vaneqe's feet, her offer to get cream to soothe the welts. She was intimately familiar with Vaneqe's treatment, and the knowledge built a rage inside him that almost rivaled his despair. Almost.

A quiet knock at the door had Jack turning. Con stood on the other side, Gabe behind him. A couple of air mattresses, already inflated, leaned against the wall. "Got your sleepover equipment," Con joked. His smile didn't quite reach his tired eyes.

"Thanks, Con." Jack ushered them in and busied himself setting up beds for Charlie and Marge. He didn't want to move Vaneqe yet, and the office had everything they'd need till tomorrow anyway. He and Maddie would stay in his office to be close by. He was pretty sure, though, from the look on her face, that having Charlie here was the best medicine Vaneqe could hope to have.

"I'll let y'all settle in, okay? You know where to find me," he told Marge a little later.

Marge nodded.

Walking over to the couch, Jack knelt next to Vaneqe and Charlie. "I'll be right across the hall."

Vaneqe reached for him, her thin arms gripping harder than seemed possible around his neck. He closed his eyes.

"I love you, Jack," the girl said.

Jack sucked in a breath, telling himself over and over that Vaneqe didn't need to witness more tears. "I love you too, darlin'." He eased back from her to ruffle Charlie's hair. The boy focused on him since the first time he'd come into the room. "And you too, little man."

Charlie stared up at him. "You kept your promise."

"I did."

Tears slid from the boy's big eyes as he launched himself at Jack. Holding Charlie's shaking body against him, Jack gave up the fight against his own tears. It was long minutes later before he could tear himself away.

"Come get me if you need anything, anything at all," he told Marge.

"Maddie better be here in the morning, Jack. I want to see her."

Jack nodded. Maddie would probably be ready by then too. Tonight she'd had more than she could handle if the look on her face when she'd gone across the hall was anything to go by.

His office was dark except for the lights of the city beyond his windows. The bathroom door was closed. Jack went to work pulling a couple of blankets and pillows from his closet and settling them on the

273

extra-wide couch. He'd spent more than one night here while working a case. Tonight he was just thankful he and Maddie weren't sharing an actual bed; he didn't think he could bear having her that far away from him for even a moment.

The bathroom door opened, the light slicing across the room to meet him. Maddie stepped into the office. "Is she settled?"

Jack held his hand out to her. "She's settled. Charlie has a pallet on the floor right beside her, and Marge is there if she has nightmares." He deliberately didn't use the word *when*. "Come here, wildcat."

The feel of her hand in his, her body curling willingly into him as he took her in his arms, sparked a wonder he hadn't realized he could still feel at his age. Maddie knew what it was to have her trust horrendously abused. That she would trust him now…it was more than he could truly comprehend, and the greatest gift anyone had ever given him. He breathed in the soft scent of her, his stubble catching in her hair, connecting them to each other.

Con had been right: he didn't care what anyone else thought. He was pretty damn certain he loved this woman. She centered him in a way nothing ever had. She made him feel complete. He was never going to let her go.

"You're mine, wildcat," he whispered into her hair. Maddie didn't answer, just slid her hands around his waist and held him as tight as he was holding her.

They stood like that, in the darkness, for a long, quiet moment. Finally, knowing she must be dead on her feet, he leaned back and tipped her chin up to meet his eyes. "You settle in, okay? I'm gonna grab a quick shower."

Maddie nuzzled her nose into his chest. "Okay, Jack." When she stepped away, a small smile lit her eyes. He smiled back and went to clean off as much of the ugliness of tonight as he could with mere water.

Maddie watched Jack step into the bathroom, her heart swelled so full she wasn't sure how it still fit into her chest. *You're mine too.*

She might not be able to say the words aloud, but she knew they were true. A mix of peace, pain, and desire swirled inside her. This man, with his combination of strength and protection and honor, was the one she was meant to be with. This was where she belonged. Her past, horrible as it had been, had set her on this path and brought her to Jack. And now he was hers; she had no doubts about it. The memory of his arms so tight around her earlier tonight, his pain and exultation being breathed into her skin, had healed something in her she hadn't realized could be restored.

Fifteen minutes later she watched from the couch as he exited the bathroom, a thick white towel knotted around his waist. He walked to the door of the office, locked it, then made his way to her in the dark. Stopping next to their makeshift bed, he quickly shucked the towel and crawled naked onto the cushions beside her. The small space left little room to maneuver as her bare legs tangled with his. Jack's hands went to the hem of the oversize T-shirt serving as her nightgown.

"Jack…"

"I need to feel you, Maddie. Please."

His voice was rough with the strain tonight had left on both of them. Hearing him, Maddie didn't hesitate, assisting him as he pulled her shirt over her head. The feel of her naked breasts against the rough hair scattered across his chest started a heat between her legs that shamed her considering where they were, what they'd been through today.

But Jack didn't push for anything further. His body surrounded her, blocking out the light from the windows across the room, his thick arms holding her as close as she could get. Quiet settled between them.

Jack's chest rose and fell in gentle reassurance against her. The scent of heat and need and man filled her nose, mixed with the faintest touch of the smoke they'd used on the raid. She'd never realized that the smell of a man's skin could be so powerful. It mesmerized her, made her want more. She turned her head, searching blindly, and her nose nudged Jack's taut nipple.

Jack shivered against her. "Maddie."

And suddenly she didn't care where they were. She breathed him in, felt that nub tighten beneath her touch, and every emotion she'd experienced today, every moment of tension united into a single burning need to show this man what she felt for him. They weren't guaranteed tomorrow— hell, the way they were going, tomorrow was iffy at best—but she had tonight, and she was damn well going to use it.

She took him into her mouth. Sucked lightly.

Jack arched into her touch, gasped, the sound strangled with pleasure. Strong hands came up to hold her to him. Maddie smiled against his skin. She took his nipple gently between her teeth and tugged. Jack grunted. Between their legs, his shaft jerked and stretched, nudging her belly. It only made her want more.

Pressing his shoulders back, Maddie urged Jack to lie beneath her. She sat up between his legs, her gaze trained on the way the scant light in the room flickered over the ripples of muscle along his chest, arms, stomach. He was so beautiful, and the way he looked at her, his eyes on her breasts, his hand reaching down to grasp the base of his erection and squeeze, made her feel beautiful too. She wanted to claim every inch of his bare skin, right now, make him feel everything he stirred in her at that moment.

Coming up on her knees, she planted her hands on either side of Jack's shoulders. Her breasts, full and aching, strained toward him, her nipples tight points of need. Jack caught them between his fingers, teasing, tugging, twisting, until her back was bowed, her need for his mouth on her driving her quietly insane. She licked her lips, and Jack whispered her name on a ragged breath. A thrill of feminine power shot through her.

Jack's lips surrounded one stiff nub, the hard suction of his mouth burning and exciting her at the same time. Maddie wobbled above him. Needing

277

more, she lifted her hand to the opposite breast, tugging the nipple between her fingers. They both moaned.

Jack took over, leaving Maddie free to explore him as he drugged her senses with the pleasure of his touch. She trailed her fingers along his shoulders, his biceps, his corded forearms. When her hands reached his on her breast, she threaded their fingers together and taught him what she liked, what felt good, how hard to pinch and when to flick. Rubbing the very tip of her nipple took her breath. Circling the areola had her pushing closer, desperate for more. Jack's mouth was hard on the opposite side, tight with rising desire, but he didn't try to take over or speed up the pace. He just watched and played, his eyes glittering, seeming to catch every speck of light in the dim room. That look filled her world.

When she didn't think she could take another minute without exploding, she eased back from his touch. His body called to her, beckoning her down the rippled expanse of his six-pack abs, around the shallow valley of his navel, to the straining evidence of his need. Jack's hoarse groan rewarded her as she breathed gently against his shaft. From this angle Jack's eyes were dark wells in his face. She couldn't read them, but she could read the taut expectation in the stretched skin across his cheekbones, the tightened mouth, the slight quivering of the muscles in his belly. She blew a second hot breath along his cock, and it lengthened, pushing toward her mouth as if it had a mind of its own. She rewarded it with a quick lick across the full wet head.

"Maddie." Jack drew her name out, the word strained, on the edge of shattering.

She moved her hands to his inner thighs and pushed out, widening his legs and giving her greater access. She'd read about this, been forced to do it with David, but she had never taken her husband into her mouth willingly. She wanted to now, wanted to give Jack everything she could.

Jack's tight sac waited impatiently at the base of his shaft. Maddie ducked toward it, angled her head, and licked one side of the warm, wrinkled skin. Jack's fingers tangled in her hair, gripped hard. Adrenaline spiked, but he didn't force her closer. Encouraged, she licked the other side, then pulled it carefully into her mouth with hot, moist suction. She stroked his sac, rolled it across her tongue, slid him in and out, slow and easy. The muscles of Jack's upper thighs were tight under her massaging hands, and when she repeated the attention on the other side of his scrotum, he pulled her hair in reaction.

An agonized groan rang out above her head. "Maddie…God. Please."

Yes, definitely agony. She hid her smile in a kiss, placed right at the base of his shaft. She loved doing this, pushing him, pleasing him. Loving him. In one smooth slide she traveled from the base to the tip of his cock and took his thick length to the back of her throat. The trick had been learned in ways she had no desire to remember; tonight, she was making new memories, with Jack. She swallowed around him.

"Fuck, Maddie. So good. Again." Jack tugged back on her hair, commanding her with both words and hands, and she wasn't afraid. She didn't want to fight him. She relaxed into his hold, let him guide her, trusting him to keep her safe, even lost in his own pleasure. He pulled her up his shaft until her tongue rested on the sensitive spot just under the head. She sucked hard, rubbed with her tongue, then took him deep again. He set the rhythm, but his pleasure was hers to give, and she gave it all she had.

When the skin beneath her hands was damp with sweat and Jack's every breath became a whispered curse, he pulled Maddie off him. Hands rough with passion gripped her, lifted, and then she was cradled in his arms. She could stare into those glazed, hungry eyes forever.

Without warning Jack flipped them over, tucking her neatly beneath him on the wide couch. Hard lips surrounded her nipple. Jack drew her in, showing her just how mind-destroying her mouth had been for him by using the same weapon on her. Her spine went rigid with fear for one long second, feeling his weight on her, and then Jack was on his side, Maddie turned toward him, his connection to her breast strong and sure. He sucked and licked and nibbled, the sensations sending wave after wave of undeniable pleasure from breast to clit and back again until Maddie felt drunk on desire, on him.

Arching against him was as natural as breathing. She needed him closer, surrounding her, protective and overpowering all at once. The memories couldn't have her, couldn't take this away. She refused to allow it. Instead she tucked a leg over

Jack's heavy thigh and pulled him closer, opening her body completely to his.

Rolling her hips in to make contact only intensified the ache between her legs. She rubbed herself along his shaft, caught her breath as sensation streaked up her belly. Jack shifted her up and tucked a leg between hers, the angle giving him the perfect opportunity to deliberately stroke her clit with each thrust, each long drag between her labia. She wrapped her arms around his head, holding him hard against her breast, and he nipped her lightly between his teeth.

Urgency forced a plea from her lips, the same one he'd used earlier. "Please!"

Maddie squirmed, rolled her hips, desperate to line up their bodies and get him inside her. Nothing worked. Jack chuckled, the sound tickling her skin as he slid lower on her body, farther away from where she so frantically needed him.

"No, you don't, wildcat."

Maddie growled low in her throat, but the sound choked off when he slid his teeth along the skin just above her belly button. His tongue circled, left a hot, wet trail, before dipping into her navel. She was so ready, so frantic for his entry that she could feel cream trickling onto her thigh. Jack ignored her wiggling and moved lower.

Tension of another kind started a tiny knot in her stomach.

Lower.

No, this wasn't what she wanted, what she needed. "Jack—"

281

Lower.

The knot became a rock, then a boulder.

When Jack nuzzled the curls at the top of her mound, she couldn't stop her body's instinctive reaction. She rolled to her back, her thighs slapping together, denying him access. She waited, chin tilted up enough to hide her expression, her thoughts. The need for breath burned her lungs. Now Jack would get angry. Now he'd demand what she was afraid to give. Now he'd strike out, yell, berate her for refusing him the one thing he wanted. A tear slid from the corner of her eye.

Jack did none of those things. He simply resituated himself next to her legs. He leaned down, his breath warming her fear-chilled skin, and began kissing and licking her cramped thighs. His tongue glided along her tight muscles, his lips traced the crease where her legs pressed together, and he lightly suckled the sensitive flesh above her knees. No attempts to pry her legs apart, no demands for her compliance or for the act she knew he wanted. Jack simply loved her, his mouth, tongue, and teeth working their magic as he waited.

She wanted to give this to him, almost as much as she'd wanted to please him with her mouth. But she was so afraid to fail, both herself and Jack. Afraid that, in the moment, the memories would win—and take something precious from them in the meantime. Her body had been trained and trained well to fear many things, including this. She loved him; why couldn't she trust him enough to have his mouth explore where she was most vulnerable?

"Jack?" Her voice was too constricted to be anything but a whisper.

He turned his head so his cheek rested on top of her thigh, his stubble rasping her flesh as he continued to nuzzle her while he looked into her eyes. "Hmm?"

Taking a deep breath, focusing all her attention on the tenderness shining from his eyes, Maddie gradually loosened her legs and let them fall open. "Don't…"

Jack lifted his head. His gaze followed the tracks of her tears as they fell. "Don't what, wildcat?"

His teasing nickname gave her courage. "Don't…bite me, okay?"

His brows drew together. "Bite you? Why…"

She couldn't explain. All she could do was lie back on the pillow and open her legs wide enough for him to settle between them. Both hands clenched the cushion at her hips, gripping so tight her knuckles ached. She couldn't let go, desperate for an anchor as she fought the demons gnashing inside her.

Silence fell for several moments. "Oh God. Maddie—" The words were rough with sorrow and what sounded like anger. But not at her, she assured herself. Not at her. Never at her.

And then Jack's hand settled, so wide, so heavy, and yet so very careful, on her mound. He pressed down. Maddie lifted her head and watched as he sat, hand over her, head hanging, and didn't move. At least, he didn't do anything but shake. He shook so hard she was afraid he'd bust out of his skin. She gripped the cushion tighter and told herself to breathe.

In that moment, there in the quiet beneath Jack's touch, Maddie felt like she had an inkling of what dealing with her past must be like for him. It had always been her problem, her memories, her fear. But now she realized that David hadn't just hurt her. That hurt was now Jack's as well, even though David was no longer in her life. But caring about her meant what hurt her also hurt Jack, so she waited while he dealt with the pain.

He finally sighed, his muscles relaxing as he bent down and pressed a kiss to her trembling thigh. "Never, wildcat. I'd never hurt you like that." He raised his head, his gaze searing in its power. "I know it's too soon and I know you'll fight it, but listen to me, Maddie: I. Love. You. I love you. Don't believe me; I don't care. I love you, and I promise"—his fingertips bit into her muscles for a brief moment before easing back—"no one will hurt you like that again. Ever. I promise you."

And Jack was a man who kept his promises.

There were a thousand things she could probably say, and none of them fit the miracle of this moment, so she sat up and kissed him. His taste and hers hit her tongue like a fireball. When the kiss ended, she stared into his eyes for a long time, then told him, voice hoarse, "I believe you."

Jack's wide grin was the last thing she saw before she lay back and closed her eyes. She could feel him move, feel the cushions sink and shift as he situated himself between her legs. His mouth was hot as he returned it to her skin. He kissed the crease of one thigh, then the other. He trailed his tongue along her lower belly. He circled her mound with unending patience and sadistic pleasure until Maddie was raising her hips off the couch to get more, get closer. By the time his breath hit her clit, she was too aroused to be afraid. She jumped when his first lick opened her outer lips, baring her slit to him. He repeated the caress, and she could tell when the taste of her cream registered from the moan that echoed in his throat. He delved deep, deep inside, suckling as if he could soak up every last drop. Orgasm hit her the moment his nose nudged her clit.

"That's it, wildcat. Again," he commanded. And she complied.

Gentle licks on each side of her clit brought Maddie down from her second high, but Jack wasn't done. Through the early morning hours, he brought her to the peak over and over, giving her pleasure, drowning her with his love. When finally he crawled above her on all fours, slid himself deep inside, and settled his full weight on top of her, there was no fear left, no memories of being trapped, being held down, being forced. There was only the joy that swelled inside her at his climax, and his words of love filling her heart nearly as full as he filled her body.

Chapter Twenty-Two

Carson's voice shook with fury as it came across the line. David would've been amused were it not for the reason Carson was calling: the girl was gone. Was Carson more upset about the loss of the girl and his dead men or about the fact that someone had bested him? David didn't really care. Carson had lost him a girl and a business connection and a million fucking dollars if said girl couldn't be provided. He and his clients expected results, not sniveling. His rage burned far hotter than a few shaky words during a phone call.

But rage could wait. That was the difference between Carson and himself. Patience. Patience was a necessity in what he did. It took time to play the right cards to get a murderer set free. It took patience to wear down jurors until they agreed to take whatever he offered them. When someone disappointed him, patience made the payback that much sweeter and still kept David in control. They might be partners, but David always retained the upper hand.

So he kept his voice calm, even. "And how do you plan to get her back?"

"'You'?"

"You."

There was a long pause on the line. David waited.

Carson finally seemed to get a grip on himself. When he spoke, the words were sharp, cold. His usual self. "*I* don't intend to do anything. Your bitch has already cost me enough as it is."

Something about Carson's tone told him they weren't talking about the pretty little virgin. "My bitch?"

"That's right." A laugh filtered across the line, low on amusement, high on mockery. "I don't think I'd gotten around to telling you about that, did I? I paid our contact a visit. You'll never guess what he told me."

"And what was that?"

"Turns out the shelter we grabbed the girl from has a local security guy they use for background checks, protection, that kind of thing. He should not have been an issue, except he's not just any security guy. He's Jack Quinn, from JCL Security."

David had heard of Quinn; anyone who had a stake in illegal matters staying private knew about Quinn and JCL. The man was the best in the business, just on the wrong side. And if David remembered correctly, he had a particular hard-on for abusive spouses, deadbeat dads. An unfortunate bit of coincidence.

"I see." David's mind raced, tallying implications, searching out avenues to proceed. A minute later he realized Carson still hadn't spoken. "Anything else?"

"Yeah."

David refused to ask twice.

"Quinn recently began spending a good bit of time at the local bar, same place our boy hangs out. He's picked himself up a new woman, it seems."

This could prove useful.

"It's Madelyn."

The casing on the phone creaked in his hand. "Don't be ridiculous. Madelyn Grace wouldn't be caught dead in a local honky-tonk." The first time David had laid eyes on his young wife had been at a charity ball, talking with friends. She was the epitome of refined beauty—delicate, mannered, reserved. Elegance personified. He'd taken steps to acquire her beginning that very night.

"It is her, David. I saw the pictures myself."

"Are you sure?"

Carson's impatience filtered through the line. "She's changed her hair, her clothes, but it's definitely her. And that's not all."

Jesus, how badly had Quinn—and Carson—screwed up everything he'd worked for? "What else is there?"

"One of my men is missing."

Fuck. "Then we have to assume the next location is compromised." And this little fiasco would cost him a lot more than the lost commission on his brown sugar virgin.

"I'll prepare to move the event."

David considered the options. "Don't do that yet. Give me five minutes."

He hit End Call without waiting for a reply. The phone hit the oak sideboard across the room with a crash. Glass shattered; antique china tumbled from the shelves. Jacobs hurried into the study.

"Sir?"

David walked past the butler without a glance at the mess he'd made. "Clean that up. I need a bag packed for a few nights stay out of town. And get me a new phone within the hour."

"Yes, sir."

David spent that hour in the basement. When he surfaced, the scent of blood and cum and tears coating his nostrils, it was to Jacobs presenting him with a brand-new phone. David ran through the features as he walked toward his office, making certain he had everything he needed. A few minutes on his computer researching JCL Security and he was ready to form a plan.

He dialed, not waiting for Carson to speak. "Cancel the auction, reschedule for a week from the original date. I take it the merchandise has been moved to the secondary location."

"Yes."

"Good. Move it again, just to be sure. In fact, bring them home." No location was as secure as his estate. "Then send out the notice to the buyers about the change. A week or two will just whet their appetites more." David went on to outline exactly what he had in mind to fix the current situation.

When he finished, Carson was silent for a moment. "How do you know she'll show?" he finally asked.

"She will. She'll have a helpless child to rescue; she won't forget her last lesson in that area." A visceral thrill shot up David's spine as he remembered the look on Darrel Hendley's face. That thrill turned dark as the rest of that night played through his mind. He still hadn't forgiven Madelyn Grace for the loss of his slave. "Best of all, she has a chance to get back at me. She'll show."

He would have the opportunity to teach Jack Quinn to keep his hands off what belonged to David Reed, and after her lover was dead, David could rid himself of the pesky issue of his legal wife—after a little fun, of course.

Nothing could be more perfect.

* * *

Jack was waiting when Gabe came into the hallway. His friend had spent the past few hours "talking" to their guest, getting the information they needed. Jack hadn't asked how he planned to do it, and Gabe hadn't shared. They both knew it was necessary, so it didn't matter.

Gabe didn't look at him, just turned and walked down the hallway toward the bathroom. He pushed his way inside and went straight to the sink. Turned on the water. Washed his hands.

"Kinda cliché, ain't it?"

Gabe managed to crack a small smile. "Shut up, asshole."

They didn't say anything else; they didn't need to. Jack waited while Gabe splashed water on his face and drank a couple of handfuls, then dried himself with careful precision. Wiping away every last drop— and, Jack knew, wiping whatever had happened in that room from the front of his mind. They couldn't stop the nightmares that came back to haunt them, but they could make sure they weren't front and center.

He and Gabe made their way back down the hall to meet with Con.

Jack had just seen Marge and Maddie off. They were headed to the shelter to get Vaneqe settled into familiar surroundings. Roger would go out this afternoon and visit, continuing to treat the girl until her wounds were healed. Once again Jack thanked God for the twist of fate that had saved Vaneqe from an even worse experience than she'd actually endured. Who would've believed those bastards' greed would be the one thing that had protected her? The sad irony was, it wasn't a hymen that was worth a fortune; it was the girl it belonged to that was worth her weight in gold. That some men couldn't see that, Jack would never get.

"Did he give you anything helpful?"

"Unfortunately nothing on the auction," Gabe told him. "Reed might be a sick bastard, but he's smart."

"We already knew that."

Gabe chuckled, the sound more an acknowledgment of Jack's point than an indication of amusement. "He keeps information compartmentalized. The guards at the warehouse knew the girls were destined for a sale, but not when or where. Apparently when they're shipped out, the transport crew is contacted after their departure with information on where to go. They meet another team at that location, drop off the girls, and that's it. The second team delivers them to their final destination."

"Clever fuck."

They moved through the lobby into the second wing of JCL's offices. At the far end, the sound of squeaking equipment and hoarse grunts said the workout room was currently in use. Jack and Gabe veered into a conference room about halfway down. Con waited inside.

"What did he know then?" Jack asked.

Gabe gave him a knowing grin. "The name of their local contact."

Jack stopped halfway into his chair. "Who?

"Bart Symmons."

"You're fucking kidding me." Con shot Jack a look that was just as confused as Jack was. If he'd been forced to bet on who would have enough balls to work with Reed and his cohorts, he sure as hell wouldn't have put money on Bart. Philip, yes, but not Bart. Jesus.

Gabe looked confused by their reaction. "Seems he had a penchant for younger girls. The job came with all-you-can-get access to his favorite pastime."

It made sense, but still…

"All right, unless you have anything that needs immediate attention, I want him picked up. We'll cover everything else after."

Gabe nodded, turned toward the door.

"Not you, idiot." Con was already gathering his things. "You've been up most of the night as it is."

Gabe shrugged. "Psychological warfare takes longer than shoving stakes under fingernails."

"Yeah," Con agreed, "sometimes having morals sucks ass." He headed for the door. "I'll take a team to pick him up. He's a weasel; it won't be that hard."

Jack called his friend back before he could leave. "Considering he was working for Alexander, prepare to be surprised."

Con hesitated in the doorway, one brow raised. Jack didn't want to admit that Bart of all people could get a drop on them, but he wasn't risking Con for some stupid manly boasting. "I mean it."

Con grinned, but Jack could see the seriousness in his eyes. "All right. We'll pop smoke in fifteen."

Jack wished Con luck and turned back to Gabe. "Well, shit like that makes for a short meeting. Why don't you catch some shut-eye in the extra office until they get back?"

Gabe didn't argue, for good reason. Where others probably wouldn't see beyond the man's enigmatic expression, Jack could clearly see his one-time subordinate's fatigue. Leaving Gabe to sleep, he returned to his own office, prepared to finish some of the work that had piled up over the past week before he went out to pick up Maddie. Tonight would likely be spent with Bart's weaselly ass.

Jack was shutting down his computer when Lori buzzed his office later that afternoon. "Boss?"

"Yeah?"

"You have a drop-in, says it's urgent."

The tension in Lori's normally sweet Southern accent raised the hair on his neck. "Who is it?"

"David Reed."

Son of a bitch.

Red-hot rage rushed over him. Jack wanted to charge into the lobby and kill the motherfucker where he stood. A gun was too good for Reed; only Jack's bare hands choking the life out of him would be enough to punish the man who'd hurt so many people. Tear him into pieces and bury him in a shallow grave—

But Jack couldn't. Much as he wanted to kill the bastard, it was too much of a risk, at least here and now. Maddie could disappear for years at a time and Reed could claim illness and the need for privacy. If Reed disappeared, Jack would likely spend the rest of his life in jail unless he could create a foolproof alibi—and with Reed, nothing was probably foolproof. Jack had to shove aside fantasies of a shallow grave in the Appalachians and figure out what Reed's plan was before the man fucked them all.

He forced his voice to neutral. "Show him in."

The door opened far too soon and yet not soon enough. The man who entered was cool, elegant, his suit thousand-dollar crisp and cutting edge fashion. David Reed strode toward Jack as if he owned the building. The man was well-known, well moneyed, and his attitude showed it.

This was the man who had raped Jack's woman.

Reed had raped her, not once but hundreds of times. Not just physically, but mentally and emotionally. Lord knew what all the man had actually done to Maddie. That she was coming alive again was testament to her strength, not the weakness of this man's actions. Why was he here, now? He had to know they were on to him; why risk walking into the lion's den?

Because the man has big damn balls, that's why.

Jack clamped down on the animal rage surging through his system. The important thing was to keep Maddie safe and protected, and to do that, Jack needed information. The only source for that was stretching out a manicured hand toward him, nails neatly trimmed and buffed to a high shine.

"Jack Quinn, I presume? I'm—"

"David Reed," Jack said, keeping his tone neutral.

"Yes, that's right. We've met before?"

Jack shook his head, taking the man's hand in a brief greeting—resisting the urge to crush every bone in his grasp—before ushering Reed into a seat. Jack remained standing. "Your name's hard to miss if you follow regional news."

"True," Reed said. He unbuttoned the single button on his suit jacket before making himself comfortable in one of the two leather chairs situated before Jack's desk. Jack stayed behind the heavy oak monstrosity, though even it might not be enough to keep him from attacking. It would have to do for now.

Reed took the lead. "I apologize for the last-minute nature of this visit, Mr. Quinn, but I've come into some information that needs to be taken care of immediately."

Jack just bet he had. "What can I do for you?"

Reed templed his hands in front of him, resting his lips against them, the epitome of Southern charm and killer instinct rolled into one. Jack guessed the slender frame, broad shoulders, and classic good looks would appeal to any woman. Close-shaven brown hair emphasized the keen intelligence in his eyes. This wouldn't be an easy man to fool, yet Maddie had managed it.

Only the thin cut of his lips hinted at the cruelty Jack knew lay beneath the surface. The Maddie whose innocent, shining eyes had peered out at him from her wedding portrait would never have guessed what lay beneath that smooth, refined surface.

Reed's lips curved into a thin, humorless smile. "I have a somewhat...delicate...matter in need of attention, Mr. Quinn." Reed leaned forward, elbows resting on the arms of the chair, hands still held in front. "I need you to return my wife."

Jack clamped his muscles tight, unwilling to give his surprise away by even the slightest jerk. Reed had bigger balls than Jack had realized. "Excuse me?"

"My wife. You know her, I've been told. Maddie...what is the name she's using...Baker?"

"I was given to understand your wife left you."

Reed waved away his comment with a casual flick of a hand, settling back into the depths of the chair. "Yes, technically. But technicalities can't sway the heart, can they?"

Jack forced back a laugh. If Reed even had a heart, Jack would eat his truck tires.

"My wife has been missing for over four years."

"Get in your way, did it?"

Reed continued as if Jack hadn't spoken. "Of course there's no formal record of her...departure. I sought to avoid the embarrassing consequences should she ever return. Her disappearance wasn't reported. Nothing is more important to me than bringing her home."

I bet. He clenched his teeth, breathing through his nose to keep himself focused, calm.

"Now, I know from my informant that you are in possession of my wife, and I want her returned. I think a million dollars should suffice, don't you?"

"What I think is that you are fucking insane. A million dollars?"

"Mr. Quinn," Reed stated in the same tone he might use with a not so bright child, "my family practically built the South on their backs—or rather, the backs of those they owned. I assure you, I could afford that and much more where the happiness of my wife is concerned."

If he calls her his wife again, I just might kill him.

"Mr. Reed." Jack mimicked the man's tone. "This is not the pre–Civil War South, and you don't own Maddie or anyone else. Nor can you buy her with a million dollars or even two million. She's a person, not a commodity."

"And that's where you are wrong." Reed stood, taking his time as he rebuttoned his jacket and stared down his nose at Jack. "After last night, I know you now have two somethings that belong to me. Though the...merchandise was worth much more than a million, I am willing to forgo that particular possession on the condition that Madelyn Grace is returned to me immediately. I'll also supply the money, though if you quibble much more, I'll make certain you never see a penny of it—or anything else—and I'll take her anyway. Which will it be?"

When hell freezes over. "How soon?" Jack asked.

"Within the week."

Jack stared at this epitome of wealth and privilege and wondered what had managed to twist the man into this. It was incomprehensible, and yet Reed stared back at him, seemingly unaware that he was in fact demanding a human being in exchange for money. All Jack saw in his eyes was a cold calculation that chilled Jack to the bone. The lack of emotion gave Jack a weird sense of being off balance, almost as if he was in a fun house with the lights dimmed.

"No." Jack leaned forward, wishing he hadn't put the desk between them. "I wouldn't give Maddie to you if you were offering me your entire fortune." He gave the man his meanest smile. "I'd be happy to make sure *you* never see anything again, though."

Reed's chuckle was his only reply. He turned to walk toward the door to Jack's office. Before he turned the knob, he said, "Be sure and give Madelyn my love, won't you?"

"No way in hell."

Glancing at Jack over his shoulder, Reed shook his head. "You don't understand, do you? You'll give Maddie to me very soon. You might even be begging me to take her." His eyes lit with promise at that idea. "Good afternoon, Mr. Quinn."

Chapter Twenty-Three

Maddie's worried eyes stared at him from across the conference table. "Jack, I'm telling you, he's got something up his sleeve, and when it comes out, it's going to be bad."

It wasn't that Jack didn't believe her; it was that there was nothing he could do about it. He refused to compromise on this. He wasn't handing Maddie over to David Reed. "We'll deal with it when it comes, Maddie. Now, tell us what you know about Reed's property."

Con had called in every team member with the training to handle this kind of situation. Between their men, Jack, Con, and Gabe, that brought them to eleven—a good-size team, but a team without a mission, and waiting for the other shoe to drop was putting them all on edge.

News of Reed's visit had blown through the office like exploding C4. Jack was still in awe at the man's arrogance to walk right into enemy camp and demand Maddie be returned to him like she was a lost puppy. A lost *abused* puppy. Then Con had returned that afternoon with the news that Bart Symmons had been murdered. When the team arrived to bring the man in, they'd found him floating facedown in the luxury pool in his backyard. Reed was cleaning house, it seemed, making certain Jack couldn't follow the trail back to the missing girls. Jack would find them, but right now they were a little short on leads. He was also very aware of the time frame Reed had given him: by the end of the week. It was already Saturday. Time was ticking away while they waited for Reed to make his move. It wasn't a position Jack was happy with.

Maddie stood and walked up to the whiteboard currently serving as a projector screen. Sketches of the interior of Reed's Nashville mansion, all four levels including the basement, were displayed for their perusal. Pointing to the first sketch, Maddie traced a path through the rooms. "This is the entry level, mostly public areas—not that any public actually comes in. This area here, just inside the front door, is all open floor, no walls. I always wondered if that was so David could see whatever was coming for him."

Jack gritted his teeth at the man's name on Maddie's lips. He knew she was intimately familiar with Reed, but the reminder bothered him more than he would admit aloud.

"This long hallway here leads to the back of the house and what used to be the outdoor kitchen but is now a garage. Right here"—she pointed to what looked like a small alcove near the end of the corridor—"is the entry to the basement."

"Does the basement extend the length of the house?" Con asked.

"I don't know. We weren't allowed in there, and I've only been as far as the first two rooms. An entry and a…training room." She pointed them out on the much smaller second sketch.

"What's the security like? How do you get in?"

Maddie began describing what she'd seen during her one visit to the dungeon, leaving out the personal details. Jack was proud of how controlled she was, the details she could recall even though that night had been a nightmare for her. She knew better than any of them how important this was. Reed could very well have the girls Vaneqe had told them about in his Nashville estate for safekeeping if he hadn't sold them already. They had no proof the auction hadn't already taken place, not with Bart dead, but Jack wasn't taking a chance on maybes. They would find a way into the mansion, and if the girls were there, Jack and his team would get them out—and anyone else they found. The question was, how?

Jack rubbed a hand over his tired eyes.

Gabe filled a pause in Maddie's intel to point out, "We don't even know for certain Reed is in Nashville. He could still be in Atlanta for all we know."

They'd managed to track Reed from JCL to a downtown hotel using security and traffic cameras Jack hacked, but after that they'd lost him. No sign of him on the hotel's CCTV, though he was registered and presumably stayed the night. The registration records confirmed an early morning checkout, but though they'd covered all the exits, there'd been no sign of him leaving. The bastard had been a ghost ever since.

"If he isn't on the property, all the better," Jack said. "Would security be more lax then, Maddie?"

Maddie shrugged. "After this many years, it's hard to tell what he might have going on. When I lived there, the answer would've been yes. David's men are well-trained, but without their master present, they tended to slack off as much as the next guy, especially when there were women around."

Maddie's grim tone said the men's attentions hadn't necessarily been welcome. Jack opened his mouth to ask more, but his phone beeped on the table in front of him, the alert for an incoming text message. He picked it up.

The text flashed on his screen: *I have the boy. Contact me when you're ready to talk.*

The number was unknown. Jack stared at the screen for a long moment, a feeling of dread roiling in his gut.

The phone rang in his hand.

The room went quiet around him.

Marge.

"Hey, darli—"

"Jack, he's gone!"

"Who's gone?"

"Charlie. He went outside; I figured he was in the tree house. I went out a while ago to call him in for dinner and he's not there. I can't find him!"

The frantic note in her voice told Jack how worried Marge was. She didn't get hysterical. She didn't fuss for no reason. Jack muted the phone. "T. C., get out to the shelter ASAP. Take your gear." In other words, be ready for trouble. "Zach, go with him."

The two men nodded and left on a run.

"Jack?" Maddie's gaze tangled with his, wide with knowledge and worry. She'd warned them, but he hadn't expected this. After what she'd told him about Nashville and Amber, he should have, but he hadn't. That pain in his gut got worse.

He held up a finger, asking her to wait, and unmuted the phone. "Marge, I've got two of my men on their way. Tell me what happened."

Marge went through the story again, but there wasn't much to tell. Charlie had vanished as easily as Vaneqe had, except this time it had happened on the shelter property, not on the way home from the corner store. And this time he didn't need to know what had happened; he already knew. Reed had taken Charlie—and just as the man had warned him, Jack now had to consider the distinct possibility that giving Maddie up might mean the difference between the little boy living or dying.

Jack planted a fist on the desk, leaning onto it as he struggled for control. He was gonna kill Reed; Jack wouldn't let anything stand in the way of that. The fucker was going to die. Charlie was the last child Reed would terrorize.

He urged Marge to stay inside where it was safe, lock all the doors, even though it was too little too late. Reed's men hadn't had to breach the walls to take his revenge. "They'll be at your place in a few minutes. Let me check on some things and get back to you. Just a few minutes."

"Okay, Jack. Please—"

He closed his eyes at the frantic worry in his friend's voice. "I haven't let you down yet, darlin'."

"And you won't now; I know that."

As he hung up, he could only hope her faith in him was justified.

"I don't think we'll have to figure out where Reed is," he said aloud.

"Why not?" Maddie asked. Jack glanced up, and in her eyes he could see she already knew.

"Because Reed's going to tell us. So we can bring you to him...in exchange for Charlie."

The room erupted. Jack was aware of it on some level, but his gaze was glued to Maddie. Dark memories swam in her eyes alongside sudden tears, tears she refused to let fall. Jack wanted her in his arms, wanted to comfort her and be comforted, assure each other Charlie would be fine, that she would be fine, but now wasn't the time. He had a phone call to make.

"Con, run an inventory. I have a feeling this will go down quick." Reed wouldn't want to give them much time to plan.

Maddie was on her feet and following him into the hall. "What are you going to do?"

"Call your husband."

She stumbled over nothing, and when he glanced back at her, she looked as if she'd been slapped. He hadn't meant it that way, but there was no time to explain. He strode down the hall and across to his office as fast as his feet and his fear would take him.

"I would say I told you so, but it seems much too clichéd, don't you think?" David said when he answered his phone.

Jack's fist clenched around the handset, imagining it was Reed's neck. "You bastard."

"I don't think I'd antagonize me if I were you, Mr. Quinn. There's a sweet little boy here that might not like it. Not as pretty as his sister, and he definitely doesn't come with my normally required body parts, but I think I can make do." A muffled whimper came across the line.

Jack let the threat hang in the air, frustration and a terrible need to comfort Charlie tightening his throat. *You're not alone, Charlie. I'm coming; I promise.*

"See," Reed said, "he likes me already. I'm not sure how long I can hold out, Quinn."

Jack squeezed his eyes shut, not even daring to breathe. Reed chuckled into the silence. "Good call."

Jack forced himself to respond with a calm he certainly didn't feel. "Just give me the time and place."

Reed tsked. "And Madelyn Grace? Does she agree with this as well, lover boy?"

Jack couldn't answer that. He didn't know what he'd do about Maddie—anything but give her back to her husband, but right now he couldn't think, couldn't plan. He needed the details; then he'd decide what to do.

"You're learning, Quinn. Excellent. I just arrived home, and I don't believe I feel like leaving again so soon. You will bring Madelyn Grace here in, say, ten hours? Dawn is lovely this time of year; I'm sure my wife will think so as well. Don't be late. And come alone."

Reed cut the connection before Jack would respond.

"How long do we have?"

He hadn't realized Maddie had followed him into the office. Staring at the now blank phone, he told her, "Ten hours."

He expected her to come to him; instead, she walked over to the window to look out. He watched her warily, unsure what to expect, but it wasn't the softness of her voice when she finally spoke.

"What I told you about finding Carson in the basement...that was true."

Of course it was true; why would she think he'd believe otherwise?

"That night, before I could leave, David...woke up. When I came back upstairs, he was waiting for me."

Jesus, Jesus, Jesus.

"He said I needed to be trained in obedience. That I should be disciplined for sneaking around, needed to finally learn who my master truly was. So he...gave me to Carson." Her voice cracked over the last word.

Everything inside Jack screamed at him to go to her, to hold her, to make the flow of quiet words stop before they tore his heart from his fucking chest. He didn't. Something about the way Maddie stood, the way she refused to look his way, just stared out at the setting sun, told him not to.

She lifted a hand, her fingertips tracing shapes on the glass. "They took me up to the guest room. I'd always been afraid of Carson, and David knew it. Carson knew it." A shiver shook her hard, head to toe. "He enjoyed what he did to me that night, how he hurt me, and David— He just stood there and watched. When I fought, he laughed."

"Maddie…" He couldn't think of a curse strong enough to release the pain bursting inside him. Nothing would help; nothing could take away the memories. What she'd endured—he just couldn't fathom. It was unimaginable.

She didn't seem to hear him. She stared out the window, her breath speeding up, coming so fast, so hard Jack feared she'd hyperventilate. "They took turns. After a while I couldn't even cry. I was just so tired, so scared. I wanted to die. And then they…together they—" She choked. "You can't imagine," she said, voice shattered, shattering. "You can't imagine what it's like to lay there and endure, knowing it's your spouse, the one person you should be able to trust, who's doing that to you. Who's letting someone else do that to you."

He moved then; he couldn't not. He was behind her in an instant. Maddie turned, eyes dazed, and reached for him. He couldn't get her close enough, couldn't force the comfort he needed to give her into her shivering body hard enough for it to ever make up for what she'd been through, but everything in him demanded that he try. He pressed her back into the glass. Maddie's nails dug deep into his ribs until he was sure they were carving his skin apart, but still he stood and held her and breathed as the sun set outside.

"How…" He sighed, hating to ask but needing to get all the details out, needing to get past this and never have to return to it again. "How did you get away?"

Maddie shifted between him and the window. "When they were through, they left me handcuffed to the bed. I managed to get my hands through the cuffs and escape."

"Maddie." He eased back to look at her hands, took one in his, rubbing over it. She had small hands but not that small.

"They're okay now." She tucked her fingers around his. "A couple of pulled ligaments, a lot of bruising, but they healed. I'm fine."

And even if she wasn't, she'd claim she was.

"You know he'll never go to trial," she said, tipping her head back to look him in the eye. "They'll never even file charges. He's too good for that."

He knew. He'd known from the minute he'd discovered Reed's identity.

"He has to die, Jack. He has to. This can't go on. I can't constantly be waiting to turn the corner and see his face, feel his hands on me. There can't be any more…" Maddie shook her head, her words dying, but she didn't have to say it; he knew what she meant. The long line of victims had to end. "He has to die."

Jack cupped her cheek. "I can make sure that happens."

"It's not enough." She took a breath, her breasts pressing against him, her exhale warm on his skin. She stared into his eyes, the need for him to understand blazing up at him. "I'm going with you. Give me a weapon, tell me what to do. I'll follow your instructions to the letter, but...I have to see him die, Jack."

He tucked her head back under his chin. "Okay."

All the fight left her, and her body melted into his.

She nodded. "Okay." And then, still with her head down. "I love you, Jack."

He couldn't answer; his heart was too full. So he did the next best thing and kissed her there in the twilight. No matter what happened, he'd have those four words forever. Now he just had to make sure he had Maddie too.

Chapter Twenty-Four

"Are you sure this'll work?" Maddie asked, struggling to situate the too-big body armor on her smaller frame.

Jack adjusted a strap, but even at its tightest, the vest sagged more than she knew he wanted it to. His frown told her that. Still, he kept at it. "It'll work, even if it's a little big."

She was small enough that *a little big* was a misnomer, but custom ordering wasn't an option on such short notice. A lot of things weren't an option. After pushing so hard to get Jack to offer her up, or at least seem to, she was beginning to wonder if she hadn't overestimated her ability to handle this. Maybe she hadn't been as strong last time as she seemed to remember. The calmer and more focused Jack and the other men became, the more the reality that this was going to happen hit her full force.

He adjusted another strap. "How's that holster?"

Instead of a weapons belt like he and the other men wore, Jack had strapped a thigh holster high on her leg. The butt of the gun—a Glock something or other, he'd said—rested just below her fingertips when her arm was extended. She was used to reaching down for her knife; the automatic response should make it easy for her to pull the gun if needed. Jack swore it wouldn't be needed. She would

311

probably be disarmed as soon as they walked in anyway.

"Draw it," Jack said.

"You already showed me—"

"Then you show me. Come on, wildcat. I need to know you know what you're doing."

Maddie gripped the gun firmly and drew, keeping it close to her body, barrel pointed down. At belly height she raised the barrel and aimed, making certain it pointed toward the opposite wall of the busy supply room, away from the men.

"Check it."

She checked the slide, the safety, the clip. Aimed again. Reversed the path and reholstered the gun. Turned back to Jack.

"There is nothing hotter than a woman handling a gun," Gabe said as he filled his weapons belt nearby. When she glanced his way, he winked. A spark of gratitude lit her insides.

"You're supposed to be packing. You shouldn't be watching me; you should be gathering guns and ammo or something."

"Guns and ammo *or something*?" Gabe chuckled.

Jack popped his friend on the back of the head. Gabe laughed harder. Turning back to Maddie, Jack asked, "Where's the knife?"

He knew her so well. She reached for her boot. Not her usual high-heeled ones; these were her well-worn motorcycle boots, not that far off from the combat boots Jack's men were wearing. They were heavy, thick-soled, but she was used to them so she had no fears about maneuvering in them during the mission.

The mission. I'm turning into one of them. Despite the tangle of emotions worrying away at her, a warm glow settled in her chest. She was turning into one of them. Now if only she could make it last longer than just tonight.

Two fingertips were all it took to slip into the side of her boot and smoothly extract the folded knife. She lifted and flicked at the same time, the knife open and locked between one breath and the next. The five-inch carbon-steel blade gleamed in the fluorescent lights.

"Okay, I changed my mind," Gabe said. "That's way hotter than a gun."

Jack shot Gabe the hundredth impatient look of the night and lifted his middle finger high enough for Gabe to see over his shoulder. "How hot is that?"

"Sorry, Boss. Doesn't do a thing for me."

Her laugh bubbled up out of nowhere, the sound startling when she felt like her insides were full of Pop Rocks and Coke. She met Jack's eyes. The emotion that welled there brought a lump to her throat. "I'm riding the emotional roller coaster from hell," she told him, keeping her voice low. Her audience didn't need to know how twisted up she was inside.

"That's normal." Jack cupped her cheek, his thumb stroking along her cheekbone. "I'll be right beside you, wildcat."

She knew that. It only made her nerves worse. Not only was she in danger, but she had lives on the line, people who would pay the price if this didn't go right, and whether Jack wanted to acknowledge it or not, he was one of them.

The plan—or what little of one they'd had time to put together—was for four teams, each with three men, to come at the house from four directions: front, back, and both sides. The intel they'd obtained on David's property the past two days helped, satellite and system info along with what Maddie had given them from her time there. Jack had done some hacking that was far above her head that gave them details about David's security system, which they intended to use to get the other teams in. Jack and Maddie would walk up to the front door.

Jack had been in touch with ICE the past couple of days as well, not the local office but the one in DC. They had no idea whom David might be buying off, but they couldn't just do nothing. Unfortunately bureaucratic red tape wasn't making things easy, and they were out of time. Maybe after the fact was better than nothing, but if they didn't come out alive, if David won, the thought that he could just continue as he had been was unbearable.

Guess you'll just have to stay alive, right?

Right.

The men began filing out. Maddie watched and knew time was up. No more prep work. As Gabe said, their plan was a go.

She shivered inside her Kevlar vest.

"Ready?" Jack asked.

Hell no. "Sure." She gave him a little smile and moved toward the door before he could analyze it too closely.

The hallway seemed to stretch on forever, like a walk to the gallows. Jack took her hand, and Maddie squeezed it hard, wanting to go back to the last time they'd lain together, to forget this was happening, to do anything but take the man she loved into harm's way. She recognized on some level that she was panicking. It was normal, Jack had said; she just had to walk through it and come out the other side and this would all be over. But she couldn't make it stop. Her breathing got quicker and quicker as the elevator went from JCL's floor to the basement garage. There were too many people too close, too little air. By the time the elevator dinged and the doors opened, she was seeing ugly black spots in front of her eyes.

The men filtered out into the garage. When Maddie instinctively stepped forward, Jack's hand on her arm stopped her just outside the elevator.

The cool air of the garage started her shivers all over again.

"Maddie?"

"I can do this, Jack. I'm not a coward."

"No, you're not."

She waited, but he didn't say anything else and she couldn't open her mouth with all the chaos jumbled inside her. As they stood there, one fact rose above all the others: This was all just too much too fast. She wanted him safe. She wanted a few more hours with him beside her, inside her. Maybe then she could face the danger without panicking.

A quick glance up at Jack's face and she knew he was feeling about the same way. Of course. She knew Jack's heart. If she was afraid for him, he had to be the same for her; she'd just been too tunnel-visioned to register it, or maybe he was used to toughening up in combat situations.

She shied away from that description. This wasn't combat; their mission was to get Charlie back. *And kill her husband.*

The thought sent her into Jack's arms.

"It's all right, Maddie," he told her, voice quiet in the cavernous space. "It's going to be all right. I'll be fine, and so will you. Stop worrying."

An anemic laugh escaped into his body armor. "Right. And I'll stop breathing while I'm at it."

He tipped her head up, forcing her to see all that he felt shining out of his eyes. "That makes two of us. Just thinking about taking you into this makes it hard to breathe, much less think. But that's the mission, and we'll get through it. Together."

She mimicked Jack's touch, rubbing her fingertips along the healthy stubble that graced his cheek. There hadn't been time for the melding of their bodies since they'd said *I love you*, much less the melding of their hearts. Now she worried that they would never get that time, and she needed it, damn it. She wanted it with a fierceness that left her feeling off balance after so many years alone. And just this once, she was going to give in to what she felt. If neither of them could breathe anyway…

Jack's mouth opened the minute her lips met his. His kiss was hard, demanding, his tongue pushing in without apology. She accepted, feeling his fear, his worry, his love in every stroke and thrust. The thick vests they both wore kept their bodies apart, kept her from feeling him against her one last time. And she needed him against her. She tried to tell him with her mouth, her breath, her hands clutching him closer. He got her message.

A low growl rumbled from his chest. Ignoring her groan of protest, he stepped back. Without dropped her gaze, he called to Con, "Hey, bro, give us a minute, okay?" And then he was leading her by a fistful of vest in the opposite direction of their team.

Somehow she didn't think a minute was going to be enough. She wanted to stop, to squeeze her legs together, bring her hands up to massage her suddenly aching breasts, but Jack was pulling her along. She caught a brief glimpse of Con and Gabe walking toward the SUV before Jack rounded a concrete pillar and pulled her into a darkened recess.

Jack tucked her back behind the barricade, her spine against the concrete wall, blocking them from sight. Maddie's heart thumped in her throat. "This is ridiculous. It's not the time…"

"It is ridiculous, but we both need this."

Just the tone of his voice had her creaming her panties. He was right, so damn right.

The wall took her weight. Jack loomed over her in a way she never would've tolerated a month ago, so big, his chest a solid, safe wall protecting her from everything around them. He slid his palm under the hem of her vest, down the front of her jeans, to cup her between her thighs, watching every move with need-glazed eyes. That look burned her up inside. He licked his lips. His nostrils flared as if he could scent her arousal across the small space, and his fingers clenched against her mound.

Her hands went to Jack's zipper.

Instant conflagration.

Jack kissed her, his growl low and hungry, lips hard as the *hiss* of metallic teeth opening filled the air. Seconds later his naked shaft was in her hands. Maddie moaned his name.

"Shh, wildcat," Jack whispered against her lips. Maddie kissed him again, her need flaring out of control as Jack's fingers slid beneath her panties. They didn't have time for this, it was crazy—she knew all the reasons they should stop, but she didn't. If this was going to be their last time together, if even the possibility existed, she needed this as much as Jack did.

His hard cock was in her hand, hot skin and thick muscle. She stroked him as he stroked her, the direct contact of his rough fingers with her clit sending her up on tiptoe. "Jack, Jack…"

"That's right; come on, Maddie."

She tried to concentrate, tried to please him, but the feel of him touching her so intimately, in so public a place, blew away her awareness of anything else. Jack tapped his calloused fingertip against her clit, slid two more back just enough to enter her, and with breath-stopping speed she went right over the edge.

Jack's harsh breathing brought her back to the surface. She'd gone still as she savored her climax, but now Jack leaned over her, his hand on the wall behind her head, his eyes closed tight as he wrestled for control. Knowing he needed more, she knelt in front of him. Without giving herself time to think, she guided him to her mouth. Jack gave a shattered groan at the first hard suck.

"Take it, wildcat. Take me inside."

She sucked him again. His shaft jerked in her mouth, spilling salty precum onto her tongue. They both moaned.

Jack buried a hand in her hair, his grip loose, and thrust carefully into her mouth. Each push took him deeper and deeper until her lips met her hand on his shaft, tugging in rhythm with her mouth. Jack cursed fluently the entire time, and Maddie could hear his breath becoming ragged. He swelled in her mouth. She pulled and sucked, desperate for him to fill her. It couldn't have been more than a minute before he spurted into her mouth.

Maddie swallowed around him, then again, until finally Jack muttered her name on a shuddery breath. When his eyes opened, he grabbed the shoulders of her vest and pulled her up, his grip shaky and rough and somehow as evident of his pleasure as her name on his lips.

"I didn't plan that, wildcat. This was supposed to be for you," he said.

She loved it when he called her that. "I know, Jack. That was for me."

The smile he gave her lit his eyes. They clung together there against the hard wall. Maddie thought she could've stayed there forever, but that wasn't possible. Jack tucked himself away and then helped her straighten her clothes, which she was sure smelled of sex despite their not going all the way. When they got to the SUV, she expected Gabe and Con to give them a hard time, but neither man said a word as she and Jack got in the backseat, instead pretending extreme interest in the GPS and the route to Nashville. Con slid her a single understanding glance in the rearview mirror, and then they were racing the dawn north to Tennessee.

Chapter Twenty-Five

They dropped Con and Gabe off a mile outside of David's estate. Dawn was just peeking over the hills as she and Jack drove the rest of the way alone. With just the two of them inside, the SUV seemed deathly quiet.

The winding road took them right to the gates. The Reed family land spread out to both sides and behind the stately mansion she could see at the horizon, five hundred acres of evil. That house dominated the landscape like David had dominated her life for so long. She couldn't quite fathom that in the next hour that domination would end, one way or another. All she'd known for so long was the drive for revenge, for justice. Fixated on the gate, the moment, Maddie didn't notice Jack move until his hand grasped hers. She jumped. Jack squeezed down.

The gate opened.

Maddie choked back a whimper.

They drove forward, the lights blazing in the Reed mansion guiding their way. Maddie closed her eyes, focusing on Jack's touch, filling her lungs, and just plain holding it together. As the SUV came to a stop outside the massive front door, Jack spoke.

"When we walk inside, the nerves will stop. Sometimes the hardest part is getting there."

"Promise?"

She heard the smile in his voice. "Promise."

"Okay."

They got out. Jack came around to her side of the vehicle and took her hand again. Together they stared up at their enemy's stronghold.

"You stay safe for me, wildcat," Jack said softly.

She turned to him, ignoring the guards that stared, stone-faced, at them, ignoring the feeling of her husband's eyes stripping her bare. She couldn't see him, but she could feel him. "Jack—" She wanted to kiss him, wanted to hold him. The time for that was past. Instead she met his eyes, trying to tell him without words everything she couldn't say aloud. "I'll make you proud." She swore she would.

Love filled his face as he stared down at her, and then, as she watched, a veil fell over his eyes, blanking everything out like a chalkboard eraser. She'd prepared for this, knew he had a role to play, but that didn't make it any harder to witness. When he let go of her hand, she wanted to cry, but she didn't. She sucked it up, even when his rough grip circled her biceps and he shoved her forward.

The two men at the entrance crossed thick arms and stepped into their path as she and Jack approached. She didn't recognize them. Jack ignored their posturing and kept striding forward. Just when she thought they'd run into each other, one guard stepped aside, taking the front door with him. It swung open, and the rush of light and air and memories blinded her as Jack led her into the room.

It was just as she'd remembered, only with more guns. The massive entry, big enough to be a ballroom, was lined with upward of thirty men, every one armed, every one at the ready. "Oh shit."

Jack kept moving forward as if the show of force was exactly what he'd expected. She hoped to God it was. And then the small group in the middle of the vast room came into focus, and Maddie almost sagged in relief. "Charlie!"

All seventy pounds of determined kid flew toward her. A sharp yank on the boy's shirt stopped him so hard his feet flew out from under him. Maddie surged forward. Jack yanked her back, much like Carson had Charlie, only Maddie kept her feet.

"Not till I see the money," Jack warned, his voice gravel and heat.

Maddie clenched her fists and waited, her gaze on Charlie. The little boy struggled and fought despite the stranglehold Carson had on him. A hard slap rang through the air. Maddie choked on her fury as Charlie slumped, dazed, in Carson's grip.

"I told you, didn't I, Mr. Quinn? My wife is a sucker for a kid. It works every time."

For the first time in four years, Maddie was face-to-face with David Reed. Her throat went tight at the sight of him. "Not every time."

The reminder wasn't appreciated. The dark expression that flitted across his face would've had her cowering in the corner a few years ago. Thank God she wasn't that woman anymore.

Still David didn't address her. "Grown a backbone, has she? I'm sure you had something to do with that, Quinn."

"Just give me the money and the kid and I'll be outta here."

Confusion knotted Charlie's eyebrows. Maddie willed him to see through Jack's ruse, to understand that they were trying to get him out, no matter what. Hurt could be fixed later, but the last thing they needed was Charlie refusing to go with Jack to safety.

David grunted. One of his men stepped forward, a massive guy that could give John a run for his money. Maddie wondered a bit hysterically if they could set up a prize match between the two men, and then the guard was lifting a steel suitcase for Jack's perusal, flicking open the locks as he came to a stop a few feet in front of them.

"With Mr. Reed's compliments," he said and lifted the lid.

Maddie registered the empty case at the same time as the sound of dozens of cocking guns reached her ears.

Jack laughed. "Very good, Reed. Too bad I was expecting that."

The door behind them burst open. Maddie dropped into as low a crouch as she could. Shouting filled the room, running, and finally gunfire as Jack's team swarmed inside seemingly from all directions. The bombardment disoriented her, the once-open space becoming a maze of fighting clusters and running bodies. Jack moved quick, dragging her along, heading for the nearest wall and its iffy cover. His grip on her arm hurt, but then it was torn away in the chaos.

"Shit!"

Maddie turned back to him, but Jack was already engaged with two guards who'd decided teaming up was the way to take him. Belatedly her hand went to her thigh, pulling the gun with an automatic smoothness she'd never have guessed she could achieve in this chaos. Jack rolled forward, right under one guard's grab, coming up for a strike to the second's jaw. Maddie aimed, waited for Jack to get clear—and a massive weight barreled into her from the side.

Her face hitting the ground hurt worse than the brute's grip on her body. The gun went skittering off—hell, she was surprised the bastard hadn't knocked her out of her boots. She kicked, hit, punched, but the guard who had her seemed impervious to her struggles. She wished she could see his face, claw his eyes out. No such luck. He had her from behind and, once he'd dragged her up off the unforgiving floor, carried her in a strong-armed grip toward the opposite end of the room and the man she knew awaited her there.

David eyed her with the intent satisfaction of a snake about to strike as her captor joined him at the entrance to the hall. Maddie never stopped squirming, struggling, hauling her legs up to throw him off balance, extending them straight to hinder his legs—anything she could think of, she tried, but still they closed the distance, step by inexorable step, toward David. A quick look around told her most of the fighting was concentrated around Jack and the front door. No exit that way, but Maddie knew David must have a plan B. He always had a plan B.

Sure enough, her hulking captor followed David down the hall to the entry to the basement. Maddie couldn't stop the low moan as memories slammed into her, reminding her how much David could make her hurt, how he could make her wish she was dead. She only prayed that it was worth it, that somehow Charlie would make it out of this hell and away to safety. As the basement door closed and the lock beeped behind them, she realized she might never know, but she would fight like it was worth it till her last breath.

They made it to the bottom of the stairs despite her best efforts to knock the guard's feet out from under him. The man dragged her, literally kicking and screaming, into the dimly lit training room. He stopped a few feet away from David and fisted his hand in the back of her hair, forcing her to look up.

"Wife," David said, smiling at her. "Welcome home."

God, her husband hadn't changed even a little bit. Four years should've wrought some evidence of the man's evil nature, but no, he looked exactly the same. Those same scary eyes, same vindictive cast to his smooth face, same degrading smile that had made her want to punch his teeth out even when she hadn't thought herself capable of punching someone. He stalked closer, every inch, every centimeter making her pulse jump. When he reached out to touch her, she lost it.

Pulling both feet up to her chest, she kicked out with everything she had. David managed to jump back at the last moment, but she caught his hand with her boot, the pop of impact giving her some small satisfaction. Her legs dropping bent her over the guard's tight grip, the pressure on her ribs threatening to crack them.

"Bitch!" David closed the distance before she could recover. A sharp backhand to the face had her seeing stars. "I can't wait to have you back underneath me," he snarled, finger wagging right under her now bloody nose. "I'll enjoy reteaching you manners before I rid myself of you once and for all."

Maddie raised her head and, before David could step back, caught his finger in a vicious bite. She, who had been too timid to bite, too scared to fight back for most of her marriage, held on like a dog with a bone, sinking her teeth in even when it made her gag, refusing to let go until another hard blow grayed her vision out too much to do anything but sag. Unfortunately her captor had a firm hold, keeping her upright. A second punch, this time to her belly, forced bile up her throat. Maddie swallowed it down with the pain and grinned up at David.

"I'm not your weak little wife anymore, David. I'd watch your fingers and any other important appendages you might not want damaged if you bring them close to me."

David's face went tight with anger, and the next thing—the only thing—she knew was his fist aiming for her face. Fortunately blackness obliterated the rest.

* * *

The bastards were getting away. Jack watched first Maddie and then Charlie being carried down the hallway to his left. Reed had obviously instructed his men to keep that area clear, because a barricade of bodies was slowly building in front of the hall opening as they fought to keep Jack's men back. All Jack could think about was getting to Maddie, and obstacles or not, he fought with every ounce of viciousness he could muster to achieve his objective. Pain didn't register. Time didn't register. The only thing that did finally get through his fixation was the knifepoint digging into his throat.

He stopped fighting then. He couldn't win if he was dead.

The battle continued around them, but Jack and his new buddy marched into the hall without interference. Ahead he could see the door to the garage Maddie had mentioned swinging to a close, but nothing else. No Maddie, no Charlie. His guard pushed him in that direction, and Jack stumbled along.

Through the far door was a garage big enough to be a stable. Carson Alexander stood beside the only vehicle in the space, a black Hummer one of his men was stuffing Charlie into. Still no sign of Maddie. Everything in him screamed to find her, to break free and storm the castle until he killed every last dragon he could find, but Charlie needed him. He clamped down on the raging in his brain and allowed the guard to shove him to his knees. Alexander made his way across the garage toward them.

The man had an elegance to his frame that spoke more to a runner's strength than a warrior's. He might wield a whip with ease against a tied, helpless woman, but that didn't make him a match for Jack's superior training and muscle. Jack watched and waited and knew his opportunity would come. He just had to be patient.

"Jack Quinn." Alexander greeted him with a little bow, incongruent given their surroundings. The man was practically licking his lips as he stared at the knife digging into Jack's throat.

Jack didn't bother returning the greeting. "Where is Maddie?"

"Don't tell me you let that little cunt get to you. Do you know"—Alexander dipped his head, eyes unseeing, as if reliving a favorite memory—"she was the most delicious pussy I've ever tasted. And do you know why? Because she fought me the entire time. There is nothing more satisfying than overcoming resistance."

The guard with the knife to Jack's throat chuckled.

A red haze coated Jack's mind. "I'm gonna kill you slow," he promised Alexander. The man behind him could die fast; Jack didn't care as long as they both went straight to hell.

Alexander unbent, his smile wide and not the least bit worried. "I doubt it." Brushing imaginary lent from the lapels of his expensive sports coat, he tsked. "You already took one of my girls. You didn't think

I'd just hand this little runt over to you, did you? And pay you for it?" His chuckle grated along Jack's tense nerves.

"I didn't think you'd be smart enough not to."

Those snake eyes narrowed on Jack. "I guess you underestimated me, didn't you?"

"Not likely."

Jack heard a *click* through the tiny earpiece hidden in his ear canal, the signal he'd been waiting for. ICE had been very interested in the possibility of bringing in Carson Alexander. That they might also nab his mysterious partner and reveal his identity had been a bonus. A mad scramble of coded messages and lots of hemming and hawing had ended in a pseudopromise to show. Apparently ICE had made good on that promise. They were on their way in; Lori's signal told him that much. Thank God his men upstairs were finally getting backup. Now to get rid of this motherfucker. There was just one more piece of information Jack needed.

"Where are the other girls?"

"Oh, they're here," Alexander said. "Or at least, they were." He glanced at his watch. "David should be moving them right about now."

That was all Jack needed to know. Without warning he brought his hand up to grip the fist surrounding the knife. A twist and quick pull down—at the wrong angle—snapped the guard's wrist. Jack dropped the hand and struck out simultaneously, hitting Alexander with a left-handed punch to the groin that doubled him over, right into Jack's web strike to the throat. Cartilage gave way. Air ceased to flow. The dropped knife was in Jack's hand and he was turned, slicing across thigh, belly, and throat, before the guard ever knew what hit him. Jack was gone before Alexander ran out of breath. He died quick, far too quick for Jack's taste. That was a promise he was truly sorry he couldn't keep.

"Charlie!"

The guard standing before Charlie's door drew his weapon too late. Jack was on him fast. He caught the shorter man around the throat, spun him around, and used the momentum to snap his neck. Jack dropped him without a second thought.

"Jack!" Charlie's door flew open, and the boy was in his arms. Jack crushed him close, so damn thankful the boy was safe. But he wasn't the only one Jack needed to keep safe.

"I need you to do something for me, Charlie."

"Okay."

"I need you to climb back in and lock all the doors."

"But—"

Jack set Charlie on the ground and knelt to look him in the eye. "I have to go get Maddie."

Charlie's eyes widened, and he nodded.

"Okay, lock the doors. If anyone comes, you hit the horn and don't let go, okay. Don't open the doors unless it's to me or Con."

"Got it."

Charlie climbed back into the car with the dignity of a full-grown soldier. Jack waited until the locks sounded, and then he sprinted back to the house.

* * *

She woke in what seemed to be a dark corridor, wider than most, almost wide enough to drive a truck through. Which was precisely what David had done. Just ahead, a heavy 4X4 similar to Jack's waited, a horse trailer hitched to the back. This trailer didn't have slats in the sides for air, though, and Maddie had a bad feeling it wasn't for horses.

One of David's men was opening a massive garage door behind the truck. Another closed the trailer. When he walked in her direction, David spoke from somewhere behind her.

"Leave us."

The man hesitated, glanced at her, and walked back to the truck. Maddie gathered her feet underneath her, prepared to follow, but a hand digging into her hair held her down.

"Don't bother, Madelyn Grace. You're not going anywhere."

She'd heard many tones in David's voice over the years. This one was new, the resigned sound of someone who'd realized they weren't going to get exactly what they wanted. He wasn't afraid or rushed, not angry, just…reconciled to the loss.

Of what?

"What do you want, David?"

"Have you forgotten how to greet your husband, Madelyn Grace?"

She wouldn't voluntarily get on her knees for this man ever again. Of course, it hadn't been voluntary to begin with, but… "I'd rather greet you with a knife to the groin, but hey, we can't have all our wishes granted. Or even one." She rolled her head up, but David was just a shadow; she couldn't get a good look at him. "What do you want?"

"I want a son, of course, the same thing I've always wanted. And since I can't trust you to provide me with one, I want you dead."

She snorted, the sound full of bravado and bluff. "Yeah. Not gonna happen."

"Don't be so sure." David loosened his hold. His fingers snagged her hair as he removed them, the pain bringing tears to her eyes. "You've changed. Blonde hair. Boots." He circled her, coming to stand in front but far enough away that she couldn't punch him in the groin. Too bad. "I even heard something about a bar. You're not the woman that once graced my bed."

"I never graced your bed, David. I was tied to it."

David smiled, and Maddie's skin crawled. "And how beautiful you looked with those ropes around your body, my marks on your skin. Do you remember, wife? Remember how good it was."

"We obviously don't have the same memories. You're delusional if you think I'd ever lay down and let you touch me again."

"But it's the resistance that makes it so good."

Maddie surged up, going for surprise, and came face-to-face with the business end of a handgun. She settled back down.

"Wise choice."

"You're good at pushing the odds in your favor, aren't you, Reed?"

She heard a step behind her, felt that change in the air that always signaled Jack's presence. Relief flooded her.

"Beating on helpless women half your size. Pulling guns on unarmed men. Where's your sense of fair play?" Jack taunted.

Reed gave a tight, strained chuckle. "Madelyn never got what she didn't deserve."

She heard Jack advance, the heavy sound more of a lunge than a normal footstep. The shift of David's finger from the stock of the gun to the trigger convinced him to stop.

Reed laughed. "It's hard to be a tough guy when you're facing down a gun, isn't it, Quinn? But then Madelyn can bring out the savage in any man, can't she?" He stepped closer to her, so close he was only a few feet away. Almost close enough to reach. She concentrated on his steps and the feel of Jack somewhere behind her. "Is that what happened? Did you fuck him, Madelyn Grace? Did you open up that tight little cunt, let him get a whiff of you? She sucks dick like a pro, doesn't she?"

The words sent a wash of humiliation over her. She closed her eyes, bowing her head like she couldn't bear for Jack to hear them. David moved closer.

The door to the truck opened. "Everything all right, Boss?" a guard called.

"Of course." Even if he couldn't handle it, David would tell them he could. Or order the men to sacrifice themselves for him. They were nothing more than bought fodder, after all.

"Are you sure about that?" Jack asked. "Because last I checked, Alexander was dead and your men were on the run. Oh, and ICE wants a word with you."

David narrowed his gaze on Jack.

Relief flooded her. Carson was dead. She hoped Jack had made it as slow as possible. The man deserved so much more than a quick death. When she glanced up to see David's reaction, her husband's face had deepened to an ugly brick red, veins popping out on either side of his forehead. He rushed forward, waving his gun. "What did you do?"

Three things happened almost simultaneously: the guard at the truck shouted a warning; men in black gear, men she didn't recognize, swarmed the room, both from behind her and in front; and she pushed to her feet practically underneath David, knife in hand.

There was no time for David to stop. He hit the blade full force, and Maddie gagged at the feel of it sliding in almost like slicing butter. David glanced down, saw the knife in his belly, and staggered back. Maddie kept the knife.

Blood splashed from David's gut. He staggered back. The gun went off.

Jack watched the whites of Reed's eyes flash as he fell, the impact to his intestines reflected in his face. Then the single shot of gunfire. Like moving through molasses, Jack fought his muscles, his instincts, trying to gain every millisecond he could to get to Maddie, to protect her. He saw the check in her stride, saw her continue forward, and then the knife was at Reed's throat and Maddie slashed across with a triumphant howl that echoed in the underground chamber for long moments after she went silent. Reed fell to the floor with the grace of a rag doll. Maddie followed him down, landing in the puddle of her dead husband's blood.

Taking no more than a second to consider the end of the human being beside her—and savoring the sharp satisfaction of the knowledge—Jack raced to kneel beside Maddie. The sight of her eyelids fluttering worried him. "Maddie?"

She writhed on the floor, panicked, struggling, gasping for air. Her hands clutched at her chest, where Jack could see a hole and powder burns in the heavy outer shirt she wore. Goddamn it, she'd taken a direct hit. Thank God for Kevlar. The bullet hadn't penetrated—there was no blood on her other than the patches where she'd landed in David's—but an impact like that would knock the wind right out of a person.

"Maddie, don't move around, okay? You may have injured ribs." He grabbed her shoulders, trying to hold her still.

She wasn't tracking. He got up on his hands and knees and put his face right above hers. Maddie zeroed in on him like she was drowning and he was the rope.

"Breathe with me, wildcat. I know it hurts. Just breathe with me." He prayed a frantic prayer that she could hear him through the roaring that must be rushing in her ears.

Jack kept his eyes on hers, kept her focused, kept himself from totally freaking the hell out until Maddie finally calmed, and though she still struggled to breathe, he didn't hear the wheezing sound that meant a lung was punctured.

"Where does it hurt?"

One hand gestured toward her chest.

"Nowhere else?"

She shook her head, then winced.

"Okay, easy does it." The vest dispersed the force of the bullet somewhat and prevented penetration, but that didn't mean it couldn't cause other injuries. With Maddie so small, he worried about broken bones. "Let's get you out of there."

Blood pooled around her. Jack lifted her into his arms, moving her away from Reed and the growing mess and the swarming of cops and agents and Jack's men. In a relatively quiet spot to one side, he set her down. Maddie's arms went around his neck and refused to let go.

Jack returned the hug, then pushed her back to lean against the wall. "Let me see, wildcat."

She smiled a small, wobbly smile and winced again. "Hurts." Her hand moved to touch her chest, but Jack moved it away.

"Yeah, I know it hurts." He swiped a soft kiss across her lips. "Just hold still. Help will be here soon. We'll get you checked out." The damn straps were refusing to cooperate. Jack finally retrieved a knife off his belt and cut them, lifting the vest and her T-shirt underneath to check her out.

A massive red welt covered one side of her ribs. *Damn it.*

He tapped his comm. "Con?"

"Yeah."

Relief that his best friend was all right flooded him. "Get to the garage. Charlie's in the Hummer."

"Already there, Jack. Little Man is doing fine."

Blessing number two, or maybe two thousand. "Good. Need a medic downstairs as soon as they arrive. Maddie's bruised up pretty bad, and it looks like the girls are down here." Probably drugged like Vaneqe had been. There hadn't been a peep from the trailer despite all the noise.

"Affirmative."

Maddie squeezed his hand. "David?"

"Dead," Jack assured her.

Her eyelids slid closed. "Jack." A tear fell onto her cheek, meandering down to linger on a dark smudge at her jawline.

"I'm here. Just stay calm. It'll make breathing easier." He couldn't tell if the color in her face was from crying or better airflow. "Don't cry," he said, the laugh that followed a bit watery.

"The…girls?"

"They're here."

She shook her head. "Hate basements. You don't have one, do you?"

Now was not the time to tell her he did. Instead he leaned close. "Woman, what am I gonna do with you?"

Her eyes didn't open, but a small smile tugged up the corner of her mouth before she gulped in another lungful of air. Jack kissed her again, carefully. "You did good, wildcat," he told her, whispering against her lips. "Even if you did scare the hell out of me."

Her eyes did open then. "Did you expect me to do anything else?"

"God, no. You're everything I expected"—he brushed another gentle kiss across her lips—"and so much more."

Chapter Twenty-Six

"So here we are in the middle of the friggin' dessert," Gabe said, "not a soul in sight but our men, and Boss is insisting we carry the mangy cur all the way back to base camp so the medic—the medic for *people*—could set its leg."

The small crowd encircling the fire pit in Jack's backyard all stared at Gabe, enthralled. Jack couldn't figure out if it was the story or the man's natural Texas drawl—which he was laying on pretty thick, by the way—that drew them, but whatever it was, Jack knew there was no way he would get out of the embarrassment of this retelling.

Jess and Con seemed to be taking particular pleasure in his pain. "Did the dog live?" Jess asked. He shot her a look that promised retribution. She sent him a sassy little smile in return.

Minx.

"Of course he did. None of us went against the boss's commands, not even that scruffy old dog." Gabe laughed, the sound echoing in the wide-open space of the field behind Jack's house. A touch wicked, Maddie called it. Jack could see every woman around the fire preparing to swoon.

Except Maddie. Her eyes were on Jack, full of shadows and promises. He loved her eyes. Easing closer, he slid his arm around her and turned a scowl on Gabe as if he were revealing national secrets. "Dog was a damn nuisance, is what he was."

Maddie groaned. "Tell me you didn't name the poor thing Dog."

"Of course he did." Gabe's tone shifted from Texas drawl to a scarily accurate imitation of Jack's Southern twang. "'Can't have the damn thing gettin' attached, ya know.'"

Jack punched the man in the arm with a hard slam, enjoying Gabe's pout as he reached up to rub the spot. "Hey!"

"That's what you get," Jack told him.

Maddie chuckled at their boyish banter. Jack wasn't ashamed to admit he felt a quick rush of pride at making her laugh.

His backyard was full of people. He hugged Maddie to him and stared out across the expanse that just a few weeks ago had been so empty he did everything possible not to come home. Now the crowd surrounded a new fire pit at the bottom end of his property. Chairs and blankets were full of adults and kids, and noise and laughter filled the night air. It was pandemonium. Craziness. The exact opposite of his life that night he'd slammed into Halftime and run into the woman of his dreams.

Jack loved it. And he loved her.

Almost a month had passed since the night they'd brought down Reed and Alexander's empire. Of course, it was hard to have an empire when both the heads of state were dead. There'd been an investigation, and though it would take many more months to untangle the webs both men had left behind and hopefully uncover more of the victims, free more women from their cold dead hands, JCL's part in what had happened had been dismissed. Not without a tongue-lashing—and a federal agency could do plenty of tongue-lashing—but Jack and his friends were through it and out the other side.

In fact, life was damn near perfect.

A small stick flew over Jack's shoulder. Sasha, Jess and Con's new golden retriever puppy, flew after it. A scramble ensued that sparked even more chaos.

Lori stood. "Come on, T. C. We better build up this fire if we want to roast marshmallows."

"And hot dogs!" Charlie yelled. He jumped off his blanket to run around the yard, followed by a couple of friends. Marge yelled after them to stay out of the creek unless they took their shoes off.

"Vaneqe," Jess asked, "how is school going? Are you caught up with your chemistry class?"

As the women started talking science and lockers and high school, Jack stood. Maddie grabbed his hand. He turned to look down at her, sure his heart was in his eyes, but who the hell cared? "I'll go get the food," he said.

Maddie nodded. Her hand slid from his slowly, and he could feel her eyes on him all the way to the house.

Gabe followed him into the kitchen. Jack ignored him as he dug in the fridge for packets of hot dogs. When he turned to set them on the counter, Gabe was staring.

"What?"

Gabe shrugged. "I was gonna ask you the same thing."

"Oh." He put the packages on a platter and turned to the pantry. "Nothing's wrong."

"Right. Did Maddie talk to her parents again today?"

Their conversations always made him a little uptight. They shouldn't, he knew that, and Dr. and Mrs. Brewer, as they preferred to be called, were perfectly nice people. More importantly, they loved their daughter with a fierce devotion that soothed something broken in his own heart when it came to the issue of parents. Still, every time they called, he worried.

Gabe's look was sympathetic when Jack returned with several bags of marshmallows. "She's not leaving you, you know."

"I know."

"Do you? I see it in your eyes every time she talks about her parents, that worry that she's gonna decide she'd rather be with them than you. She hasn't left yet, and I don't think she plans to. She loves you, stupid."

Maybe it was stupid, but something inside him just wouldn't let it go. In fact, the worry had made him do something that was probably even more stupid. "I bought her a ring."

Gabe choked on the swallow of beer in his mouth. "You what?"

Jack felt himself getting defensive. "It's not an engagement ring; it doesn't have a diamond." But it was a ring. He'd thought about returning it a million times since he'd bought it a week ago, but he just couldn't bear to. He had to see it on Maddie's finger, see *his* ring on her finger.

"Well hell." Gabe stood, coming around the island to shake his hand. "Congratulations, Boss."

"She hasn't said yes yet."

"She will; I don't doubt it. Besides, a ring is a little more permanent than naming her Dog."

Jack laughed and threw a package of marshmallows at Gabe's head. Gabe tore it open and stuffed a handful in his mouth.

"Those are for the children, dickhead," Jack said.

"I am a children," Gabe said, cheeks looking like a squirrel in nut season. Then he smiled wide, marshmallows in full view. Jack shook his head and went back outside.

It was late when everyone left. After Gabe told them good night, Jack lay beside Maddie on a blanket out by the fire, watching her as she watched the stars. The rush of the creek and crackling of the fire played a calm accompaniment to the banging drum of his heart as he stared at Maddie's profile in the dim light.

"Tired?" he asked her.

"Yes." Her tone said it was a good tired, and part of his tension eased. Another part of him got tighter. For a moment the constriction in his jeans took his breath. He shifted his hips to a better position.

She was beautiful in the moonlight, the fire's faint glow flickering over her skin. Jack couldn't breathe, looking at her. Knowing she belonged to him. Knowing she'd chosen to stay instead of running, to trust him when everything in her world had taught her that trust meant pain. He reached out, tugging the hem of her tee up to allow his lips access to the smooth skin of her stomach.

"What is that for?" she asked.

"What do you think?" He nipped her in a particularly ticklish spot, then ran kisses over the place where Reed's bullet had left such a horrible bruise. She'd healed, but he'd never forget it. He never wanted to see her in pain again. He wanted to love her, pleasure her. Right now.

But there was something else he had to do first.

For once words escaped him. He dug in his pants pocket, gripping the jewelers' box tight before pulling it out for Maddie to see, only she wasn't looking at him, so he placed the box carefully on her breastbone, right between her perfect mounds. Then he went back to kissing her.

"What's this?"

He couldn't answer; he was too afraid his voice would crack.

Maddie stared at him for a long moment. When he still didn't speak, she sat up, the velvet-covered square in her hand. He held his breath when she opened the lid.

"Oh Jack."

He sat up too.

Inside, nestled on a satiny white pillow, lay a narrow gold ring. Chocolate diamonds nestled in clusters along the band, formed into small rosettes that sparkled in the moonlight. His throat got tight as the same chocolate sparkles stared up at him from her eyes.

"I know it's too soon to get engaged, but I wanted—"

But Maddie was already shaking her head. "You're always worried about too soon, you jackass. Who cares about too soon? Worry about what you want instead." She dug the ring from the box and slid it onto her left ring finger. "It's beautiful."

"You're beautiful." And his ring on her finger... His breath got choppy. "Strip for me," he said. Without waiting for an answer, he unzipped his jeans, the relief bringing a sigh to his lips. He pushed the stiff material down and lay back to watch as Maddie removed her clothes one piece at a time. The little tease was making him wait. Only when he circled his stiff erection and pumped roughly did she hurry up.

"Did you need something?" she asked teasingly.

He growled as she got to her knees, her breasts bobbing in the moonlight. "You on my dick."

"Aren't you charming."

"Always." He gripped her by the waist and tugged her atop him. Maddie spread her legs, and hot liquid settled against his needy shaft. They groaned together.

Jack swore his voice went so rough it scratched his vocal cords. "I want you, Maddie."

"You've got me." She rocked atop him, coating him in her sweet cream.

"Forever?"

Maddie went still. She stared down at him for a long time, her eyes too dark to read in the dim light. Jack held his breath. Finally she leaned forward, her full breasts coming to rest on his chest, her lips a whisper away from his. "Forever, Jack." She kissed him. "Forever."

Fierce emotion filled his chest until he thought it would split right open. He kissed her back, only his kiss was lips and tongue and teeth and breath—everything he could give her, every way he could give it. When they were both panting and restless, he rolled them over and sat up.

Maddie stretched out on the blanket, showcasing her beautiful body for him. Jack groaned. He curved his fingers over her mound, cupping her, digging the tips into the valleys on either side of her clit. He began to rub, to circle, teasing her with the rough rasp of his fingers and the smooth slide of her hood, up and down, up and down. Her breath hitched in her throat.

"There you go. I want you to come, wildcat. I want you to set all that fire free, right here in the moonlight." He kept up the movement, encouraging the thrust of her hips against his hand. He massaged her breast, rolling and rubbing her hard nipple, squeezing the plump flesh, raking his nails over the pebbled areola.

When she was gasping with pleasure, he drove two fingers deep into her channel. The wash of liquid need over his palm told him she was there, ready, willing, waiting. He removed his fingers and replaced them with his thick, throbbing cock. When she was full to the absolute brim, he leaned down to take her mouth in a harsh kiss.

Maddie jerked her hips up, begging silently for Jack to thrust, to take her. Her muscles clamped down hard, and Jack's eyes crossed with the pleasure.

"Good. Good girl," Jack said. The *d* was soft, his drawl close to the surface. But he didn't thrust, even when she whined, even when she started to beg. Instead he pushed her legs out, opening her to him in a way he never had before, completely vulnerable. Snugging himself right up against her body, he pressed himself as deep as he could go and held himself there, absolutely still. Maddie squirmed, impaled on his cock, unable to achieve the climax she needed until he laid a single finger against her sensitive clit and pressed.

She wailed out her release.

Jack wasn't done with her yet, though. When her body no longer clamped down around her, he met her eyes. "Again, wildcat." Holding her gaze, he licked his finger, savoring the taste of her essence, and then he placed it on her swollen clit again. That single finger circled, circled, making her wet, coaxing her response when she swore there was none to give. He teased and flicked and held himself tight and deep, and Maddie rose once more until she spasmed around his cock. He shook with the need to find his own release, but not yet.

Finally, tilting her head, Maddie looked up into Jack's eyes, her own luminous with tears, and gave him a little smile. "Jack," she breathed. It was the only word he needed.

The inches that divided them surrendered to his kiss just as her mouth did, opening to the warmth of his tongue, his possession. He tapped her nipples, hardening them, drawing them out to play. Long swoops of soothing motion eased her shaky muscles before he returned to the apex of her thighs to play. When he slipped back and then forward, driving himself deep inside her, Maddie arched up off the blanket, her cries echoing in the quiet of the night.

"Jack, please! It's too...too much. Harder! Yes, harder."

Jack tilted his pelvis forward, and her clit struck his pubic bone as he thrust deep to her womb.

Maddie's breath stopped; her body clenched up so tight he thought she might break him in two. He watched as the pleasure took her, and then it was taking him too, pulling him down in a perfect swan dive of release where all he knew was the warmth of Maddie surrounding him and the peace of knowing she was his.

Surfacing long moments later, he dragged air into his constricted lungs and looked down at his woman in amazement. She was quivering like a racehorse after a five-mile run, sweat glistening across her stomach and thighs.

She was crying.

He pulled her up into his lap and smoothed his hands along her spine. "Wildcat?"

Maddie tipped her face toward his. The soft smile shining through her tears reassured him. Her soft lips went on a journey along his jugular, adding a tiny lick at the bottom as she nestled her breasts against him. "I love you, Jack."

His heart swelled at her words. A couple of months ago he'd never thought to hear them; now they were the bread and butter on which he subsisted. He couldn't live without them. There were times he thought he might explode with the joy they brought him, with the wonder of holding this wild, passionate woman in his arms and loving her, receiving her love in return.

Ducking down to kiss her, he pushed his tongue deep, trying with desperation to convey the depth of the emotions he felt for her. When he pulled back, words poured out. "That very first night, the minute I saw you, I knew. I fought it, but I knew right then—you were mine. I'll never want another. Never need anyone but you. You're mine, wildcat. I love you."

He had no idea what else he whispered into her hair as he held her close, every thought, every sigh tied up in the woman in his arms. He wouldn't have it any other way. And when he turned her to her back and made love to her one more time, he knew—this was forever. His wildcat didn't have to fight anymore, and neither did he. They had found home in each other's arms, and they were here to stay.

Epilogue

Gabe reset the alarm before walking out the door and closing it softly. He could still see Jack and Maddie together, their bodies molded into one as they made love on the blanket in the backyard.

He envied them. A lot.

Stepping to the edge of Jack's porch, he looked up into the night sky. The moon shone through dense clouds obscuring the stars. It never mattered where he was—here in Georgia, in Texas with his twin brother, in some godforsaken war-torn country no one had ever heard of—the stars were the one constant. They sparked in the sky, reminding him of the need to find his way, to navigate this life he'd created and figure out how to survive it.

They reminded him of when he'd lost his own guiding star through his selfish desires, his need to share with his brother, his twin, the joy of a woman between them.

Sighing, he hefted his go bag over his shoulder and stepped off the porch, headed for his rental car. His time here was over, though he'd been able to do some good. Now it was time to return home. To Sam. To the countryside that used to soothe him but now left him empty. To a life that held no meaning, no desire.

It was time to return to being alone.

Did you enjoy TRUST ME? If so, you can leave a review at your favorite retailer to tell other readers about the book. And thank you!

To find out all the latest news on the Southern Nights series and other upcoming releases, sign up for Ella's newsletter today at http://eepurl.com/IJkRf.

Also available from Ella Sheridan

TEACH ME
Southern Nights Book One

A woman determined to heal…

Shy researcher Jess Kingston spent the last eight weeks recovering from her ex-boyfriend's brutal attack. Body healed, she's ready to put her life back together—except her ex isn't ready to let go. She won't cower in a corner while Brit tortures her, but she's powerless to fight back.

A man determined to resist…

Ex-military security specialist Conlan James avoids commitment like the plague. His job, his Harley, and the occasional one-night stand are all he needs, until the day he rescues Jess from a tense situation and realizes he can't get her off his mind. He can teach her to protect herself, but protecting his heart is another matter.

A madman determined to win…

As the deadly game of cat-and-mouse with Brit heats up, so does the hunger between Con and Jess. Safety might be found in numbers, but in bed, all bets are off—and the wrong move could lead to heartbreak. Or death.

And don't miss the third Southern Nights book, TAKE ME, coming Summer, 2015.

* * *

Ella Sheridan

DIRTY LITTLE SECRET
Secrets To Hide Book One

Cailin Gray transferred to the new Atlanta branch of her company to work for the senior vice president, Alex Brannigan. But before her job begins, she allows the anonymity of the big city to lure her into a night of dancing—and the arms of a mystery lover hotter than anything this country girl could imagine. When she wakes alone, his absence hurts more than she thought it would, but not nearly as much as walking into the office Monday morning and discovering her lover is her new, *married* boss.

Alex has one goal: help his best friend, Sara Beth, keep her inheritance. Their plan included a marriage of convenience—check—taking over the vice president's position—check—and keeping the platonic state of their relationship secret until their position of power is solidified. That last takes time, but the resulting solitude weighs heavily. Until Cailin. He told himself a single night would have to be enough, but fate had other plans. Now he must choose between keeping his dirty little secret and fulfilling his promise to Sara Beth, or finding the strength to free them all from the secrets that bind them.

* * *

NAUGHTY LITTLE CHRISTMAS
Secrets To Hide Book Two

Harley Fisher's life changed forever when her twin sister gave birth to a baby one month before she died. This Christmas, Harley wants her adopted daughter to have the very best gift possible: her real father. Determined to discover if Damien Adams is worthy of being a part of the baby's life, Harley forces her way into a job as the manager-in-training for his new nightclub, Thrice. Damien is blunt, challenging, and sexy as all get-out. Desiring him is wrong, but when he touches her, it's oh so right.

Damien needs a manager for Thrice so he can return to overseeing all three of his clubs. Harley's too young, too hip, too damn tempting—and perfect for the job. Wanting her violates every rule he's laid out for his life, but even the strongest convictions can falter under the mistletoe.

Harley's keeping one hell of a secret. When Damien finds out, will Harley and his daughter be the best Christmas gift he's ever received, or will her secrets leave them with nothing more lasting than a naughty little Christmas this year?

* * *

JUST A LITTLE MORE
Secrets To Hide Book Three

Six weeks ago Angel had it all—a brand-new master's degree, an apartment with her best friend, Brad, and the chance to take their friendship to a whole hot new level. But on the night of their first kiss, a would-be rapist ripped her bright future apart. Stuck in a never-ending cycle of fear and depression, Angel is determined to find herself again, even if it means putting herself at risk.

Brad has loved Angel since he saved her from a playground bully in the fifth grade. But just as it seemed Angel's eyes were opening to the true feelings between them, it all fell apart. When Angel disappears on the night of a freak snowstorm, Brad is determined to find her. And when he does, he won't let her hide any longer. It's time to wake her up—to a life without fear, and to a love that can heal the deepest wounds.

About the Author

Ella Sheridan grew up in the Deep South, where books provided adventures, friends, and her first taste of romance. Now she writes her own romantic adventures, with plenty of hot alpha men and the women who love and challenge them. With a day job, a husband, two active teenagers, and two not so active cats, Ella is always busy, but getting the voices in her head down on paper is a top priority. Connect with Ella at:

Connect with Ella at www.ellasheridanauthor.com or: Facebook (Ella Sheridan Author)

Sign up for Ella's newsletter at http://eepurl.com/IJkRf